A DISTANT HORIZON

Ireland, 1851. After enduring years of the devastating potato famine, Ellen Kittrick is a survivor. To put food on the table, and to stop the landowner's agent from tearing down their cottage due to unpaid rent, Ellen defies her family and works at an Englishman's manor. But with an unemployed husband, and a secretive brother-in-law wanting her for his own, she must face every challenge with new strength.

With aid coming from the unlikely source of Englishman Rafe Hamilton, Ellen leaves Ireland with what is left of her family to start again in a new country. But will the colony give her the security and happiness she longs for, especially when she has left her heart behind? Can Ellen thrive in a strange land — or has she made the greatest mistake of her life?

ANNEMARIE BREAR

A DISTANT HORIZON

AURORA
Leicester

First published in 2021

First Aurora Edition
published 2021

A catalogue record for this book is available
from the British Library.

ISBN 978–1–78782–840–7

Published by
Ulverscroft Limited
Anstey, Leicestershire

Printed and bound in Great Britain by
TJ Books Ltd., Padstow, Cornwall

This book is printed on acid-free paper

For my Irish ancestors

1

September 1851. Louisburgh, County Mayo, Ireland.

Ellen Kittrick brought in the washing as the wind was picking up, blowing straight off the coast of Clew Bay, across the green undulating fields and up towards the ridge of low mountains behind her. The gale threatened to tear her family's few remaining clothes into shreds.

With the clothes in the worn basket, its handles broken, Ellen placed it on her hip and stared out over the jade landscape where it dipped and flowed like an emerald blanket to the wind-tossed bay. Beyond the bay stood Clare Island, the last piece of land before the wide and wild expanse of the dark blue North Atlantic Ocean.

Stone walls divided the fields like a patchwork quilt she'd seen in the shops in Westport once long ago. Those same fields once grew plump with rows and rows of potatoes or were flecked white with sheep.

It seemed a lifetime ago when their own fields were bountiful with crops of potatoes and their sheep used to graze alongside the two cows they owned. The one remaining house cow, Snowflake, named by her daughter Bridget, was the only beast left on their land and they had to lock her up each night to stop thieves from stealing her. The ewes were long gone to pay the rent as the blight destroyed all the potatoes they grew. The potato crop failures each year had destroyed lives, ruined once happy homes, and wiped out a landscape

1

she'd always known as lush and plentiful and crowded with friends and neighbours.

Ellen sighed deeply, lifting her face to the blue sky with its flat pale clouds. The potato crops had failed again this year, and the devastation of another dark winter with no income from their major crop rendered her speechless.

How had it happened?

Within six years their prospering farm and happy, contented life had dwindled into a nightmare she couldn't wake from. Her four children, who used to be lively little things, now resembled haunted walking ghosts a far cry from the children they once were.

In their short lives they'd seen too much horror, too much suffering. The walk from their cottage to her parents' farm was strewn with empty and ruined cottages. Neighbours had long since died or emigrated or left for the workhouse too starved or wracked with fever to stay in their homes.

Now strangers looking for work roamed the lanes and were so emaciated they would curl up under the hedges and never wake up. These were the images her children had witnessed, and she couldn't shield them from it, for everywhere they looked desolation blossomed as easily as weeds.

Six years ago, when the first crop of potatoes failed, there was alarm, for a crop blight had happened in years past, but people had enough potatoes stored to last that winter and replant in the spring. Yet, when the next season failed, destroyed by a blight that turned healthy potatoes into rotting, stinking black mush, panic set in. Farmers didn't have enough seed potatoes to plant for the next season, and so for a third year the fields didn't provide food or income.

Hunger and desperation walked hand in hand across the countryside. What food was grown was shipped from Ireland's shores while the people wasted away.

Ellen's gaze grew vacant against the beautiful scenery that hid the reality of death. The wind chilled her, cutting through her threadbare shawl and thin dress, whipping her long hair from the black ribbon that held it secure. She quickly tugged the ribbon from her hair and tucked it up her sleeve. It was the last ribbon she owned and was loathed to lose it to the wind. Pride kept her from using twine to hold her hair back. They were poor, but not yet reduced to living as paupers in ditches . . . not yet . . .

'Ellen!'

She spun at her name being called and raised her hand in acknowledgement to Father Kilcoyne, her uncle and the parish priest, as he came down the slope beside the cottage.

'Dia dhuit,' Father said in greeting as she joined him.

'Dia is Muire dhuit,' she replied in Gaelic and led him inside the grey stone cottage, her stomach rumbling with hunger.

'It's quiet.' Father Kilcoyne looked around the sparse room.

'The boys have gone down to the beach to collect seaweed and of course Bridget had to follow.'

'They need to be careful. The English are everywhere. It takes nothing for them to round up children and have them put into the workhouse or sent to Canada.' Father Kilcoyne sat on the stool before the peat fire, which smoked into the room until Ellen closed the wooden door.

'We have to eat, Father,' she defended.

'Where's Malachy?'

Ellen busied herself in pouring a glass of milk for her uncle, not sure how to answer him. It shamed her to acknowledge that her husband was spending his days squandering what little money they had on drink. He was no longer the dependable man she'd married twelve years ago when she'd been an independent, strong-willed sixteen-year-old girl with a head full of dreams.

'Ellen?' He pushed, then sighed knowingly. 'Tell me he's not gone to Westport again.'

'He has.'

'To gain work?'

'I hope so, Father.' But she couldn't speak positively, for they both knew her husband would splurge what few coins he had in his pocket on ale.

'This can't go on, Ellen.'

'No . . . ' She fought back the tears — tears she refused to cry. Crying used too much energy, and she had to be strong for her children.

'I hear the public works system is helping families. Has Malachy tried to find work with that?'

'I believe so. He mentioned it on his last visit home. Only, working a day or two here and there isn't enough money. Sometimes he only gets soup for payment.'

'Will he not replant in the spring?'

'Potatoes?' Ellen gave a mocking laugh. 'No, Father. We are done with potatoes altogether. The blight has broken Malachy. Five years of planting only to find months later the entire crop is a squelching stinking black mess. No, he's done with that. Besides, we have no money for seed potatoes.'

'What will he do instead, pray?'

Ellen shrugged. 'Sure, and I don't know, Father.

4

Anything. Something. I keep us alive with the money I earn for the few days I work at the manor. Da gives us fish when he gets a decent catch, so he does.'

The door flung open and on a gust of wind her children clambered into the cottage with high voices of achievement.

'Look what we got, Mammy!' Austin, her eldest son, held up a netted bag full of wet seaweed. He'd turned twelve two days ago, and she'd only been able to give him some milk and a corn patty to celebrate.

'And these!' Patrick at ten refused to be outdone by his older brother and showed her two tiny crabs.

Ellen took the sea produce from them. 'What clever boys you are.'

'Me too! I'm clever.' Thomas's gapped-toothed grin melted her heart. As the third son, he was often doing his best to catch up with his brothers.

'So clever.' She brushed his over-long dark hair from his forehead before turning to her only daughter, Bridget. 'Did you behave for your brothers?'

Bridget nodded and sidled up to Ellen's skirts, her eyes large in her thin face as she stared at Father Kilcoyne. Usually, her daughter talked non-stop. At six-years-old Bridget was quick-witted and quick to temper.

'Now, my children,' Father Kilcoyne focused their attention onto him. 'Have you been saying your prayers?'

Austin instantly stiffened. A rebellious look came into his grey-blue eyes, but his siblings nodded dutifully. Ellen watched her eldest, alarmed by how quickly he was maturing. It was becoming harder to make the boy go to church these days. Too many times Austin had too much to say, especially to his da, who didn't hesitate to slap the boy into place. How soon would it be before Austin was too old to be chastised by his father, a man who was barely here? Many times, over the last year, Malachy insisted on taking the boys with him to find work, but Ellen refused. Their thin, malnourished bodies and ragged clothes wouldn't keep them alive when working manual labour in all weathers.

'Can you tell us a story, Father?' Thomas asked, sitting before the fire.

'I'm afraid I've not the time today, my child. I have many people to see, so I have.'

'Can I stroke, Blaze?' Bridget's large blue-grey eyes implored him.

'Course you can, my child.' Father smiled.

'Be careful,' Ellen warned as her young daughter slipped outside to pat the old nag Father rode around the district. Bridget adored animals, and despite her tiny size, she never seemed scared of any large beast. The family said she was gifted with understanding animals and whereas with people she could be snappy and volatile, with creatures she was patient and tolerant.

'I'll go mind her.' Austin followed his sister out.

Father stopped him. 'Austin, you've not been to Sunday school for the last two Sundays.'

Austin shrugged. 'I know my letters. I can read. Sure, and it's better I use my time more wisely, Father?'

'Learning is for the wise, my child,' Father reproached.

'But it doesn't put food on the table, does it?'

'Austin!' Ellen snapped, ashamed of her son's manner.

Father held up his hand in peace as Austin stepped

6

outside. 'The boy is growing up, Ellen.'

'He is, and he feels the loss of our crops and beasts keenly. He sees and hears too much. His friends are dead or in the workhouse . . . '

'Austin would remember this place when it was a prosperous farm and when his da was around to care for the land.'

'He's also seen the family and neighbours lose everything and he's worried, so he is.' Ellen ignored the jibe about Malachy. She folded the washing, needing something to do with her hands. 'Only yesterday we said goodbye to the Riordans. They've set off on their journey to Canada. How many more friends and neighbours will leave their homeland for goodness knows where or enter the workhouse and be never seen again?'

'If it keeps their body and souls together, then it must be done.' Father shook his head. 'But the parish will never be the same. Fewer and fewer people sit in my church now. Some travelling to distant lands, some in the poorhouses, some living in ditches and some to meet their saviour. I'm surprised Malachy hasn't mentioned leaving.'

'He hasn't yet.'

'Would you go if he did?'

'Sure and abandon Mammy and Da? It'd break me.'

'Sometimes staying breaks you, too.' Father finished his milk and passed a small parcel to Ellen. 'Sell it for the rent,' he said quietly. 'Your mammy and da send their regards. I saw them this morning, so I did.'

'How are they doing? I've not been to see them in a few days. I've had work at the manor.' She took the parcel from him, knowing he'd not want her to open it until he was gone. She didn't know what she'd have done without her uncle's help in the last few years, or her cleaning position at Wilton Manor.

His expression fell as he stepped nearer; his voice lowered. 'They're not good. The rent can't be paid next week. The fish haven't been running into your da's nets. I've done what I can, but my brother-in-law is too proud and refuses any offer I make. I managed to give your sister some pennies, but Riona has to hide them quickly before Fionn sees them.'

She nodded. Her da, Fionn, struggled even harder than she did to keep the family safe from eviction, but his potato crops had failed each season as well, and he'd sold all of his animals to pay the rent over the years. Being a fisherman, his catches of fish saved them from total starvation. Without Da's boat and his small catches, and her work, Ellen didn't think they would have survived as long as they had.

'I'll go and see them tomorrow,' she said.

'I've done as much as I can for my blessed parishioners, but my resources are limited.' Father sighed. 'I hate to see my family reduced to this state. Fionn always prided himself on paying his rent and providing for his family.'

'As we all do.' Ellen glanced at Patrick and Thomas, quietly huddled before the peat fire, which today had more smoke than flame.

Father kissed her forehead. 'God bless you, child. I'll see you in church on Sunday. Bring Malachy.'

'I'll try . . . ' She didn't need to tell her uncle how her husband behaved. He knew too well. Her entire family knew exactly how weak Malachy was where drink was concerned.

'God bless you all.' Father Kilcoyne made a sign of

8

the cross and left the cottage.

Once the door had closed behind him, Ellen unwrapped the parcel. Inside was a fine piece of lace-work, a collar for a dress, but not for her. She'd walk into Louisburgh and try to sell it, and if not successful there, then she'd walk the four hours to Westport.

Many of her uncle's parishioners didn't have money to pay him for his services, and many times they paid him with something made, or produce, or livestock, or whatever could be spared. Since the start of the crop failures, even those offerings had diminished. Now the people of the parish could barely feed themselves, yet their Catholic faith was stronger than ever and giving Father Kilcoyne something often gave them as much comfort as his prayers.

Ellen stirred the milk-soaked cornmeal in the pan and began making patties to fry over the fire for the children's' meal. Gone were the days of having three hearty meals a day. Instead, they ate one meal at noon and that depended on whether they caught something in the wild or she was given some food from the manor to take home.

At least Malachy's regular disappearances meant she had more food to spread further for the children. The hated cornmeal had never been a part of their diet until the crop failures. The British Government thought sending Indian maize would satisfy the Irish rabble, but it took a long time for them to get used to the taste and how to cook it well enough not to be riddled with stomach pains.

Still, at least she could give her children something to eat, and it gave them a respite from eating boiled nettles from the roadside or seaweed.

Her boring task gave her time to ponder on her

husband's whereabouts. This time, he'd been gone two days. She prayed to God he found work. She prayed every night that he would be successful in earning enough money to keep a roof over their heads. Perhaps then the happy, loving man she married would return and replace the haunted stranger she lived with now.

The change in Malachy in the last few years alarmed her. Gone was the provider, the laughing, witty young man who had captured her heart at aged fifteen. They'd married on her sixteenth birthday when she'd been the young and pretty Ellen O'Mara and nine months later Austin had been born in this very cottage, which they had managed to rent due to Malachy's hard work.

They believed themselves to be blessed in finding such love with one another and although the early years were tough with toiling the land and raising beasts and babies, she looked back on those first few years of her marriage with deep gratitude at the happiness that filled their days.

Malachy's family, the Kittricks, were one of the largest tenant farmers in the district. His parents both died of fever last year, leaving their farm to his oldest brother, Colm, but Malachy had been given some acres to farm upon his marriage and Ellen, who also coming from her da's good sized tenant farm, had been happy with that. Together they had worked hard to make the farm pay its way. Potato crops were planted, they had a few sheep grazing, a milk cow, chickens, a pig, and some geese.

Before long, Malachy whined that their acres weren't enough. Colm needed to give him more, but Colm refused. Tensions rose between the brothers, but then the blight came and ruined everything. Now they couldn't farm the land and the only income they had was her small wage from cleaning three days a week and the odd days Malachy gained work as a labourer.

Ellen fried the patties she made, again her stomach rumbling with hunger. Austin and Bridget came back inside, and Bridget helped to set the wooden table with tin plates.

'Milk, Mam?' Austin asked, holding up the jug. 'Yes, there's enough for you all until morning.'

Snowflake was milked every morning and evening and Ellen thanked God each night for the bounty that was their blessed cow, but how much longer could she keep her? The loft above their heads no longer held a store of potatoes, or any other vegetables they managed to harvest at the end of summer. Ahead was a long winter and empty shelves. Ellen prayed Malachy would find work to tide them over until the good times came again.

She looked at those empty wooden shelves and winced. Once those shelves held tea, sugar, flour, salt, oats, slabs of bacon and cured ham. She'd never gone without potatoes, onions and carrots. Now she'd be hard pressed to remember when she last owned such bounty. The hated cornmeal was cheap and filling once soaked in milk and she knew she should be thankful she had it, for thousands and thousands of people had much less or nothing at all.

She couldn't walk into Louisburgh without passing beggars in the ditches, too weak to move, skeletons on the roadside, left where they dropped and died or silent empty cottages, most reduced to rubble when the landlord's men caved them in when the rent wasn't paid. For years she'd stared at death and had night terrors of the devastating scenes she'd witnessed of desperate people begging for food or homes being destroyed or bodies on the roadside.

Somehow, she and her family had struggled through so far, but she no longer took it for granted that their crops would grow, and they'd have fleshy white potatoes in abundance. So, she lived day to day, hour by hour, and prayed she'd not lose her position at Wilton Manor. Working at the manor provided her with a midday meal, and sometimes, the odd basket of leftovers to take home to her starving children.

A knock on the door preceded Colm. 'God bless all in this house.' He made a sign of the cross. His tall, thick frame dwarfed the room. Colm Kittrick never looked like he was starving.

Ellen mumbled a reply, rising from in front of the fire to portion out small amounts of the cornmeal to the children. 'You are well, brother?' she asked, not looking at him.

Her brother-in-law made her nervous. A bachelor, he continually joked that he'd never marry as Malachy had married the only decent woman in the district. His jokes made her uncomfortable, as did his intense stares and lingering touches. For twelve years she had seen him watch her, smile and jest with her, yet underneath the brotherly humour lurked something deeper and she didn't like it.

'Where is Malachy?' he asked, sitting at the table, and helping himself to the last of the patties, which Ellen had saved for the children to share before bed.

'Looking for work in Westport.'

'Huh. Sure, so he is.' Colm laughed, not believing her. 'Likely to be drinking his last pennies in some

12

backstreet inn is my bet.'

'He'll find some work.'

Colm shovelled the food into his mouth. 'You're still convinced my brother will do the right thing? 'Tis madness to think so.'

'He is my husband, naturally he'll do right by us, so he will.'

Colm poured the last of the milk into a cup. 'More fool you then. My brother has lost his way. He doesn't deserve your faith in him or a fine family such as this. You picked the wrong brother, Ellen.'

Ellen turned away, fighting the anger building up inside. Grabbing the bucket, she went outside to the well for water. The wind buffeted her, but she welcomed the coldness of it against her hot face. Damn Colm. Wrong brother, indeed. She would have rather remained a maiden than tie herself to that man.

'Ellen.' Colm was suddenly beside her, his hands on her shoulders, squeezing gently. 'Forgive me for speaking my mind. I only want the best for you, so I do.'

'And that's speaking ill of my husband, your brother, and my children's da?' She stepped away from him, hating his touch, which was becoming more and more sensual.

He ran his hand through his thick black hair. 'It frustrates me that you blindly believe in him. He's done nothing in the last few years to deserve that.'

'That is for me and God to judge!' She pulled the wooden cover back over the well.

Colm took the full bucket from her. 'I care for you all. I'll look after you if you let me. Please let me. Move into my house.'

'Malachy will provide for us.'

'Malachy is incapable. My brother is no longer the man you fell in love with as a girl. He's changed. When was the last time he did a day's work?' He glanced around the neglected farm. 'What have you got left? You'll be in the workhouse before you know it.'

She lifted her chin in annoyance. 'We are better off than most. I've my position at Wilton Manor and my da still has his boat.'

'Working for an Englishman?' he scorned. 'Wilton is an old fool. He doesn't care about you or any of us. The British only want us dead in the ground so they can farm the land. Cattle are more highly prized than the Irish people. British landlords are greatly taxed if they have tenants. Why do you think they are pulling down the cottages and starving people off their land?'

'Mr Wilton is a good man, even if he is English. I need the money and that's all I care about, so keep your rebellious tongue in your head!'

'Do you know that there are warehouses all around the country full of wheat and maize? It all gets shipped to England. It's not to be borne. We must stop it.'

'What stupid words you speak. To fight the British is to rot in a jail somewhere or to flee the country to exile as many others have done before.'

'And what good men they are to have tried to free us! To fight for Ireland is all we have left!' His cheeks reddened with a vengeance.

'I'll hear no more of it, Colm. Sure, and you'll keep a civilised tongue in your head when near the children. I'll not have the boys fed rebellious language.'

He sighed deeply. 'Come to me, Ellen, I beg you. Live at my farm. Sure, it'll be grand. The cottage is twice the size of yours, so it is. I have beasts and chickens to feed the children. I hate seeing them so thin. I

14

dread them getting sick or worse.'

'I can take care of my children.' He made her feel guilty. As though she was deliberately starving them. Was she? Should she swallow her pride and go to Colm?

'Living off cornmeal like a pauper in the work-house?' he taunted.

Ellen stiffened at the insult. 'It's not always corn-meal. We'll have crabs and seaweed for supper. They have plenty of milk.'

'And what happens when the cow dries up?'

'I'll deal with that when it happens and not before.'

He took her arm, his fingers massaging her flesh. 'I only want what is best for you. I can't bear to see you reduced to this,' he whispered passionately. 'You'd be happier with me at the farm. I would treat you like a princess. You'd want for nothing.'

'I'm not your wife, Colm.'

'No, but you should be, and can be in secret.' He leaned in close, his breath in her ear. 'I'd love you properly, Ellen. Your beauty stirs me to speak openly. I want you with me. Malachy can be forgotten.'

She laughed mockingly. 'How can you say such things? To forget Malachy? He is my husband! Your brother.'

She shrugged off his hand and marched back to the cottage, wishing he'd leave and Malachy was here. Let him deal with his brother. But then she knew Colm would act differently when Malachy was around. Colm kept his manner light and happy to play the doting uncle to the children in front of Malachy. Only when she was alone did he behave in an ill-mannered way and over-stepped the boundary of brother-in-law.

He followed her. 'I care deeply for you, Ellen. Just

promise me that if it all becomes too difficult, you'll come to me first?'

'My husband will decide that.'

'Oh, Ellen.' He bowed his head.

'Goodbye, Colm.'

He took a step, then stopped. 'Before I go, a warning. You're not to speak the Irish tongue when in the village. English soldiers demand that only the English be spoken.'

'I speak our language at home. I know it's better to speak English when abroad. I have eyes and ears, Colm, and I work for an English master. I'm not a fool.'

'Tell the children. English only. Major Sturgess is looking for ways to punish us, but his soldiers are comprised of local men and some of them I know, and they tell me things.'

'Perhaps you know too much?' she snapped. 'Best that you stay by your fireside more and not roam the district listening to things that don't concern you?'

'What I learn is to help us all. Austin is of the age he could be sent to work on the road gangs in chains if he gives abuse. Sturgess needs no excuse to round you all up for the slightest offence and have you put into the stocks.'

Ellen knew of Major Sturgess and his band of soldiers who travelled the area for the absentee British landlord who owned the land here. She had seen evidence of the work Sturgess did. The cottages destroyed, the people flogged in the street, dogs shot, men hunted down on the slightest charge. Sturgess was the devil himself.

'I'll keep the boys away from the village.'

Colm nodded. 'Send Austin to me. He can kill a

16

chicken.'

'I will.'

'And think of my offer. God bless and keep you.' Colm disappeared around the corner of the cottage and soon she heard his horse's hoofbeats pounding along the dirt track.

It irked her that Colm still had a horse. How had the man managed so well through all the years of catastrophe? Were the rumours of him being a secret arms dealer true? Or worse, was he a spy for the British? He made a good show of hating the English, but too many rumours abounded that he'd been seen drinking with the soldiers that roamed the countryside. Yet was he simply getting information for the Young Irelanders? The rebellious group had men all over the country, despite past uprisings failing recently and the leaders fleeing Ireland.

She sighed in exhaustion. Colm was dangerous, and he knew too many people, good and bad, but he loved the children, she couldn't deny that. She just wished he didn't love her so much.

Rubbing the tightness from her neck, Ellen walked inside. The children were sitting before the fire, listening to Austin telling them a story about a monster who lived in the bog on the edge of their land.

Taking Bridget onto her lap, Ellen smiled at Austin. Her home and land might have been stripped bare of all comforts, but at least she had four trusting faces who looked at her with love, and for the moment, she was able to feed and home them. She had more than most.

When the sun lowered into the Atlantic, Ellen ushered the children into the other room to bed. Malachy had built one large bed for all four children to sleep in, while their own bed was up in the loft next to the vegetable storage. She listened to their prayers and then kissed them goodnight.

Ellen was adding more turf to the fire, to keep it in overnight when the door opened, and Malachy stumbled in.

'Shh!' She indicated with her head to the sleeping children in the next room.

Malachy smiled, exaggerating his tiptoeing into the room. He embraced her tightly. 'M'fhíorghrá.'

'I'm not your true love, Malachy Kittrick, drink is!' She turned her head from his searching lips. He stank of stale ale and goodness knows what else.

'Don't start, woman. I've walked all the way home to see you.'

'Have you earned any money?'

'Some.'

'Enough for the rent?'

He frowned, his handsome face losing its jollity. 'Not yet.'

'But enough for you to get senseless on?' At that moment, she hated him.

'I'll get more money . . .' He swayed, eyes half closing. 'It's hard finding work. Men, women, and children will work for nothing, just a piece of bread. I can't compete with that.'

'The rent is due next week.'

'I know when it's due, so I do. The end of every March and September, you don't need to remind me.' He dipped a cup into the water bucket and drank deeply.

'What will we do if we haven't got enough to pay it? I'll have to sell Snowflake, but then what about the next time the rent is due?'

'I'll sort it. I promise.'

18

'Malachy, you need to stop drinking. We can't afford it.' She crossed to him, desperate for some reassurance, for some tenderness and support. 'Please stop.'

He held her tightly to him and kissed the top of her head. 'I'll try, but I've lost everything, my lass. Drink helps me to forget . . .'

'You've not lost your family, not yet.'

A haunting look darkened his grey eyes. 'It'll only be a matter of time.'

She jerked from him. 'Why do you talk that way? Sure, and I don't know who you are anymore. We have managed so far, and we can continue if you try hard enough!'

'Don't be lecturing me. I'm spent. Walked miles I have. I'm to bed.'

From the settle she threw him a stitched together blanket which hit his chest and fell to the floor. 'Sleep down here, you'll not make it up the ladder. The last thing we want is you falling and breaking a leg.'

Grumbling, he bent to pick up the blanket, lost balance and crashed to the stone-flagged floor.

Ellen stood over him, knowing her love was slowly ebbing from her heart as it had done for many months now. 'Where have you gone, Malachy Kittrick?'

A snore was her answer.

She took off her shawl and placed it under his head and the blanket over him. She stared down at him, the man she had once loved so deeply, and who had promised he'd never give her reason to worry about anything.

He wasn't to blame for the blight that swept the country and destroyed the potato crops, but he'd not done enough to keep her and the children safe. He'd let the worry and the constant fear settle on her shoulders, and she couldn't forgive him for it.

In the feeble light cast by the fire, she climbed the ladder to the straw mattress above.

After saying her prayers, which each night was becoming more begging in nature, and wearing only her threadbare shift, she crawled under a cold blanket and snuggled down into the dipping mattress that needed fresh straw to fill it out. The wind howled around the cottage, finding the gaps in the thatched roof and whispered like icy fingers over her face.

Day by day, hour by hour . . .

The words swirled around in her head. She would get through this terrible time as she had been doing, and if she couldn't rely on Malachy, then she would continue to rely on herself.

2

Shouting woke Ellen the next morning. She frowned, annoyed that the children would make such a noise.

Quickly dressing, she looked for her shawl and then remembered it was under Malachy's head. Her annoyance reached a higher level. She hurried down the ladder, realising the shouting was coming from outside. Those children would feel the back of her hand, so they would.

Grabbing her shawl from where it had been laid over a chair, Ellen was ready to give a tongue-lashing to the four of them. However, opening the door, the sight before her checked her step.

In the rain, three indignant men stood fighting off her children. One of the men held the rope attached to Snowflake.

'What in God's name is going on?' Ellen demanded, storming up to the men as the boys fell back, panting, and red-faced. Bridget clung on to the rope near Snowflake's head while a man tried to prise her little hands from it.

'Missus, call off your brats!' shouted a man whose hat had fallen into the mud.

'Let go of our cow.' Ellen looked around for some sort of weapon. Thievery was ripe in the area.

'She's not yours anymore!' The man holding the rope gave a hard yank and Snowflake jerked sideways, knocking Bridget over into a puddle.

Ellen raced to pick up her daughter, but Austin beat her to it. He swung a fist at the man, who easily parried it and pushed him away. Austin gathered Bridget into his arms, his gaunt face furious.

'I will report this!' Ellen held onto Thomas, who came to hide in her skirts. 'This is theft!'

'No, it's not, missus. This cow is ours. Won honestly in a card game. Your husband, Malachy Kittrick, is it? He told us to collect this cow this morning.'

Ellen shook her head, not daring to believe it. 'A card game?

No. You're lying. I'll not believe you!'

'Aye, it was, missus, won fair and square. There were witnesses. The landlord of the Dog and Duck is one. Ask him.'

'I'll not take your word. I'll speak to my husband first. Let go of our cow!' Ellen rushed to grab the rope, but the man easily pushed her away.

'I'm speaking the truth, so I am. Soldiers were there, too. Go to the Dog and Duck, there are men there who'll tell you the truth of it. Your husband lost. He said his brother Colm would stand the rest of what's owed. We're off to see him next, so we are.'

She swayed at the enormity of what was happening. 'But this cow provides milk for my children. It'll pay our rent . . .'

'Aye, missus and us three have ten brats between us, so we have.'

'You can't take her, you *spalpeens*!' Austin growled out, his fists clenching by his side.

'Sorry, boyo, she's ours. Tell your da that cards aren't his game.' The men turned and walked away, pulling a placid Snowflake along behind them.

A rage so intense burned through Ellen. 'Where is your da?' she shouted at Austin as the rain fell faster.

'He left early,' Patrick told her in a small voice.

'Before those men came.'

'They tipped over the bucket of milk, too,' Thomas whined. 'We've none for breakfast.'

'Snowflake . . . ' Bridget's tears ran down her cheeks.

Ellen wished she could cry, too, but her throat was a large knot of emotion choking her. Snowflake was not only their milk, but she was insurance for the next payment of rent if Malachy couldn't provide it. As much as she didn't want to sell Snowflake, at least she would have bought them another six months with a roof over their heads.

What would they do now?

She'd sold everything of value over the years to pay the rent. The sheep that were Malachy's pride and joy went to auction two years ago. All the pretty things she'd filled the cottage with when times had been flourishing were now a distant memory and all homed with strangers. The fine linens her mother-in-law had made for her were sold, along with the little clock they'd received from Father Kilcoyne on their wedding day. As well as the green glassware Malachy had won as a prize for boxing at the Louisburgh fair, the gold-painted cross, her second pair of boots, the children's baby clothes, their cradle, spare pots and pans, her best coat, Malachy's hunting rifle he'd had since he was a boy, his father's fob watch . . . all gone. All the things that made them happy, that made the cottage a home were sold or pawned to pay each half-yearly rent.

Yes, they'd been fortunate to have those things to sell when so many of their neighbours had nothing but a few animals and the clothes on their backs. But both the Kittrick and the O'Mara families had been successful farmers until the blight killed the crops.

Without the early success of years gone by, they'd have suffered the same cruel fate which took many families from the area. She had watched friends and neighbours die, or enter the parish workhouse, but most had emigrated to the far corners of the world. However, the Kittricks had survived.

Until now. Now, Ellen had a great fear their luck had run out.

A horse and rider came trotting along the road, flanked by two mounted soldiers, and Ellen inwardly groaned. Major Sturgess was the landowner's agent and a slimier looking toad Ellen had yet to meet.

'Mrs Kittrick,' he acknowledged, slowing his horse before them.

'Major.' She was barely civil to the hated man.

'Was that your cow I just passed?' His large bulk strained his black suit, and the waterproof coat he wore billowed out like a black sail. Ellen always felt sorry for his poor horse carrying such weight.

'It was.' Rain plastered her hair to her head and ran down her face, but she ignored it, too sick with worry to care.

'You have sold it?' He was incredulous, and she couldn't blame him.

'Debts must be paid, Major.'

'And what of your rent? The Marquis of Sligo is a reasonable gentleman, but he has his limits as many of your neighbours have found out to their cost.'

'We haven't yet been in arrears, have we?'

'Will you be next time?' Rain dripped off his hat.

'No.' She could easily lie to a worthless man like Major Sturgess.

'I'd hate to see you and your children on the roads, Mrs Kittrick.'

24

'Who said it'd come to that, pray?'

His narrowed gaze took in the ragged state of the children and finally rested back on Ellen. 'There are ways for you to earn, Mrs Kittrick. Perhaps we should go inside and discuss it?' He pointed to the children standing in the doorway out of the weather. 'Send the children away for a time. I have a proposition for you.'

She lifted her chin haughtily, knowing exactly what he wanted from her, and he wasn't going to get it. Too many times in the past, the major had eyed her up like a prized cow. 'I think not, Major. Sure and isn't my husband due back any moment.'

The major smiled knowingly. 'As you wish. Nevertheless, should you change your mind, you know where to find me.'

She stared at him without comment.

He smiled evilly, turned his horse about and trotted away, his men following.

'We're going to your granny's,' Ellen decided. She couldn't stay at the cottage today. The loss of Snowflake was too raw, and if Malachy was to return now, she'd do him an injury, she was certain of it. The mile and half walk to her parents' cottage near the beach would give her anger time to simmer and cool. She needed to talk to her parents.

In the past, the walk usually allowed the children to scamper and chatter, but weak from hunger slowed their steps. The four of them were subdued, shoulders drooped. No one talked. Thomas didn't run off to find rabbit holes, Bridget didn't sing, Patrick didn't talk of his need for a dog, and Austin didn't regale her with the best fishing spots on the beach. There was none of that. They simply trudged along in the grey rain, cold and wet and utterly devoid of hope.

Further along the track, in the hollow of a bluff, a family of strangers made a shelter out of sticks and rocks and dried seaweed. A woman dressed in rags sat inside the opening of the structure, holding an infant that looked close to death. Behind her a man worked with an older girl trying to make a fire with a sod of peat.

Ellen wished she could help them, but she didn't have the energy and what's more, the family might have fever and she couldn't risk the children.

All around them, the land was dotted with graves and half-built shelters that collapsed in bad weather. Mangy dogs snuffled in ditches where the unburied lay, skeletons bleached white by the sun and weather. Often, Ellen would find parts of a human skeleton along the road where dogs had dug up shallow graves or gnawed on the dead where they dropped in the fields.

The sight no longer upset the children, they had grown used to the devastation and death.

The rain eased and the clouds broke apart, allowing a weak sunshine to spear the land below. Her parents' stone and thatched cottage was identical to Ellen's, though it was situated on a slight rise a half mile from Louisburgh, closer to the beach on the lowlands. Fishing was a source of income and a way to feed them all when Ellen was growing up, but as her da felt his age more each winter, the farm and the fishing were becoming too much for him, and grandpa was even older and frailer.

Her younger sister Riona was carrying a bucket of water into the cottage as they approached the rise. She held her arms out as Bridget ran to her, fresh tears coursing over her lashes.

'Nay, what's all this?' Riona asked Ellen when she reached her. 'Bridget says your cow has been taken?'

Ellen nodded as the children all spoke at once about the three men taking their beloved Snowflake.

'Come away inside.' Riona ushered them into the cottage but hung back to stop Ellen from following them. 'Where's Malachy?' 'Who can guess? He left again this morning before I awoke. Hopefully, he's gone to find work, pray that he does.'

'Da heard he was seen playing cards in a Westport tavern. He didn't believe it, but now we know it to be true for sure.'

'Aye.' Ellen walked into the cottage to kiss her elderly grandpa Ronan O'Mara in greeting before giving her mammy a wan smile.

Bridget was already on her granny Bridie's lap while the boys were hovering around their great-grandpa Ronan watching him fix a fishing net with his bent arthritic hands. Ronan, too old to live by himself, had moved in with his son Fionn and daughter-in-law Bridie when Ellen married Malachy.

'Where's Da?' Ellen asked.

Instantly her mammy stiffened. 'Louisburgh for the petty sessions.'

'That's today? I forgot all about it with everything going on with Snowflake.'

'Wouldn't it be the luck of the devil if your da is fined yet again?' Mammy lifted Bridget off her lap and attended to the fire. 'He can't catch enough fish to pay off his fines, so he can't. The great eejit of a man!'

'Da needs to stop this fighting with Martin Joyce.'

'It's a feud that's gone on since they were boys.' Mammy sighed. 'Sure, and we don't have the money for paying fines when the rent is due. Holy Mother of God, your da will send me to the grave, so he will.'

Riona set out cups and poured weak flavourless black tea into them. 'Da says Mr Joyce has gone too far this time. He's assaulted him for the last time.'

'But wasn't that because Da was seen in Mr Joyce's fields? Carrying something in a sack and suddenly Mr Joyce is a piglet less in his stye?' Ellen shrugged, knowing the long history of animosity between her father and Mr Joyce. Sadly, they were neighbours, and each man found the slightest thing to accuse the other, hoping that one day the other would be sent to prison.

'He has no proof it was Fionn. So, was it reason to call the constable?' Mammy grumbled.

'Father Kilcoyne is tired of being stuck in the middle of it all, trying to make them see sense.' Riona gave the children small cups of water to drink.

'Sure, and it's never going to stop,' Mammy said. 'A time in prison might make them both see sense. They're a pair of old fools, so they are.'

'Tish now, don't speak of prison,' Ronan said in Gaelic. 'I can't manage the boat by myself.'

Mammy looked at Ellen. 'Enough of that. What is this about your cow?'

'She is gone.'

Mammy crossed herself. 'Holy Virgin Mother. How are you to cope now? It's all you have left.'

'I can't think of it, Mammy, for it fair breaks my heart, so it does.'

'Malachy gambling?'

Ellen could only nod.

'Jesus, Mary and Joseph.' Mammy crossed herself again. 'What was he thinking?'

28

'Sure, and thinking is something he does little of these days.' She sipped the weak tea that had no flavour left or colour from the overuse of the same tea leaves.

'You'll have to let go of the land and move in here with us.' 'Another five people in this place?' She looked around the cramped, dark cottage she'd grown up in. 'That'll make it nine in two rooms, Mammy.'

'It's been done before.'

'I'll think of something,' Ellen mumbled. 'I still have my work at Wilton Manor.'

'Well, pray to the Holy Virgin then that Malachy finds some work and let's hope She hears your prayers.' Mammy spun to Austin, taking him by surprise. 'And you, my boy, where were you last Sunday? For you weren't at Mass!'

'Rabbiting, Gran. Someone needs to put food on the table.'

Mammy raised her eyebrows at him. 'Will you look at that, a man he be now. Be careful with that sharp tongue of yours, boy, or you'll cut yourself with it.'

Ellen watched her mother and her son eye each other up, but the love between them was too strong for there to be any hard feelings. Austin was her mother's favourite and could do no wrong.

'Can we come with you tonight, Grandpa Ronan?' Patrick suddenly asked as Grandpa folded the fishing net.

'Sure, and I can't be taking you all. You'll capsize my little currach!' He grinned; his lined face weatherworn like old leather. A clay pipe hung out of his mouth, not lit, for there was no money for tobacco.

'Whose turn is it?' Ellen asked.

'Mine!' Patrick said.

'No, it's mine!' Thomas pushed his brother.

'Whist the pair of you! Sure, and neither of you'll go at this rate!' Mammy frowned, which instantly quietened the boys.

'Austin, who's turn is it?' Mammy asked.

'It's Thomas's.' Austin would never lie to his grandmammy.

'That's settled.' Mammy prodded the fire. 'Thomas goes out tonight and you mark my words, they'll return with a great haul Jesus himself would be proud of.' She turned to Ellen. 'You'll stay the night?'

Ellen nodded. She had nothing to return home for.

★ ★ ★

Howling wind woke Ellen as it thrashed against the cottage, finding its way in through the ill-fitting window shutters and sending the wisps of smoke back down the chimney.

She turned on the flat straw mattress, careful not to fall off as she was right on the edge with Riona on the other side and Patrick in between them. Austin and Bridget were sleeping with their gran.

For a while she listened to the wind, hoping that out to sea the weather wasn't as wild. Earlier, her da had come home, shouting, and cursing at being fined two shillings for trespassing, but not found guilty on the theft of the piglet as there was no proof. Hatred for Mr Joyce only intensified with each of his curses. His stomping about the cottage got on everyone's nerves and they were glad when at sunset he and Grandpa, along with Thomas, headed down to the beach to go night fishing in the currach.

Grandpa said the weather wouldn't be a concern,

and the family believed him, for hadn't he been fishing in Clew Bay for all of his seventy years?

As the shutters rattled, Ellen, still fully dressed, rose and crossed to the window and opened them. She shivered as the cold air hit her. A thin streak of grey light showed on the horizon, but looking towards the beach all she could see was darkness.

'Close the shutter and keep the cold out,' Mammy said, coming into the main room, making Ellen jump.

'It's blowing a gale out there.' She did as she was told while her Mammy raked at the fire's ashes and added small clods of turf.

'Aye, it's the devil's work, so it is.' With licks of flame flaring, Mammy swung the pot over the fire to heat the water. 'I've cornmeal soaking for the children, but nothing for us until they bring up the fish haul.'

'No, Mammy, save the meal for you all. Da and Grandpa will be hungry when they return. I'll take the children home once it's light. I've cornmeal for them.'

'I'll feed the children.' Mammy was adamant. 'And God be praised they'll have a good catch of fish and you can take some with you.'

Ellen watched the flames, not able to bear seeing the haggard strain on her mammy's dear face. Mammy had been touted as the parish beauty in her younger days, a role that Ellen herself took over as she grew up, but all that remained in memories now as grey had washed out her mammy's ebony-coloured hair and deep lines crisscrossed her pale thin face.

'Our kin, the O'Malleys from Killeen left two days ago for America, may the Holy Mother protect them,' Mammy murmured.

Ellen glanced up. 'You never said. I would have

come and said farewell to them.'

'They didn't want a fuss, God bless them.' Mammy swallowed and made a sign of the cross. 'That's the last of my mother's kin. Those not buried in the church grounds are over the sea. There aren't many left of the Kilcoyne's either.'

Remaining quiet, Ellen thought of her O'Malley cousins. Dozens of faces she'd known growing up and who she'd never see again. Hundreds of families were displaced or wiped out altogether. No longer did she see distant members of their kin. The O'Malleys joined the families of O'Mara, Kilcoyne, Farrell and others who would never been seen again.

The wind rattled the cottage's two small windows.

Suddenly, Mammy stood, frowning. From the mantelpiece, she took out her rosary beads from the little box which always held them.

'Mammy?' Ellen shivered.

'Pray with me!' Mammy dropped to her knees, dragging Ellen down beside her.

'Mammy?' Ellen asked, frightened.

'Pray to the Holy Mother with all your might, sure, and it'll be a day of horror if we don't.'

Ellen remained on her knees, praying beside her mother until the children and Riona woke. Morning light filtered through the cracks in the shutters.

When a loud knocking startled them, Mammy straightened from her position. She took a moment and then looked at Ellen; her face drawn. 'It wasn't enough.' She crossed herself.

'What do you mean?' Ellen followed her to the door.

Paddy McLoughlin stood outside, bent over, and panting. 'You're to come!'

'What's happened, Paddy?' Ellen asked him. The

32

young man had once been her brother Tommy's friend until fever took Tommy at just fourteen. It was he who she named her own Thomas after.

'Boats have gone down. At least five.' Paddy made a sign of the cross against his chest. 'They say your da is one of them.'

As though someone had thrown a bucket of cold water over her, Ellen jerked, staggered backwards, shaking her head. No. It couldn't be true. She wouldn't let it be true. Thomas!

'Come!' Mammy grabbed her elbow and pulled her along.

In a daze, Ellen followed her mother down to the beach, which as the sun rose higher in a wind-whipped pink and grey sky, showed the gathering of folk down on the sand. People from Louisburgh and the farming lands of this far eastern corner of Mayo came streaming out to help or to witness what could be another disaster to hit their parish.

Refusing to believe anything had happened to her father's boat, Ellen searched the choppy waters of the sea as they ran. Waves crashed onto the beach, churned up and frothing a foam that the wind blew into everyone's eyes.

Her footsteps sunk into the cold sand, faces she knew looked away in pity, many hands made the sign of the cross as she passed by. Heart pumping, she dutifully followed her mammy to where the wreckages of the smashed boats were being washed onto the shore. Debris and fishing equipment ebbed and flowed in the shallow waves.

She spotted the black cloak of Father Kilcoyne. He knelt beside the body of a boy . . .

Someone was screaming, a keening sound that hurt

her ears.

Ellen ran, the sand and her long skirts tripped her up. She tried to catch her breath, but there wasn't any air. She had to reach the boy.

'Dear child.' Father Kilcoyne grabbed her arms. 'I'm so sorry.'

She stared down at her darling son lying on the damp sand next to his grandfather. Both of them had the ghastly white pallid faces of death.

She fell to her knees beside her son's head. Carefully, she cradled his wet body against her and held him tight. He was white, cold, and limp. 'I'm here, Thomas. Mammy's here, my darling.'

The world around her ceased to exist as she rocked her son in her arms. Dimly, she was aware of her mammy sitting near her, smoothing the clothes of her da, making him look tidy, while Father Kilcoyne prayed over them and the other men who had drowned during the night's storm. Grandpa Ronan's body hadn't washed ashore.

3

The muted voices of the children alerted Ellen to their presence as they entered the cottage. She turned from staring at the small flames in the fire, trying to focus on what they said.

'Mam?' Austin crouched down before her and held her hands. 'I'm taking Patrick out with me to hunt for rabbits as we've nothing to eat.'

'I want to go!' Bridget demanded.

'No!' Ellen snapped.

Austin fell back at her harshness.

'You are to stay here. Sure and no one leaves the cottage.' She couldn't protect them if they were out of her sight. She'd failed Thomas, she wouldn't fail her remaining children.

'But we've no food, Mam.' Austin stood and Bridget slipped her little hand into his, her frightened eyes stared at Ellen. Patrick sat at the table, his bones protruding as his body wasted away from lack of food.

Ellen began to shake. Would God take Patrick, too? He was so thin. They were all too thin! Was she to lose all her children? Why was God punishing her like this?

'I'll find us food.' She rose from the stool and swayed. Dizziness overwhelmed her. When had she last eaten? She couldn't remember. Yesterday? The day before? She didn't even know what day it was.

'Mam?' Austin touched her shoulder. 'Mam let me go. I'll catch us something.'

Dazed, she glanced around. She couldn't remember much of anything since they buried Thomas and her da three days ago. Of Grandpa Ronan, they had no resting place for him. His body still hadn't washed ashore with the others, and he was listed as lost at sea. However, his name had joined her da's and son's carved onto the wooden cross in the churchyard.

Ronan O'Mara
Fionn O'Mara
Thomas Kittrick
Died 21st September 1851
May God hold them in His arms

They were low on turf sods for the fire, but the bucket was full of water. The shelves on either side of the chimney were still bare though. Jesus, Mary and Joseph, what was she to do?

Austin added the last sod of turf onto the fire. 'Da came home yesterday when you were sleeping, but he left again straight after. He gave us a small bag of cornmeal, but I've used it all.'

She nodded, not even remembering sleeping or much of the last three days and certainly not Malachy coming and going. All she knew was the burning pain of Thomas dying. The wretched feeling ate away inside her, blocking out her ability to think or act. Her little boy had been flung into the cold black water and drowned. Had he called out for her? He must have been so frightened, his little body sinking beneath the rough waves, gasping for air, wanting his mammy.

Nightmares of his last moments plagued her. After the funeral Father Kilcoyne had given her brandy to drink and she was sure Riona had given her something, some herb to help her sleep for she hadn't been able to stop her tears and then she remembered nothing.

But when she woke, the pain returned. All she wanted to do was curl up into a ball in bed and hide from the truth that her precious son no longer breathed. She'd never hear again his soft laughter, his gentle voice as he pleaded to go out on the boat with his grandpa. How would she bear going through life not having him in it?

A knock on the door made her jump.

Colm entered, his face solemn. 'God bless all in this house,' he murmured.

'God bless you,' Ellen replied, as did the children.

Colm placed a plucked and trussed chicken on the table. 'Austin, start cooking that in the pot.'

Ellen stiffened. Over the years she had always refused Colm's gifts, stating that she'd not be beholden to him when she had a husband who could provide for them. To her it felt as though his gifts came with a price, a price she didn't want to acknowledge.

'Now don't be saying you're not accepting it, Ellen.' Colm raised his hands. 'Not this time, when you're all suffering such loss. I'll not have it, do you hear? It's just a chicken, that's all.'

Just a chicken. She could have laughed at him. She'd not had a chicken boiling in her pot in over a year or more. 'Thank you, Colm.'

'Where's my brother?'

She shrugged. 'I've not seen him since we . . . we laid Thomas to rest . . . '

'I know he got drunk that night with me, but I thought he'd have come home to stay.'

'He did for a while,' Austin said, busy at his task of raking the fire to create more heat. 'He left again yesterday.'

37

'You must come to me, Ellen. I can look after you and the children.'

She shook her head. 'I'll go to my family. Austin don't put the chicken in the pot. We'll take it to your gran's so we will.' She pulled her shawl over her head and taking Bridget's hand, led the children outside.

'Ellen, please.' Colm followed her out. 'Malachy would want me to take care of you all.'

She turned, finding an anger simmering in her chest. 'Malachy? The husband I never see? I no longer care what Malachy wants, and that's the truth of it. May the devil take him for all I care.'

'Let me help you. I have friends who will keep you fed. I'll take Austin and Patrick with me. I've need of them.'

Ellen's rage snapped. 'You've need of my sons? Really? In what way? For you have a labourer work on your land while you gallivant all over the countryside doing secret business. Is that what you want my sons for, to help you with your clandestine meetings?'

'I don't know what you mean?' He looked shocked, yet guilty.

'I'm not stupid, Colm. Stay away from my boys and stay away from me!'

She marched away down the rutted dirt track towards the curve of the beach and to her parents' cottage. She walked in silence, an angry silence that the children dared not break.

Entering the cottage, she noticed the coldness of the room. The smoking fire gave no heat yet Riona and her mammy huddled around it with Mammy clutching her rosary beads.

Riona stood and embraced Ellen. 'I'm glad you came.' She turned to Austin. 'What's in the basket?'

38

'A chicken from Uncle Colm.'

'A chicken.' Riona's eyes widened. 'Goodness. We'd best cook it for our supper then, hadn't we? Shall we go down to the beach and get some seaweed to add to it?'

Austin nodded eagerly. 'We might find a crab or two in the baskets. I sank them this morning.'

Mammy lifted her head as Riona ushered the children outside. 'Go careful!' She sighed as the door closed behind them. 'Sit down, daughter. You're blessed to have such generous kin.'

'His gifts come with a price, Mammy.'

'Colm Kittrick seems well set up.'

Ellen gave her a sideways glance. 'I'm not sure how Colm manages it. He seems to become wealthier as we grow poorer.' Ellen sat on the bench seat beside her mammy and took her hand.

'You married the wrong brother, girl.'

'Don't say that. I get enough of that from Colm.'

'Well, he has a point. Malachy was all good looks and charm when you were younger and worked hard at the beginning, but where is he now when you need him the most?'

'I have no answer to that, but I have never liked Colm.' Ellen glanced at her da's chair opposite and a fresh pang of loss enveloped her. She'd never receive her da's loving smile or his soft touch on her shoulder.

'Malachy is the head of this family now,' Mammy said. 'He's needed here, not God knows where.'

'He thinks he's doing good being out there looking for work.' Ellen gazed down at the floor. 'Sure, and what good is it for him to make money only to spend it in a tavern?'

'The rent is due next week, and we don't have it.'

Mammy sighed.

Ellen paled. The rent. She didn't have it, either. She'd not given it a thought for days. She had nothing to sell either. 'You must come to me, Mammy. One rent is easier to find than two, so it is.'

'To you?' Mammy looked affronted. 'Leave my own house? Sure, and the very thought is a devil's curse.'

'You and Riona can't stay here alone. The rent is due. Give up the cottage and come to me. Riona might find work in Westport and with my position at Wilton Manor and whatever Malachy provides, we'll manage just grand.'

'You only get work when the manor has guests. I'll not be a further burden to you.' Mammy glanced around the room as though listening to past voices, remembering get-togethers and times when the room was full of people and laughter. 'This place holds so many memories. I've lived here for nearly forty years. I first came as a young bride, so I did.' Her blue eyes so like Ellen's misted. 'Here I gave birth to ten children and I only have you and your sister left. To leave would be to leave them.'

'No, Mammy. You take them with you in your heart. They are safe there and will never leave no matter where you are.'

'I feel so tired, lass. So tired of burying those I love or saying goodbye to those that have crossed the water to start new lives elsewhere. This is my home. I want to die here.'

'Aye, but without the means to pay the rent you'll have to leave, anyway.'

Mammy nodded to her spinning wheel, sitting in the corner of the room. 'It's to be sold for the rent.

Father Kilcoyne says he'll get a good price for it in Westport. It's not enough though.'

'Oh no, Mammy, not your wheel.'

'Sure and haven't I had it longer than I expected to? We only kept it as your da still managed to bring in the fish. Now that income has gone . . . The wheel is the last thing we own worth anything. It is to save us from going into the workhouse.'

'And what will happen in March when the rent is due again? You can't waste any more money on this place, Mammy. You must come to me, please.' Ellen stood and paced the room. 'I'm your daughter, it's my duty to care for you.'

'And a dutiful daughter you are to me.' Mammy wiped her eyes with a scrap of lace that had once edged a linen handkerchief. Lace making was a special talent Mammy had and one which her two daughters hadn't mastered to the high standard she expected. 'In truth, this place is too quiet without your da and grandpa here.'

'You and Riona will come then?'

Mammy nodded, beaten by the knowledge that life had changed. 'I'll get Father Kilcoyne to sell the wheel and it'll help towards your rent.'

'Mammy — '

'I'll not be changing my mind, so I won't. It's done. Shall we start packing then? We might as well return with you this evening after we've eaten.'

'I'll be away to work in the morning,' Ellen murmured, taking baskets from a shelf in the other room which had been her and her sisters' bedroom when Ellen lived at home. Her brothers had slept in the loft and her parents had slept on a bed in the corner of the main room.

41

'Aye, at least you have that.' Mammy filled the baskets with the pitiful amount of remaining kitchen utensils while Ellen packed the few items of clothes and thin blankets.

Ellen thought of the elderly Mr Wilton, the man who owned Wilton Manor and who, despite being a wealthy Protestant Englishman among a countryside of Catholic Irish, was kind and considerate to his employees. She knew Austin had run to the manor and told them about Thomas. She hoped Mr Wilton would understand why she hadn't turned up for work this week.

'What will Malachy say about us coming to stay?' Mammy asked.

Ellen shrugged and rammed an old duck-down filled pillow on top of the basket. 'Malachy has to be home to notice.'

★ ★ ★

Ellen slipped into the large kitchen of Wilton Manor the following morning just as dawn broke.

'Hey now, Ellen.' Mrs O'Reilly, the manor's cook, gave Ellen a look of sympathy. ''Tis good to see you, so it is. What a time of it you've had. It shocked us to hear of the loss of lives from the storm and you and your family hit the hardest of them all.'

'Thank you, Mrs O'Reilly.' Ellen swallowed, not wanting to dwell on Thomas, for tears were never far away and she couldn't break down this morning. 'Has Mr Wilton mentioned anything about me? I've still got my position?'

'Aye, he spoke to Mr Israel saying he was sorry to hear of the tragedy and that your place is secure here

42

while you mourn.'

Ellen relaxed and unwrapped her shawl from her shoulders. 'He's such a kind man. I'll set to work straight away.'

'Aye, get the fire going in the dining room first and then his study and then come back and have a cup of tea. Mr Wilton's last guest left yesterday, and Kathleen cleaned the bedroom since you weren't here.'

Ellen donned a large apron over her black dress, a dress that was becoming more threadbare by the day, and grabbed her box of cleaning materials and another bucket full of screwed paper and kindling.

From the kitchen she followed a narrow corridor past the stairs and taking the first door on the left entered the dining room with its long mahogany table, polished to a shine which reflected the room's contents. She flung open the heavy red damask curtains, letting in the weak sunshine.

Quickly setting to work, Ellen cleared out the ashes from the previous evening, swept the green-tiled hearth and laid the paper and kindling in the grate and set a match to it. Coaxing the flames, she added a few more sticks, allowing the air to draw the fire. While she waited, she used a damp cloth to wipe the tiles clean and then added small pieces of wood from the brass wood store beside the fire.

Satisfied the fire would take hold, she settled the fireguard around it and began polishing the surfaces. The mantelpiece was cleared of ornaments and wiped down before everything was replaced upon it. Next, she shook the curtains and made sure they hung in neat pleats. In summer she would open the window to listen to the birdsong, but with a cool day such as today she kept them closed.

'There you are,' announced Kathleen, the other housemaid, who came in carrying a sweeping brush and a box of cleaning materials. She gave Ellen a timid embrace and then stepped back. 'Your dear heart must be broken in two.'

'Something like that.' Ellen nodded, gathering up her bucket and box.

'Poor dear Thomas, such a sweet wee lad.'

Ellen briefly shut her eyes as the sudden the image of her son filled her mind. 'I'd best get on. Keeping busy helps.'

'We'll have a cup of tea shortly.'

In the study, Ellen closed the door and leant on it. Her chest squeezed with pain whenever she thought of Thomas. When the children sat at the table, she looked around for Thomas before remembering he wasn't there. Last night, she'd washed them in front of the fire with a rag dipped in water warmed from the fire and then tucked them into bed. She kissed three faces instead of four, and it had been almost too much to take. Thankfully, she had Mammy and Riona to fuss over and settle in before climbing the ladder to her own bed, which she shared with Riona while Malachy was away.

Malachy.

Pushing away from the door, Ellen knelt before the fireplace and started to clean out the ashes.

What was she to do about Malachy? They couldn't go on as they were. His fleeting comings and goings had to stop. He had to find suitable and secure work. Maybe she could ask Mr Wilton about a position for him here on the manor. When she'd mentioned it before to Malachy, he had flatly refused to consider it. He had every intention of rebuilding their own

44

farm, but how he'd manage that with no money to buy beasts or seeds for crops she didn't know. And now his drinking took control over him, leaving nothing left of the man he used to be.

Successfully lighting the fire, Ellen set to tidying the study. She opened the curtains, cleaned the cigar ash from the crystal ashtray on the desk and collected the newspapers from the floor and piled them onto a chair in the corner.

The door opened and Mr Wilton ambled in, only to stop on seeing Ellen.

'Mrs Kittrick. This is a pleasant surprise. I wasn't expecting you back here so soon.'

'Forgive me, sir, for not coming in for the last few days . . .'

'Nonsense, there is nothing to forgive, dear woman. You've lost your son, father, and grandfather in one treacherous night. What a state you must be in.' He walked to his desk and faced her. 'I hope you didn't think I would dismiss you for not turning up?'

'I had hoped you wouldn't. I know you to be a kind and decent person.'

He smiled. 'The same could be said of you, Mrs Kittrick. You're hard-working and punctual no matter what the weather. You're a credit to your family.'

'Thank you.' Ellen gathered her cleaning products. 'Do you wish for me to polish in here now, sir?'

Mr Wilton ran a hand over his sparse grey hair. 'No, Mrs Kittrick. By the look of you, I think you should return to the kitchen and have something to eat. You cannot afford to become ill. Your children need you.'

'I'm grand, so I am, sir.'

He raised his eyebrows, not believing her.

Ellen twisted the cloth in her hands. 'Sir, I was

45

wondering if I could speak to you about a position in one of your establishments for my husband, Malachy?'

Mr Wilton's expression was full of pity. 'I'm sorry Mrs Kittrick, but I've employed as many people from the area as I can, more than I should, really. I've tried to do my best to keep people alive during these difficult times.'

'Yes, of course.' She knew of his generous spirit. He employed many people at his farm a few miles away, as well as the small factory he owned in Westport.

He suddenly looked horrified. 'You are not for the workhouse, are you?'

'Oh no. No, sir, it's not come to that yet.' She dreaded the thought of the workhouse. For her family to end up in that institution would be the end of her.

'So, your husband is still out of work?'

'He manages the odd day here and there, sir.'

'But it's not going to be enough, and as winter approaches, he might have even less than that?'

She nodded. 'Malachy has lost his way a little. He means well but . . . ' She hated that she had been reduced to begging for work for her husband, the man who once had been her rock, her anchor, and who had worked his fingers raw to improve their lot.

'I'll see what I can do, Mrs Kittrick.'

'Thank you.' She paused, not wanting to push her luck.

'Is there anything else?'

'Just if it's not an inconvenience, if you should hear about any work for my sister, Riona, that would be grand.'

'I will let you know should I hear anything. Go to the kitchen. Polishing can wait. I am away for the rest

46

of the day and Mr Israel is also out running errands for me so you and Kathleen can have the place to yourselves to do what must be done. Go along now and eat something. You're a walking skeleton.'

'Thank you, sir.' Ellen made her way back to the kitchen and found Mrs O'Reilly and her kitchen maid, Patsy, ladling eggs, and bacon into warming silver bowls to take into the dining room.

Ellen's stomach rumbled at the delicious smell.

'You have done for the moment?' Mrs O'Reilly asked, adding a toast rack to the tray.

'Mr Wilton said for me to go to the kitchen.' Ellen looked up as Mr Israel joined them from his butler's pantry. 'Good morning.'

'How are you, Mrs Kittrick?' the butler asked stiffly, not being one to be friendly.

'Well, thank you, Mr Israel.' Ellen helped Patsy finish the tray in readiness for Mr Israel to take into the dining room as Kathleen came in humming a tune.

She stopped humming on seeing Ellen. 'Sorry, Ellen. I didn't think of you in your mourning.'

'Don't be sorry. You're allowed to hum, Kathleen. It's fine to be happy.'

'What have you got to be happy about, Kathleen?' Mrs O'Reilly asked, pouring out cups of tea for them all.

'Nothing.'

'Liar.' Patsy grinned. 'I saw you walking with Jamie Curry last evening.'

'So? Sure, and it's not criminal to walk with a man now is it, Patsy Donnelly?'

'Hush the pair of you.' Mrs O'Reilly glared. 'Just you be careful, Kathleen. Jamie Curry is known for his antics with young lasses, so he is.'

47

Kathleen tutted. 'Not with me, he won't. Not until we've said our vows before Father Kilcoyne.'

''Tis getting married you are now?' Patsy scoffed. 'Not likely if his mammy gets a say.'

'Well, she don't!' Kathleen huffed.

'Girls, enough. Go out and get some more water, Patsy. Kathleen empty those buckets of ash, too.' Mrs O'Reilly sat down opposite Ellen. 'There's never a minute's peace with those two.'

'Altogether it's nice to hear normal chatter, so it is. At home we all speak in whispers, in dread of what the future will bring.'

'Nay, lass, it's a troublesome time. How's your man doing? Found work yet?' The cook handed Ellen a bowl of warm creamy porridge.

Again, Ellen's stomach rumbled with hunger. 'No. He's never home though.'

'Can you keep your farm?'

'I don't think we can. We might make this rent payment if Malachy returns with some money, but how we'll make the next rent I don't know. Malachy refuses to put potatoes in the ground again. He says it's a waste of good coin, but how else will we survive? The blight can't continue forever, surely?'

'Who can say?' Mrs O'Reilly sipped her tea and gave Ellen a few minutes to eat her porridge. 'Have you thought of emigrating?'

'Emigrating?' Ellen glanced up from the delicious porridge, wishing she could take the pot of it home to the children. The meals she ate at the manor had kept her alive during the past few years. Eating at the manor allowed her to give what little food she could grow or scavenge to the children. Sometimes, Mrs O'Reilly sent her home with a basket of leftovers, but

48

not often as Mr Wilton asked for all spare food to be handed out to those walking the roads that came to the back door begging and were barely alive.

Mrs O'Reilly refilled her teacup. 'My cousin and his family are out in Canada now. Left last year and another side of the family sailed to America three years ago. They're doing very well. They've a farm and settled into a small community. The wee children go to school and are growing like weeds, apparently. You should think about it.'

'I've no wish to go to America.'

'It might be the fresh start you all need. If I didn't have this good position, I'd join my cousins for what is left for us here? The landlords are tossing people out of their cottages quicker than the blight can ruin potato crops. All around us is the legacy of years of devastation and loss and graveyards full of headstones and crosses. What have we got left to stay for?'

Ellen scraped the bowl clean as the girls returned, filling the room with chatter. Rising to her feet, Ellen gathered her cleaning box and fresh cloths, her mind repeating Mrs O'Reilly's words. *What have we got left to stay for?*

4

Tossing and turning, Ellen gave up on sleep as the sun rose the following morning. She dressed quietly, so as not to disturb Riona, and climbed down the ladder.

Her mammy still slept, so she gently poked at the fire and added peat to it before going outside to relieve herself.

The chill of the frosty morning woke her fully and she shivered. Returning inside, she drank a mouthful of water from the bucket and tugged on her dusty black boots that hadn't seen new soles or been polished for several years now. She sighed at the other boots by the door. Her children's footwear were in a sorry state as well. Austin had outgrown his and needed a new pair. How would she get the money for those? Patrick had Austin's old pair, but the sole was coming away from the rest of the boot and had been tied together with twine and poor Bridget had never owned boots and instead wore wooden clogs Da had made for her.

Winter would soon freeze them, and she didn't know how they'd survive it. Last winter the children spent every day by the fire as snow piled up around the cottage, shutting out the world and shutting them in. Malachy had dug them out on his return and brought a bag of cornmeal and a string of fish Da had given him as Malachy passed their cottage, but the smell of brandy on Malachy's breath had soured Ellen's enjoyment of her husband's return. It had only worsened as time went on and Malachy became more unreliable.

How would they survive this winter?

Wrapping her shawl around her closer, she closed the door behind her and started the long walk to Wilton Manor. Along the road she kept hoping to see Malachy walking home, but she was disappointed in that. She needed him home and with the rent money.

Perhaps it was a good thing he wasn't about? She doubted she could speak two civil words to him, such was her anger towards him. He had left her when she needed him the most. Their son had died, and he had gone. They hadn't comforted each other or shared their grief as parents should. No, he had gone the minute the dirt left his hands that he threw on Thomas's coffin — a plain wooden coffin that Colm had paid for.

Malachy's only saving grace would be to return with pockets loaded with coins, anything less, and she feared she would do him harm.

The sun lifted above the mountains, spearing the landscape in golden arrows. A rabbit, its white tail bobbing, ran for cover as she rounded a bend in the road. Aside from the rabbit, she was alone. The countryside she'd grown up amongst which once was filled with sheep and cows and cottages with chimneys of smoke spiralling out of them no longer existed. Instead, she was surrounded by wasted fields, ruined cottages, stone-mounded graves and the smell of death.

How long could she hold on to the farm?

Rent was due tomorrow. She'd have to walk into Louisburgh in the morning and report that she couldn't pay it. How would she stand the humiliation?

The added care of Riona and Mammy weighed heavily, too. Riona needed to find work. With Da gone and no fish to sell, Riona might need to become a domestic servant as Ellen was. It was a discussion they'd have tonight, whether Riona wanted to or not.

In the manor's kitchen, Mrs O'Reilly was rolling out dough on the table as Patsy and Kathleen scurried around preparing the breakfast, a look of concentration on their faces. The smell of pork chops frying made Ellen's mouth water. She'd eaten nothing since her porridge yesterday, eking out the limited food Mammy brought with her to feed the children.

'Oh good, you're here,' Mrs O'Reilly said. 'There's a cup of tea over there for you.'

'Thank you.' Ellen sipped at the sweet milky tea, wishing she could savour every mouthful but knew she'd need to hurry.

'Mr Wilton returned last night with a guest who is unexpectedly staying a few days. Will you start in the dining room first? Mr Israel says the front parlour needs opening up. You might need to stay longer today.'

'I'll get started.' Reluctantly, she gulped the rest of the tea.

'Oh, and Ellen . . .'

'Yes?'

'You might want to go into the scullery and freshen yourself up a bit. You've a dirty mark on your face.'

Embarrassed, Ellen hurried into the scullery and looked in the mirror that was there for the maids to check their appearance before entering the main house.

Her dark auburn hair was lank and in need of a wash. She tied it up and then taking a cloth washed her face clean. She stared at her reflection, noticing her dark blue eyes and shadows beneath them. Her

52

cheekbones protruded. Once she had been a beauty, everyone said so. Like her mammy, she'd turned men's heads when she'd been a girl ripe for marriage. Now she hardly recognised the woman looking back at her.

Ellen donned her apron and grabbed the box of materials and headed into the dining room. She worked quickly, cleaning out the fire and relighting it, before polishing the mantle as Mr Israel came in to set the table for breakfast.

'Did Mrs O'Reilly mention you are needed longer today, Mrs Kittrick?' he asked, placing knives and forks on the table.

'Yes, Mr Israel, and I'm happy to, of course. My mammy and sister are at the cottage so the children will be fine.'

He set out the plates and bowls on the sideboard. 'Good. Mr Wilton's guest, a Mr Rafferty Hamilton, is staying and so the front parlour needs to be ready for use. We all know how Mr Wilton likes to close off rooms when he is at home alone.'

'Aye, I'll see to it.'

'Do it before going into the study, as the men may sit in there after breakfast before they go out. Oh, and Kathleen will need help with the upstairs, too. Mr Hamilton's late arrival meant Kathleen had to quickly make up the bed, but we attended to nothing else. We need the room cleaned and a fire lit.'

'Very good, Mr Israel.'

He nodded and left her to fetch the food warmers.

After finishing in the dining room, Ellen hurried into the parlour. She liked this room best of all in the house. Mr Wilton was an enthusiastic traveller, and he'd filled the room with books and keepsakes from his travels.

Opening the heavy drapes, light flooded the room, warming the green silk wallpaper and highlighting the furniture. A cream damask sofa sat before the fire, and Ellen brushed it down and plumped up the cushions.

She polished the two small occasional tables, carefully handling the porcelain ornaments of birds and horses. She took the lamp into the butler's pantry for Mr Israel to refill and clean, before returning to set a match to the paper and kindling in the fire grate.

As the flames took hold, she tidied the cushions on the padded window seat and then swept the large oriental red and blue rug and the polished timber floor. The small writing desk, not used by Mr Wilton but there for his guests, received a polish and she couldn't help but gaze at the globe sitting on top of the desk.

With a fingertip, Ellen turned the globe, reading the names of countries she'd heard Father Kilcoyne mention, foreign sounding places thousands of miles away. Her finger paused on the lower side of the globe. Terra Australis. Australia.

In the rare times she had studied the globe before when cleaning this room, she often wondered about the country that people spoke about in whispers. The place where fellow countrymen had been sent in chains. A British colony on the other side of the world where no convicts returned from, at least none she knew about. How did they fare, so far from Ireland and home?

'Good morning.'

Ellen spun on her heel, alarmed at being caught looking at the globe. She bobbed her knees, lowering her head. 'Good morning to you, sir.'

'I was looking for Mr Wilton.' His smile reached his

light blue eyes the colour of a midsummer's sky and which were framed in long black eyelashes.

'Oh, he'll be down shortly, sir.' She stared at the tall, black-haired man in a tailored pewter-grey suit, the colour of which was never worn in this area of brown and black. 'He goes straight into the dining room,' she added, and felt it was a foolish thing to say.

'Which is where?' Again, the charming smile.

'Down the hall and the first door on the left.'

He studied her. 'You were looking at the globe?'

'I was,' she admitted.

'The world is a fascinating place, is it not?'

'Yes.'

He walked closer and turned the globe. 'It's hard to imagine those countries so far away from us filled with people who speak different languages and have different colour skin to us.'

She nodded, watching him and not the globe. He was tall with striking features. There was something about him that caught her attention. She'd seen many of Mr Wilton's guests before, but never spoken to them at any length.

'Where would you like to go? If you had the choice?' he asked her.

'I don't know. Father Kilcoyne says there is nowhere better than Ireland.'

'Has Father Kilcoyne ever travelled?'

'He's been to Rome as a young man, and England.'

Mr Hamilton glanced at her. 'Perhaps Father Kilcoyne is correct. For Ireland does have incredibly beautiful countryside.'

'But you think there are better places?' she dared to ask. Why was this gentleman talking to her as though she was his equal?

55

He straightened, his gaze on her. 'I have travelled to many countries in Europe and yes, there are many excellent places to see.'

For several moments they simply stared at each other.

'I should go to breakfast.' He bowed his head and left the room.

Cheeks hot, Ellen took a deep breath as though realising she'd not taken in air. So that was Mr Rafferty Hamilton. He was English, his accent told her that much, and her eyes told her that he was one of the handsomest men she'd ever seen.

A glance in the mirror above the fireplace made Ellen groan. Her lank, greasy hair had escaped the ribbon that held it. Her white apron had ash dust smears on it, and her ancient boots poked out beneath her worn black skirt.

Sighing, she left the room and entered the kitchen to collect clean cloths and an empty bucket.

'What's he like, Mr Israel?' Kathleen asked.

Mr Israel gave the sparkling silver teapot another wipe with his special polishing cloth just for the silver. 'He's a gentleman from England. Mr Wilton met him on one of his visits to London last year. They are in business together, have shares in the same company, shipping I believe.' Mr Israel inspected the silver teapot and satisfied it met his standards he took off the lid and warmed it with hot water, then allowed Mrs O'Reilly to pour in the tea from the plain brown earthenware one she used for the kitchen staff.

'I saw him just now,' Ellen said, heading for the door.

'You did? He's down so early?' Mr Israel quickly added the teapot to the tray and carried it out to the dining room. 'He didn't ring for me to help him dress.'

'What's he like? Young or old?' Kathleen asked, slicing the bread loaf.

'In his thirties, perhaps.' Ellen thought of the man's friendly smile and couldn't but help to feel happier for it. It was rare to see a genuine smile these days from anyone.

'Come along then. We've a lot to do today,' Mrs O'Reilly chivvied them back to work.

Ellen went along to the study and began to clean the room, her thoughts on the Englishman seated in the next room enjoying his breakfast of sausages and pork chops, kippers, and eggs. Her stomach rumbled at the thought of it.

Did he know of the hardship in this part of Ireland? Did he care? Of course, he wouldn't care, why would he? He was English, and they saw to themselves and ignored the poverty and plight of the Irish, especially those as poor as Ellen and her family.

She wasn't into the politics that filled the local men with anger and hate. She had enough to worry about keeping her children fed and warm to weigh in on the state of Irish politics. In the past, she'd heard enough of it from Colm. She wasn't stupid, and she knew they were the unforgotten part of the British Empire. Being able to read meant she understood the articles in the newspapers in Mr Wilton's study that spoke of taxes on the landlords, which was why they wanted the tenants off their land and replaced with sheep. Every building a landlord had on their land was taxable, sheep were not.

She knew the world wasn't fair or just, but she left it to those who could fight, who could have a voice. Whereas she, Ellen Kittrick nee O'Mara, wife and mother only needed to look closer to home for her own fight. Rent money and food was all that concerned her.

Was Malachy at the cottage?

The thought that he might have earned some money gave her the spurt of energy to complete her tasks in record time.

Back in the kitchen after she'd finished, she wearily sat at the table with the others and ate toast and kippers for breakfast, trying not to eat too quickly and savour each mouthful. Staying longer to clean upstairs would mean she'd have a midday meal here, too. Maybe she could save it to take home for the children as she had on other occasions. They enjoyed the little treats she was able to bring home for them.

Kathleen chatted away as they cleaned upstairs, and Ellen knew she didn't have to add to the conversation. Her energy was draining away as the hours ticked by. Together they stripped Mr Wilton's bedsheets and remade the bed before cleaning the room and setting the fire ready for the evening.

In the guest bedroom, Ellen noticed Mr Hamilton's tidiness. His blankets had been straightened, but she took care to remake the bed again for him, while Kathleen dusted around the room. Nothing personal was left out, and Ellen left the bedroom no more the wiser about Mr Hamilton.

Downstairs, Mrs O'Reilly carved a ham to go with their boiled cabbage and carrots.

'May I take my meal home, Mrs O'Reilly?' Ellen asked, washing her hands as the clock on the wall chimed one o'clock.

'Sure, you can. For the kiddies?'

'Yes.' Ellen sipped a cup of tea, allowing herself that

58

much.

In the scullery, she took off her apron and wrapped her shawl around her. From the window she saw the trees swaying in the wind and sighed. Rain looked ready to pour down any minute.

'Will you bring back the basket tomorrow?' Mrs O'Reilly handed Ellen a basket with a cloth covering the top.

'Tomorrow? It's Saturday. I don't usually come in on a Saturday.'

'Aye, I know, but Mr Wilton saw me before he left after breakfast and requested that you come in as he's having a few friends over for dinner and with Mr Hamilton staying, I'll need extra help in the kitchen.'

'That'll be grand.' Ellen peeked under the cloth and saw a generous amount of ham slices, half a loaf of bread, a few eggs, carrots, and the other half of the cabbage. 'You're very charitable, Mrs O'Reilly. God bless you.'

'You've got lovely children, Ellen. I can't see them go without. We've lost too many young 'uns as it is. I heard only this morning from Billy O'Hara when he delivered the post that the Hastings family from Louisburgh lost two children overnight from fever. The family had been sleeping rough since losing their farm. My grandma was a Hastings.' Mrs O'Reilly made the sign of the cross and Ellen followed suit.

'God bless the family. Thank you for the basket. I'll see you in the morning, so I will.' Ellen nodded; her chest tight with gratitude.

Although the basket was heavy, Ellen didn't mind in the slightest. She swapped the basket to each arm as she tiredly trudged home in a wild wind that whipped her hair into her eyes and the skirts about her legs.

The children would be excited to see the basket's contents, and there was enough to feed Mammy and Riona as well.

A couple of horse riders came thundering up the dirt road behind her, and Ellen moved aside to give them clear passage.

The front rider slowed down, and Ellen groaned as Major Sturgess grinned down at her. He kicked his horse to step so close to her that she had to jump into the road's muddy ditch to avoid being trampled on.

'May the devil take you, Major!' she shouted, suffering the cold mud seeping through the holes in her boots.

He laughed at her. 'Mrs Kittrick, why are you standing in a ditch?'

She scrambled out only for him to nudge his horse into her. Ellen jumped back, losing her balance, and landing with a thud on her back in the ditch. The shock of falling rendered her speechless. The basket lay by her side, the contents flung amongst the mud.

Sturgess roared with laughter, as did his man on the other horse.

Ellen glared at them both, then realising the ham slices were covered in mud, she screamed her anger. Quickly, she collected the items and placed them back in the basket, including the ruined ham. 'Does it amuse you to see my children starve, does it?'

'Do you have your rent money for tomorrow?' he jeered. 'Will I get the satisfaction of pulling down another cottage? As of tomorrow, your parents' cottage will be nothing but a ruin. Yours will be next.'

Not leaving the ditch, Ellen lifted her chin in defiance. 'I curse you, Major Sturgess. May you never have the comfort or love of a living offspring.' She made the sign of the cross.

He jerked back in the saddle. 'I don't believe in your peasant religious curses, you Catholic slut!' He swung his horse around and leaned down to spit at her. 'You'll soon be in the workhouse and I'll laugh like a fool when you are!'

She watched him canter away, the wind blowing in her face. Sturgess had ruined the slight happiness she had at presenting food to the children. She glanced down at her mud-splattered skirt, grimacing at the cold wetness of her backside where she landed in the bottom of the ditch.

Slowly she made her way home.

At the cottage, Riona was bending over the fire, stirring something in a pot. Ellen looked around for any sign that Malachy was home.

Riona smiled at Ellen. 'I'm boiling up some nettles for supper. I found some on a walk . . . Look at the state of you. What happened?'

'Major Sturgess, the devil's spawn.' Ellen placed the basket on the floor. 'There's food in there. You'll have to sort through it. He made me fall into the ditch and it spoilt the food.'

Mammy came in from the bedroom. She tutted at the sight of Ellen. 'Strip off those wet clothes, *a leanbh.*'

'Here.' Riona splashed some water into a bowl from a jug and handed Ellen a clean cloth. 'Have a wash.'

'The children?'

'Colm took them for a few hours to his farm.'

Ellen stiffened. 'I don't want them going there.'

'Why in God's name?' Mammy frowned. 'He's their uncle and can give them a decent meal. If you had any sense at all, you'd have accepted his offer to move

61

in with him years ago.'

'And forever be wary of his looks and touches?'

'And can they harm you?'

'Mammy! He'll not stop at looks and touches if I'm under his roof. He'll want me in his bed too.'

Riona gasped. 'You're his brother's wife.'

'Sure, and why should that stop him?' Ellen snapped.

'Would it be so bad if it means keeping your children alive? They are nothing but skin and bones,' Mammy said angrily. 'Do you want to see them die?'

'You're suggesting I whore myself, Mammy!' Ellen couldn't believe her mammy.

'I'm suggesting you survive.'

'I'll not sell myself to Colm Kittrick for a piece of bread.'

'Then we're all going to be on the road by tomorrow night then, aren't we? For I don't see your husband here with the rent money, so I don't.'

Rage burning, Ellen climbed the ladder one handed, carefully holding the bowl of water with the other hand. She stripped off her filthy clothes and washed herself, fighting the tears that threatened. *Please, Malachy, come home.* The words spun around in her mind repeatedly.

62

5

Standing outside McDermott's Hotel in the soft rain that cast a grey light over the buildings of Louisburgh, Ellen huddled in her shawl awaiting her turn to enter the building. She'd been lining up for over an hour to see the clerk, Mr Harris, who accepted the rent payments and recorded the names and amounts in his ledger.

Ellen spent the time talking to people she knew, which were pathetically few now. The famine had taken so many lives, leaving the parish filled with ghosts of past faces, empty homes, and empty streets.

The clerk's assistant came out to her, his gaze unable to meet hers. 'Mrs Kittrick, is it?'

'Yes.' From the corner of her eye, she saw Major Sturgess come out of the hotel, smirking at her.

'Sorry, madam, but we've been informed that you've not got your rent with you today. Mr Harris says he'll mark it down that you haven't paid. You've got two days' grace to pay.'

'Two days.' She swallowed. 'Sure, and it's not enough time altogether. I need another month or more. I'm saving my wages, as God is my witness, I am.'

The small man winced. 'I'm only telling you what I've been told. Forgive me.' He bowed and returned inside.

Ellen glared at the major. No doubt it was him who told Mr Harris. He made her blood boil. She turned on her heel towards Wilton Manor.

63

'Two days, Mrs Kittrick,' Sturgess taunted.

Ellen clenched her jaw, refusing to yell back at him and make a spectacle of herself in the middle of town.

She arrived at the manor and went straight to work, helping Mrs O'Reilly peel vegetables as Patsy basted the roasting chickens.

'Did the children enjoy the ham?' Mrs O'Reilly asked.

'They did,' Ellen lied. She hadn't the heart to tell her what happened with the major. Riona and her mammy had washed the ham slices and ate them ravenously. Colm had brought the children home with bellies full of mutton stew and tales of walking along Bunowen River with their uncle. The three of them had fallen asleep the minute she sent them to bed. It brought a lump to her throat to think that Colm had provided for them what their own father hadn't. At least they would have the vegetables from the basket for this evening's supper, so she wasn't letting them down today.

But what of tomorrow and the next day and the one after that? Was she being selfish in keeping them away from Colm and all he could give them?

'Ellen?'

Hearing her name called, Ellen jerked back to the present. 'Forgive me.'

'Miles away was you?' Kathleen joked.

'She should be if she had any sense,' Mrs O'Reilly muttered.

'Anyway, I was saying, can you take Mr Wilton's coffee tray into the parlour? Mr Israel has gone into Louisburgh on an errand, so it's left to us, so it is.'

'Yes, of course.' Ellen checked her apron for dirt and washed her hands. She straightened her woeful black skirt, which she'd washed and dried by the fire last night. She tidied her hair the best she could.

Her stomach flipped a little on seeing the tray set for two people. Mr Hamilton would be in the study as well. She mustn't look at him and his endearing smile.

Balancing the tray, she knocked and opened the door. The fire crackled, lighting the room invitingly considering the gloominess of the grey rainy day outside.

'Ah, Mrs Kittrick. Coffee. Excellent.'

Ellen smiled and placed the tray down. 'Shall I pour, sir?'

'Yes, please, and what delights has Mrs O'Reilly given us?'

'Your favourite, sir. Apple tartlets and cream, date pinwheels and lemon cake.'

'What a feast.' But the light fell from Mr Wilton's eyes. 'It is a travesty really, isn't it, Rafe? In regards to what we were just discussing about the state of the parish poor. I feel most put out by the bounty before us when outside my door people starve.'

Mr Hamilton sighed. 'It does put many things into perspective. But we cannot work miracles. We do what we can, which I believe is helping hundreds of desperate people. When I return to England, I'll use my influence to do what I can to improve the situation in this parish.'

Mr Wilton nodded and sipped the coffee that Ellen passed to him. 'I feel whatever we can do still won't be enough. I provide staples for two soup kitchens, but there's never enough food for those poor unfortunates who line up.'

'Emigration is a key component to survival.' Mr

Hamilton accepted the cup and saucer from Ellen, giving her one of his charming smiles.

'It is an enormous undertaking. So many of those that voyage to a new world suffer such wretched journeys. Many don't survive. Coffin ships they are called.'

Ellen shivered at the name.

Mr Hamilton tapped his fingers on his leg. 'We must do better than that with our ship. We take the passengers and cargo out of Ireland. Australia needs imports of so much. We need to be in that supply chain. And on return journeys we ship cargo from Australia, grain and wool. My business associate in Sydney, Mr Emmerson, is coordinating everything on that end. Sydney is desperate for good workers and cargo.'

'It makes sense.' Mr Wilton nodded, selecting a date pinwheel. 'Other companies are doing it. Why shouldn't we?'

'We will make money. However, it also eases my conscience that I have done something worthwhile for these people in this current situation. Visiting the workhouse this morning in Westport was atrocious. Seeing the empty farms, the starving people living in ditches and fields like animals, living off nettles and grass, babies too weak to cry . . . ' Mr Hamilton shook his head. 'You and I must work quickly. Helping people start a new life with one hand while expanding the import and export business with the other is the least we can do. Australia is the key, not America, for the competition is too fierce for the American market.'

Listening to Mr Hamilton, Ellen forgot to cut the slices of the lemon cake. His passionate words filled her head. Not all Englishmen were evil like Major Sturgess. Some like Mr Wilton, and now Mr Hamilton, wanted to help her people. She took a step back.

'Is that all you'll be needing, sir?'

'Indeed, yes, thank you.' Mr Wilton dismissed her.

Ellen walked out of the room, wanting to listen to more as the two men discussed the business venture. The last she heard was them talking about the ship Mr Hamilton had purchased.

Later, instead of going straight home, she diverted to her parents' cottage. Standing on a slight rise, with the rain on the wind, she watched as labourers under the orders of Major Sturgess set lighted torches to the thatched roof. The weather made the smoke swirl, but the age of the thatch soon sent flames soaring to the grey clouds above. A few mounted soldiers sat on their horses, chatting together as though destroying some-one's home was a minor inconvenience to their day.

Watching the roof disintegrate inwards, billowing out smoke through the cottage's door, Ellen remem-bered all the good times spent in her former home. The dances and singalongs, her own wedding, the summer days helping Da mend the fishing nets in the sunshine . . .

She turned away, unable to watch any more. Stur-gess's men would knock down the walls to deter vagrants from sheltering there, and she couldn't see it happen.

Once back at the cottage, Ellen gave Austin, Patrick, and Bridget kisses goodnight. They'd eaten a supper of boiled vegetables and all three looked slightly bet-ter for having nutritious food for the last two days. Their skin was still stretched tight over their bones, but they seemed to have a little energy instead of sit-ting balefully before the fire.

Mammy and Riona sat on either side of the fire as Ellen joined them. They shared a cup of the flavoured water they boiled the vegetables in for nothing went to waste. She told them of her day, of Mr Harris giving them two days' grace to pay the rent.

'And your cottage is gone, Mammy,' Ellen murmured. 'Major Sturgess set fire to it.'

Mammy closed her eyes. 'It fair breaks my heart, so it does.'

'I hope he burns in hell for it,' Riona murmured.

'If there's any justice he will,' Ellen said.

The silence stretched between them as each dwelled on their own thoughts.

'So, two days' grace we have, is it?' Mammy spoke into the flames.

Ellen stretched her legs out towards the heat. The rain had soaked her on the walk home. 'Mr Wilton will pay me my wages on Monday. It's not enough, but it might keep them quiet for a few weeks.'

'And what of food?' Mammy didn't look up. 'The children are so thin a gust of wind would blow them over.'

'You don't need to tell me, Mammy. I have eyes.'

Riona sighed. 'I've walked miles today looking for work. I'll walk into Westport tomorrow and see if I can find something.'

Mammy snorted. 'Walk into Westport? Are you a fool? You barely made the walk back from the village, never mind walking the four hours to Westport. You think you can work all day and then walk four hours back here on an empty stomach?'

'I need to do something, Mammy!' Riona cried, tears in her eyes. 'Ellen can't do it all.'

Suddenly the door swung open, and the three women stared in surprise at Malachy. He closed the door behind him and stumbled, dirty dishevelled and so gaunt he resembled a corpse.

Ellen stood and stepped to him. 'Malachy?'

His lips twitched as he kissed her. 'I had nowhere else left to go.'

She tasted the brandy on his lips. 'What do you mean? This is your home. Where else would you go?'

'I've tried, Ellen.' He collapsed onto the stool Ellen vacated. His hands hung between his knees and through his wet threadbare coat, his shoulder bones stuck up like his shirt was on a clothes hanger.

'You've no money then?' Mammy gave him a narrowed gaze. 'Or is it all in an innkeeper's purse?'

'Mammy,' Riona scolded.

'Well, sure, and you can't tell me he's not had a drink while he's been away while my daughter works for an Englishman in his fancy home full of food?'

'Mammy.' Riona dragged her mother up from the stool and pulled her into the bedroom with the children.

Alone, Ellen stared down at the man she'd married when she was just a silly, madly in love girl. 'Something has to be done, Malachy,' she murmured. 'The rent is due in two days. That's all the grace they gave us. Major Sturgess was behind it, I'm sure. I didn't even get a chance to speak to Mr Harris.'

Malachy sighed and bowed his head.

Ellen noticed the grey hairs peppering his hair. He was only thirty years of age but looked so much older, much nearer to forty.

'I'm sorry, Ellen,' he whispered, not raising his head. 'I don't know what else to do. I've walked hundreds of miles looking for work. I'd get the odd job here and there, but nothing more. I've dug ditches and laid roads. I've worked at inns and warehouses.'

69

'If that's true, then where is the money you've earned?'

'It's been pennies, not even that sometimes when I've worked for food and lodging only. No one wants to pay good wages. There are too many men out there who will work for a bowl of gruel a day. How can I ask for money against those men?'

'I think we should emigrate.' The words were out of her mouth before she was aware of them.

He jerked up. 'No.'

'Why?'

'I said no. You'll not get me on a coffin ship.'

His words made her think of the discussion earlier between Mr Hamilton and Mr Wilton. 'Malachy, please listen. I think we can do it, so I do. Father Kilcoyne will help us — '

'I *said* no.'

'And what have we to stay for? Sure, and to stay here means to starve or be thrown out onto the road within a month. Do you want that for your children, for me?'

'I'll not go across the water. I won't.'

'Jesus, Mary and Joseph!' Ellen fumed. 'We have no choice.'

'And how do we pay for the passage, pray?' he yelled.

'There's a government assistance scheme. Mrs O'Reilly has told me about. She mentions emigration at every opportunity and has done for over a year or more.'

Malachy held up his hands. 'And say we get to America, what then? Where will we *live*? Do they *give* you a *house* the minute you step off the ship?' His sarcasm grated on her nerves.

Furious, she stared him down, hands on hips. 'I

don't know, but it's worth a try. I'd rather die trying than under a hedge in the depths of winter watching my children fade away in my arms, so I would!'

'We go to Colm.' Malachy's clipped tone enraged her further.

'I'll not go to Colm.'

'Why, for heaven's sake? He's doing well. I've no idea how he's managing it, but he's coping better than most.'

'Because he's doing things underhand, against the law.'

'An English law? Who cares?'

'Malachy, don't sound like those other men who chant freedom from English rule.'

'Why shouldn't I? It's the truth. The British don't care that we starve and die in the fields like beasts. They want us off the land so they can grow their flocks of sheep or herds of cattle and make more money than they can spend.'

'Not all Englishmen are like that. Mr Wilton has been good to us. Giving me a position in his house when we lost our crops. He works hard in this parish and others to feed the destitute.'

'That's us. Why isn't he feeding us?'

'He has been. He's fed *me*. I've managed to have a meal there to save what little food we have for the children. He's done more for us than *you*.'

'Oh, has he now? So, I'm a failure again, am I?'

Ellen swallowed back the tears. The hurt in her chest tightened. 'You keep going away to find work, yet you never bring home any money. You left after Thomas . . . I needed you here.'

'Colm said he'd look after you all.'

'I don't want *Colm* looking after us. It's for you to

71

do not him!'

'We should have gone to Colm months ago. I could have worked with him in whatever it is he's doing, but I didn't want to get involved.'

'No, because you could go to jail for it.'

He stared at her. 'We go to him in the morning, give up this cottage and live with him permanently. You'll take care of the house for him. That's my final word on it.'

'No.'

'I've decided, Ellen.'

'And will he take Mammy and Riona?'

Malachy shrugged. 'We'll ask him. He's always liked them. You and Riona and the children can work on the farm for him, and he and I will continue to do whatever it is that he does.'

Shaking her head, Ellen walked closer to the fire. 'He's in with some bad men and you know it. Yet he is never in trouble, has never once been caught. Rumours are all over Louisburgh that he's an informer for the British. He's playing both sides, Malachy. He pledges alliance to the Young Irelanders but secretly meets the British and tells them all he knows.'

'Nonsense.' Malachy couldn't meet her eyes.

Ellen scoffed at his reply. 'You knew all along, didn't you?'

'You're talking gobshite, so you are.' Malachy stared into the fire. 'He's true to the Irish cause.'

'I'll not go. Not there. Not with him.'

Malachy banged his fists on his legs. 'Devil in hell! Why not? Who cares what he does as long as the children have food and a roof over their heads?'

'We can give them that if we move away.'

'I'm staying here. This is my home. Ireland.'

'Please, Malachy, please listen to me. We can start again and with hard work we can have a better life than this.'

'We'll have a good life with Colm. He's my brother.'

'Sure and doesn't *your brother* want me in his bed. Do you want to live under the same roof as the man who lusts after your wife?'

Malachy reeled back. 'You lie, so you do! He wouldn't do that to me. I'm his kin.'

'And you're never here! You don't see the look in his eyes. He's asked me to go to him many times, but I refuse because I know he wants more. Colm has always wanted me. He got blind drunk on our wedding day and cried to my sister that I'd broken his heart by marrying you.'

Wiping his greasy hair back from his face, Malachy slumped onto the stool. 'I knew he had a thing about you. I thought he'd stopped all that nonsense years ago, so I did.'

'Ha, that's because you've hardly been home for the last couple of years. You're not here when he calls. You don't see him give me lingering lustful glances or when he touches my hand or my shoulder, his voice soft with whispered promises.'

'He wouldn't do it if I was with you though.'

'Are you saying you'd stay home if we went to live with Colm?'

'Well . . . I need to work, to provide . . . '

'Sure, and that's been working well so far, so it is.' It was her turn to be sarcastic.

'I'm trying, Ellen.'

'Not hard enough!' She marched to the ladder. 'You've failed as a husband and as a father, as a son-in-law and a brother-in-law. Go to Colm if that's what

73

you want but we won't be going.'

'Ellen!'

She ignored him and stomped up the ladder to the loft. She crawled to the bed but filled with anger she couldn't lie down and instead sat on the floor. Tears fell over her lashes and she let them fall. With or without Malachy, she would make a new life for her and her children.

Below, the cottage door slammed shut, and she flinched. Malachy had gone again.

6

On her knees, Ellen scooped the dead ashes into the bucket. Outside the rain fell, tapping at the study window in a rhythmic tune. Dawn only lightened the grey sky a little, and Ellen wished for the warm days of summer. October had brought only rain and cold winds.

Once the fire was set and relit, she dusted the room and tidied Mr Wilton's desk, which sometimes could be littered with papers and books. Shuffling away days-old newspapers, she paused as a headline caught her attention.

A very extensive and urgent demand exists in this colony [New South Wales] for Married Mechanics — particularly Carpenters, Joiners, Stonemasons, Stonecutters, Bricklayers, Plasterers, Blacksmiths, Wheelwrights, Glaziers . . . Agricultural Servants, Shepherds (especially persons v/well acquainted with Stock), and Gardeners.
A LIMITED NUMBER of such persons, provided they are of competent skill . . . , of industrious and moral habits, and not exceeding 30.

'You have time to look at a newspaper, do you?' Kathleen chuckled, coming into the room to sweep the rug. 'What's so interesting?'

Ellen handed her the newspaper. 'Read this.'

Kathleen stepped back as though scolded. 'Sure, and I can't read, Ellen. I didn't have Father Kilcoyne for my uncle and his teachings.'

Her mind whirling, Ellen frowned. 'Sorry, I forgot.'

'What does it say?'

'It's an announcement about New South Wales wanting people to go there and work.'

'New South Wales? That's in the colony of Australia.' Kathleen's eyes widened. 'They sent my cousin there. It was either that or hang him for stealing a sheep.'

'They want settlers to go out there.' Ellen studied the newspaper again.

'To be with the felons? Why?'

'There's work to be had, so there is.'

'You'd not find me going all that way.' Kathleen began sweeping. 'Mrs O'Reilly is forever going on about America or Canada. I'd hate to leave my home.'

'We don't have much of a home anymore,' Ellen whispered, her mind on the idea of emigrating. Perhaps she could talk to Mr Wilton about it and Father Kilcoyne?

For the rest of the morning, Ellen only had half her mind on her work, while she pondered on the prospect of leaving Ireland. Could she do it? Was it even possible? Would Father Kilcoyne be able to help?

'Will you take this tray into the parlour, Ellen?' Mrs O'Reilly asked, setting out the tea tray. 'Mr Israel is answering the door.'

Ellen wiped her hands and checked her apron was clean before picking up the tray and walking down the hallway to the parlour. At the front door, Mr Israel was speaking to a policeman who he beckoned inside.

Turning, Mr Israel stared at her. 'Mrs Kittrick.'

'Shall I return to the kitchen with the tray?' she

asked, not wanting to intrude on the men's business.

'Wait there,' Mr Israel ordered and disappeared into the parlour with the policeman.

Ellen stood holding the heavy tray, annoyed at Mr Israel. Sure and didn't she have enough to do without standing in the hallway?

'Come in, Mrs Kittrick.' She was summoned and saying a few choice words under her breath, she entered the parlour, smiling at Mr Wilton as she placed the tray on the small table. All four men were standing. She kept her gaze down after a glance at Mr Hamilton, who looked concerned.

'Mrs Kittrick, stay a moment, will you, please?' Mr Wilton asked as she turned to leave.

Dumbfounded, she frowned at Mr Wilton, her gaze straying to Mr Hamilton who stood by the fire, his eyes full of worry.

'Yes, sir?'

'This is Constable Gordon, from the police station in Westport.' Mr Wilton looked rather upset. 'He's come to speak to you, Mrs Kittrick, after first visiting your cottage and being told you were here.'

'Me?' Ellen's heart raced. What had she done to have police visit her? Was it to do with Colm's activities? Or the rent not being paid? The two days grace had come and gone, and it'd been over a week since the deadline to pay. Was she to be arrested for not paying the rent? The thoughts whirled in her head until she thought she'd be sick.

The constable, his hat in his hands, stepped forward. 'Mrs Kittrick. I've been told that you are married to Malachy Kittrick from this parish?'

'Yes,' she murmured, tensing for the news that Malachy had been arrested.

'I'm sorry to inform you, but we have reason to believe your husband was killed in a fight at the Red Star tavern in Westport in the early hours of this morning. I'd like you to come to Westport and identify him, please?'

Ellen stared uncomprehendingly at the constable. 'Malachy?

You think it is him?'

'We need formal identification, Mrs Kittrick, by you or some other next of kin. We have been told by reliable witnesses that they believe the man who was killed was Malachy Kittrick from this parish.'

'He's been killed . . .' She couldn't think straight.

'My dear, Mrs Kittrick.' Mr Wilton took her elbow. 'Sit down, please. This must be such a shock.'

Sitting on the edge of the sofa, the men all started talking at once. Ellen gripped her hands in her lap. It couldn't be true. They were mistaken.

Mr Hamilton bent down in front of her and gave her a small glass of brandy. 'Drink this.'

She sipped the golden liquid, which burned down her throat and set a fire in her empty stomach.

'I'll help you. I can come with you to Westport if you like?' Mr Hamilton said.

Mr Wilton patted Mr Hamilton on the shoulder. 'Excellent idea, Rafe. We'll accompany Mrs Kittrick to Westport. Israel have the carriage brought around and inform Mrs Kittrick's family. Do you know where they live?'

'Yes. I'll see to it, sir.'

Ellen's shawl was brought to her by Kathleen and in a short space of time she was handed up into Mr Wilton's black carriage with its dark green upholstered cushioned seats. In a daze, she realised this was the

78

first time she'd ever travelled in a carriage.

On the journey, the rain stopped, and the sun poked out between dove grey clouds. Ellen was too numb to make conversation and the two men seemed to understand that and talked quietly amongst themselves as they trundled along the rutted muddy roads. Ellen stared out at the passing landscape, the stone walls, the bare fields, the shelters made from branches and reeds that housed gaunt, pale-faced families. The numerous stone covered graves dotting the roadside where the dead had been buried where they fell, failed to rouse any emotion in her. She felt dead herself.

Only once had she been to Westport by vehicle. Back when she first married Malachy, he treated her to a day in the bustling town and he'd borrowed Colm's cart to take her there. Since then, she'd made the four-hour long walk to sell anything of value, and then make the exhausting walk back. Sometimes, Riona would accompany her, but often she'd make the journey alone. Using the time to have some peace from the children. At least this time it'd not be a four-hour walk, but a fine carriage would take her in half the time . . . It would take her to see her dead husband . . .

They entered the town as the sun was setting into the North Atlantic Ocean. They turned their back on the sunset as the driver steered the horses away from the High Street and down smaller roads before finally stopping in front of a stone building close to the Infantry Barracks.

Mr Hamilton assisted Ellen from the carriage and into the tall building. She didn't look around or ask any questions; she let Mr Wilton do that for her. They were guided downstairs, deep under the building,

79

which was cold and damp. An officer opened a door and led them into a large room holding tables of dead bodies covered in sheets. Water dripped down the walls, beating an eerie tattoo in the stark, freezing room.

Without preamble, the officer pulled back a frayed cream-coloured sheet to reveal a man.

Ellen steeled herself to look, grateful for Mr Hamilton's strong hand at her elbow. She allowed her gaze to slide from the torso up to the throat to the chin and finally to rest on the man's face.

Her knees buckled. In death, Malachy looked handsome and young again.

Aside from the bruising at his temple and a small cut to his lip, he looked like the young man she had married. The devilish, laughing, happy man who'd stolen her girl's heart when she barely knew her own mind.

'Is that your husband, Mrs Kittrick?' the officer asked quietly.

She nodded stiffly, just once. 'Yes.'

'Malachy Kittrick?' he asked.

'Yes.'

'Thank you, madam.'

Ellen turned and stared up at Mr Hamilton.

'Well done,' he said. His blue eyes were kind and tender, and he squeezed her elbow in support.

As he led her out, she turned once more and swiftly bent to kiss Malachy's cold lips and speak to him in their native Irish language. 'Go and be with our son. Goodbye.'

★ ★ ★

Ellen sat before the fire, Bridget on her lap and Patrick sitting at her feet. They'd attended Malachy's funeral only hours before with Father Kilcoyne holding Mass. For the first time the family wouldn't hold a funeral wake, for there was no one to attend except Colm and he didn't count in Ellen's eyes. She hated the sight of him. To her it appeared as though Colm didn't mourn his brother but instead seemed rather smug that *he* still lived.

Austin was helping Riona make a basket from reeds while Mammy sat at the table with her rosary beads slipping through her fingers as she prayed. Colm sat on the stool near the door, whittling a bird from a piece of wood for Bridget. He stayed away from Ellen since he made the mistake of telling her that he'd look after her while they stood at the grave. She'd rounded on him and given him a tongue lashing, much of which implied that the wrong brother had died.

When the knock on the door preceded Father Kilcoyne, Ellen made an effort to welcome him, though her heart and head were in a fog-like state.

'God bless all in this house,' Father said, entering and taking off his wide-brimmed black hat.

'Come sit by the fire, brother,' Mammy said. 'Sure, and you must be frozen to the bone.'

'I'm fine, Bridie.' He patted Mammy's shoulder. 'Have you eaten?'

'Colm was kind enough to bring some buttermilk and a pot of stew,' Riona supplied.

'What a blessing.' Father turned to Colm and shook his hand. 'Good man.'

Colm bowed his head. 'They are my family, Father.'

With a large sigh, Father Kilcoyne took the stool Riona offered, and she sat on the floor with Austin.

Father Kilcoyne grasped Ellen's hand. 'Now, my child. What are we to do?'

Ellen swallowed, weak from hunger as she'd not eaten since seeing Malachy lying dead. For two days she'd only drunk nettle tea, her stomach rebelling at anything else. Mr Wilton had sent a basket of food for them, but she'd lost her appetite. The future weighed on her shoulders like a heavy mantle. How was she to keep them all safe and alive? Was Colm the only answer? How long could she keep him from taking her body?

'You must eat, Ellen. Bridie tells me you refuse food,' he murmured. 'Your children need you.'

'I buried my husband today, Father.'

'I know. I was there, child.' He gave a small smile. 'If you do not eat, you'll not have energy to work. If you do not work, you'll not be able to pay the rent.'

'I can't pay it, anyway. It was due days ago, so it was.' She shrugged, not really caring. She was tired of fighting to stay alive, to survive, for what? To die on the roads or to whore herself to Colm to feed her children? Both seemed the same fate.

'Then we must work out a solution to this problem.' Father Kilcoyne gazed around at them all. 'I can find you a room to stay in Westport. Ellen and Riona might have a better chance for work in Westport. Failing that, then head south to Galway.'

Colm squared his shoulders. 'There's no need for that, Father. Sure, and I can provide for them. My home is theirs.'

'Ellen?' Father Kilcoyne quizzed her for a response.

She ignored Colm and making a decision, she stared at Father Kilcoyne. 'I need your help, Father.'

'Of course, my child. What do you need?'

'Information.'

'Information? Dear child, about what?'

'Going to Australia.'

A collective gasp filled the room.

'Holy Mother of God.' Father Kilcoyne made a sign of the cross. 'It is a dangerous voyage, Ellen. If people survive it, they don't usually return to their homeland.'

'I'll have no wish to return, so I don't. What do we have here, but empty bellies and graves of dead loved ones?'

'I'm not going,' Mammy stated, clutching her rosary beads to her chest.

Ellen stared at her. 'Sure, you are, Mammy, or you'll end up in the workhouse. Is that what you want?'

Colm scratched his head. 'You're only jesting, so you are. Australia? Is it mad you are?'

She turned to him. 'This is none of your concern, Colm Kittrick.'

'You're my family.'

'Not by choice any longer.' Ellen pointed to the door. 'Go home. This discussion isn't for you.'

'I'll have a say in what happens to my own kin!' he bellowed.

'They are *my* children and I'll decide their future.'

Riona stood beside Ellen and grasped her hand. 'We go as a family. Don't leave me behind.'

'As if I would,' Ellen murmured.

'Then if we're to go, we need to be strong. You'll eat some stew and no arguments. I saved you a few mouthfuls.'

While Riona heated up the congealed stew over the fire, Ellen knelt before Father Kilcoyne. 'Will you help us?'

He placed his hand on her head. 'Of course, dear girl. I'll do all in my power.'

'And me, brother,' Mammy said. 'Will you take care of your sister when she is alone in the world?'

'Mammy, please,' Ellen muttered in exasperation. 'You're *coming* with us.'

'No, I ain't and you can't make me. I'll stay with my brother or even in the workhouse, anything is better than dying in a ship at sea. The sea has taken my husband, my father-in-law, and one of my grandsons. It'll not claim me as well. I will die and be buried in my own country, to be sure.'

'We'll talk about it later,' Ellen said, giving her attention to Father. 'There is an assistance for people. The government pays your passage, isn't that true?'

'It is, but you have to meet a certain criteria.'

'I know something about it.' Ellen pulled a torn piece of the newspaper from inside her bodice and showed it to him. 'I saw this in the newspaper at the manor.'

Father read the scrap of paper. 'Let me look into it. There have been schemes for some years to assist folk leaving our shores. It was stopped recently, for the last decade in Australia has seen a depression in land and animal value, but recent reports are more positive. The colony needs people to help it grow and prosper.'

'Yes, that is what I've read. Mr Wilton's newspapers have many articles about Australia and emigration. They want workers.'

'That is true, my child. I believe to sail to Australia you first must sail to Liverpool, England. I, we,' he glanced at Bridie, 'have distant cousins in Liverpool. They were trying to get to America but ended up staying in Liverpool. Do you want to try your luck in

84

England first? You could stay with the cousins?'

Ellen shook her head, ignoring Colm angrily huffing and puffing by the door. 'No, not England. We sail to New South Wales where they are asking for people.'

'Well, I shouldn't think it'd be too difficult to get you selected. The colonies are crying out for single women, too many men are out there you see.'

'I'll find myself a husband then, so I will.' Riona smiled, handing Ellen a chipped cup half filled with the watery stew. 'When can we go?'

'I'll make some enquiries.' Father stood and donned his hat. 'I'll call when I have some news.'

'Pray make it quick, Father, for the major will have us living in a ditch before the week is out, I'm sure.'

'I'll go to Westport first thing in the morning. God bless you all.'

Grim-faced, Colm glared at Ellen after Father had left. 'Will you look at that?' he scorned. 'You're willing to risk your *lives* crossing the seas but won't come a mile to live with *me*? Have you rocks for brains?'

Raising her chin, Ellen took a deep breath. 'I'd risk the seas any day rather than be your whore.'

'Ellen!' Mammy shouted.

'Go home, Colm.' Ellen didn't take her eyes off him. 'I'll bring the children to you to say goodbye when we leave.'

'Malachy wouldn't want this.'

'Malachy isn't *here*,' her voice broke. 'I've wasted enough time waiting for Malachy to be the man he once was, and now he never will be. So, I make the decisions.'

'You'll regret this, Ellen.' He slammed the door behind him.

Weakened by the outburst and the emotion of the

day, Ellen sipped at the tasteless stew and managed to finish it to please Riona. She put the children to bed after listening to their prayers and then impulsively climbed in with them.

Lying squashed between their thin bodies, Bridget's arms wrapped around her neck, Ellen closed her eyes, eager for sleep and the day to be over.

'Mammy?' Austin whispered.

'Yes, darling?'

'I want to go to New South Wales.'

In the dark, she reached out to find his cold hand and held it tight. 'We'll make a new life there, Austin, I promise. A life where you'll all grow as strong as trees and will have sunshine on your backs and food in your bellies.'

'I believe it, Mammy.'

Ellen drifted off to sleep thinking of lush green fields and rivers full of fish in a land she'd only seen on Mr Wilton's globe.

7

Dusting the parlour furniture, Ellen was lost in her thoughts as Mr Hamilton walked in. She bobbed a small curtsy to him.

'How are you, Mrs Kittrick?' he asked.

'Well, thank you, sir. And may I say thank you for your kindness last week with my husband . . . '

'I am glad I was of some use. In such difficult times, it is easy for a person to do or say the wrong thing.'

'You didn't.'

Mr Hamilton gazed at her for a moment, then looked around. 'I'm searching for my diary. Have you seen it? I was certain I took it upstairs last night, but it's not in my room and I can't leave without it.'

'It's here, sir.' From the bookshelves beside the fire-place Ellen fetched the brown leather book with the gold initials REBH. 'I saw it when I was dusting, and I thought it wasn't Mr Wilton's.'

'Oh, good. I must have put it there when I was look-ing for a book to read.'

'You're leaving?'

'Yes, tomorrow.' He reached to take it from her, and their fingers touched.

The impact of his touch made her stomach clench with awareness. She stared at him and he stared at her.

Ellen clasped her hands together, her breath sud-denly short.

'Have you decided on a place on the globe where'd you'd like to visit?' he asked.

'Australia.' She gave him a small smile. 'I'm taking my family there as soon as it can be arranged.'

His eyes widened. 'You're emigrating? Goodness. That is an important decision.'

'It is, and it's thanks to you and Mr Wilton and a newspaper article I read.'

'How have we helped?'

'I heard you talking of your business . . . I wasn't prying,' she quickly added.

Hamilton held up his hand. 'I did not assume that you had.'

She relaxed a little. He had a calm way about him that eased the tension in her. Since announcing the wish to leave Ireland, Mammy had been angry with her and refusing to go. 'If I can get assistance from the British Government, then we can leave. I can't afford to pay for the tickets myself.'

'It is the very thing Mr Wilton and I have been talking about. Australia is in desperate need of good people.'

'Yes, I have been reading the same in the newspapers Mr Wilton throws out.'

'Mr Wilton told me you could read. It will stand you in good stead in the colony, that's for certain.'

It thrilled her that he'd been talking about her to Mr Wilton. 'Have you been to Australia, sir?'

'Not yet, but I intend to. Like you, I wish to see the great southern land. We are destined to be adventurers, you and I.'

She laughed softly. 'I'm willing to take the risk to venture beyond Ireland, away from the death and heartache of the past.' She thought of her sweet boy Thomas, her father, grandpa, all the brothers and sisters she'd lost along the way, and of Malachy.

Praise glowed in his blue eyes. 'I believe you have the strength of character to achieve whatever you desire, Mrs Kittrick.'

She swelled at his compliment and her heart thumped. Why did this gentleman have such an effect on her?

Mr Wilton walked in, smiling at them both. 'Ah, Rafe, are you ready to visit Green Park Hall? They are expecting us.'

'Indeed. Mrs Kittrick found my diary for me.' He held the book up as proof. 'She was also telling me her plans to travel to New South Wales.'

Mr Wilton's eyes nearly popped out of his head. 'Is this true?'

'Yes, sir.'

'Well, I say. That is astonishing, truly it is.' He took Ellen's hand and shook it vigorously. 'Excellent news, madam. It will be the best thing for you and your family.'

'I hope so, sir.'

'It will be. I promise you that.' Grinning in delight, Mr Wilton let go of her hand and turned for the door. 'I shall write to some friends of mine. They will be only too glad to help you. Contacts in Australia are vital, Mrs Kittrick, vital.'

'That would be so kind of you, sir. But it depends on whether I can get the government's assistance and be put on a waiting list. Father Kilcoyne is travelling to Westport today to find out for me.'

'Government assistance waiting list? No, no.' Mr Wilton looked aghast at the very idea.

'I was going to mention it to you, Jonas.' Mr Hamilton chuckled. 'Privately, I wondered what we could do for Mrs Kittrick and her family. We are deeply passionate about helping families, Mrs Kittrick,' Mr Hamilton explained. 'I have just this morning received word from my friend Mr Emmerson of Sydney who writes that the government there have agreed to our company sending out suitable people to Australia.'

Mr Wilton clasped his hands behind his back. 'Mr Hamilton is to return to Liverpool tomorrow and begin planning the first voyage that will incorporate immigrants as well as cargo.'

'I'm pleased for you both, sir.' Ellen gave them a small smile.

'Allow us to help you, Mrs Kittrick,' Mr Hamilton implored.

'Have we time for a discussion before we go to Green Park Hall, Jonas?'

Mr Wilton frowned. 'We do not, I'm afraid. We are late as it is.'

'Then later, this afternoon, Mrs Kittrick?'

'Thank you, sir.' Ellen gathered her cleaning materials and made for the door.

Happier than she had been for a long time, Ellen entered the kitchen.

'Everything good, Mrs Kittrick?' Mr Israel asked her from where he sat at the table.

'It is.' She nodded. 'Mr Wilton is going to help me and my family travel to New South Wales.'

Mrs O'Reilly dropped the wooden spoon she was using to mix a batter. 'God in heaven! Australia?'

Ellen nodded, hardly believing it herself.

'Oh, Ellen, this is such news,' Mrs O'Reilly cried, quickly spilling the news to Kathleen and Patsy as they came in from the scullery.

The midday meal was a happy occasion as they spoke of mystical faraway countries while eating meat and kidney pie with stewed apples for afterwards.

For the rest of the day, Ellen worked with her mind buzzing with the thought of settling in a new country, of starting again, away from the despair and grief that haunted her.

When she was summoned into the study later that afternoon, she had washed and tidied herself, leaving her apron in the kitchen. She knocked on the study door and it was opened by Mr Hamilton.

'Come in, Mrs Kittrick.' His beaming smile gave her such confidence.

'Mr Wilton is not here?'

'He has a headache and gone to lie down for a while, he sends his apologies. Our visit to Green Park Hall was a little tiring for him. Our host insisted he take us on a tour of his gardens and lake, which stretches for miles. Mr Wilton is a little worn out.'

'Well thank you for seeing me, Mr Hamilton.'

'Let us get to business, shall we?' He guided her to a chair, and he took a seat behind the desk. 'I shall need some details from you for the official papers. Shall we start with your name and go from there? I will need information about all the family going with you.'

She began to tell him of the names and ages of Mammy, Riona, herself and the children.

As he wrote, Mr Hamilton would often glance up at her and smile, putting her at ease. 'And you are a domestic servant . . .'

'Before working here, I worked our land. If it's possible, land is what I'd like to have in Australia. I know how to grow crops and look after beasts.'

Mr Hamilton continued to make notes. 'I know you can read and write English.'

'And Irish, too,' she added.

'Indeed. And your family?'

'They can all read and write. Father Kilcoyne taught us all.'

'That is a great skill, Mrs Kittrick. One that will put you in a good position in the colony.'

'Is it true there is much work there, Mr Hamilton? I am making the right choice, am I not?'

He relaxed back in the chair. 'I can only tell you what I know, Mrs Kittrick, and that is Australia needs to grow its population. Mr Emmerson tells me there are many advantages to being out there. He has done very well for himself, but he tells me that folk who have excellent work ethics and the will to succeed usually do so.'

'I can work hard.'

'I have no doubt about it.' His tone was soft, believing.

Ellen swallowed, intensely aware of him. 'All I want is for my children to be safe and happy. I just need the chance to make it happen.'

'And I want to help you achieve that.' His gaze lingered on her face. 'In this life, we do not often have the opportunity to help change people's lives in such a dramatic way. It gives me a great deal of pleasure to know that I am doing something which will benefit you and your children.'

'How do I ever repay you?' she murmured, fighting emotion. For so long she had struggled alone to survive, yet here was a gentleman she'd only known a short time who wanted to help her.

'I am not married, nor do I have any children, but if I did, I would want only the absolute best for them. My visit here to County Mayo has sickened me with the loss of lives and the evidence of such devastation.

92

Thousands of people no longer exist. None of that is right or just. Today in the carriage we passed two small children sitting on the side of the road, too weak to walk and their father standing by helpless. We threw coins out to them, but it is not enough. It will never be enough.' Hamilton sighed. 'Repayment is to give those children of yours the best chance they have to grow into decent people.'

She clasped her hands in her lap, moved by his words. 'I'll do my very best to make that happen.'

'I leave tomorrow morning. I have stayed longer than intended . . . ' His blue eyes held hers. 'It has been a pleasure meeting you, Mrs Kittrick. I am glad that we will meet again in Liverpool.' He gave her one of his devastating smiles that made her chest tighten.

'I'll be happy to see you again, too, Mr Hamilton.' She meant it. Something about him made her feel like a woman again.

From an inner pocket of his jacket, he pulled out a gold embossed card. 'My office address in Liverpool. Come and see me as soon as you arrive. Mr Wilton will advise you until then.'

Ellen gripped the card as though it was a magic talisman. 'Thank you.'

* * *

A week later, on her way home from the manor, Ellen walked with a slight spring in her step despite the cold October weather. Mr Wilton had just given her the best news she could wish for.

'Hail, Ellen,' Father Kilcoyne called, coming alongside her on his old horse.

'God bless and keep you, Father.'

93

'And you child.' He looked tired as he dismounted and walked beside her in the waning light. 'Let me carry that for you.'

'No, it isn't heavy.' She carried a basket that Mrs O'Reilly had filled with leftover boiled chicken and onions and a few slices of fruit cake. Since Ellen had announced her decision to emigrate, Mrs O'Reilly had been full of advice and good tidings.

'I am sorry I haven't seen you before now. I have been busy with my work. I buried the last two Finlay children yesterday. Fever has wiped out the family, leaving only Mr Finlay left. He's gone into the work-house.'

'Yes, Riona heard the talk in Louisburgh. Mr Finlay must be suffering so to lose his wife in childbirth and then his four children from fever within a week. Poor man.'

'A sad business. I did manage to ride to Westport a few days ago, but my news isn't good, I'm afraid. To gain government assistance we'd have to apply to the British office in Dublin. Of course, I can provide an excellent letter of reference for you all, but applying will take some time. They are inundated with applications. It would be easier if you wanted to travel to America or Canada, for I could find the money to pay for you all as it's a much cheaper fare than to Australia.'

'Thank you for trying, Father. Thankfully, Mr Wilton is helping me. He and his friend Mr Hamilton are part of a committee to help those wishing to emigrate to Australia. Mr Wilton told me today that Mr Hamilton has written to him from Liverpool, and we have a place on his ship. I was going to tell you on Sunday at Mass.'

94

'How decent of them.' Father rubbed his chin in thought. 'Perhaps I should call on Mr Wilton, for I am aware of many other families wishing to try Australia rather than America.'

'Sure, and wouldn't he help them, being the kind man that he is?'

'Yes, I agree even if he is an English Protestant.' He smiled sadly. 'I will call on him this week.'

They walked in silence for a while, the only noise being the cries of the sea birds and the jingle of the horse's bridle.

'You're set in your mind then that this is the only course open to you, child?' Father asked quietly.

'It is, Father. I believe we can make a good life across the seas. We have nothing left for us here. I have to try for the children's sake. I'm excited, Father. My children have a chance to grow old out there.'

'Then this is excellent news, my dear girl. A fresh start in a country needing workers sounds perfect. It is brave that you are, Ellen.'

'No braver than the others that have gone before me.' She sniffed, smelling smoke on the cold air. 'It will be hard to leave this land for I love it, so I do, but we can't continue as we are, Father. My wages at the manor aren't enough to keep body and soul together. We'd end up in the workhouse soon enough.'

'I'd not allow that.' His earnest expression made her grateful for his continued support.

'We can't be a burden to you, Father. There are six of us.'

He glanced up as an orange glow appeared in the distance.

Ellen stared as he did, and her heart dropped to her tattered boots. 'Is that . . . ?'

'It can't be your cottage, can it?' Father quizzed as if trying to get his bearings on the landscape.

'Oh, heaven help us!' Ellen started running, the basket swinging wildly as she lifted her skirt with one hand and sprinted towards the increasing golden blaze.

Her feet slowed as she approached the cottage. Dread and fear of seeing it on fire was nothing to the anguish of searching for the children. Were they trapped inside?

'Austin! Patrick! Bridget!' she screamed their names.

Breath suspended, she ran around the other side of the cottage and sagged in relief as the children cuddled against Mammy and Riona.

'Mammy!' Bridget ran to her, and she staggered as the boys joined them in a wordless embrace.

Father Kilcoyne rode around the cottage to reach them, his horse skittish at the roar of the fire as it hungrily ate away the thatched roof.

'How did it happen?' Father asked, coming to stand with them.

'Major Sturgess and his men,' Riona said dully as the heat pushed them back a few yards. Her sister turned and pointed to the group of men standing far back in the shadows.

Anger burned deep in Ellen's body as fiery as the flames ravaging her home.

'We got a few things out, but not much,' Mammy clutched her rosary beads.

'Not my rabby,' Bridget cried, burying her head into Ellen's skirt.

'I'll get you another rabbit's foot, so I will,' Austin crooned, rubbing his sister's back. Some years ago, Austin presented Bridget with a rabbit's foot cut off

the bo
and re
Maj
her to
scene.
Swa
shook
'I'll
snarle
Fro
conce
'Yes
'I d
so bac
'Dc
my m
'Bu
He
and n
make
not to
to *any*
Elle
'If '
grabb
Fathe
hang.
Sta
the d
She s
word.
'Pro
'I p
won't

from the first rabbit he'd ever snared, and after drying it out, Bridget kept the rabbit's foot to hold when falling asleep. It was the one thing she treasured, the only thing she had that was totally hers.

'May the devil roast his black soul for eternity,' Ellen spat. Glaring into the flickering shadows where the major and his men stood chatting.

Father Kilcoyne made a sign of the cross but remained silent. He showed his anger by the stiffness of his shoulders and narrowed eyes.

The timber roof joists cracked like gunshots and fell inwards. The cottage glowed red and orange in the night sky as the flames, hungry for more, demolished the items inside.

Major Sturgess sauntered over to them. 'You have no one to blame but yourselves. You were overdue for rent by weeks.'

Ellen's fists clenched by her side. 'Hundreds of people are months overdue on their rent. Why target our cottage?'

Sturgess grinned and rubbed his hands together. 'Possibly because you're too smug, Kittrick. For years, your neighbours have been dying of starvation, have walked away from their land to look for work only to die on the roadside. But not you. Somehow, you've kept a roof over your head, your children alive. How?'

'Do you think it was easy for me? Do you think we've not gone days without food?'

'I know your brother-in-law is in an even better position than you. How is that?'

'I don't know or care what Colm does, but you've just ruined everything we have. You've destroyed my children's home.'

'Perhaps you and Colm Kittrick have some kind of

97

skirt, which nearly fell back down again.

'We'll get Kathleen to fix that. Do you not have a corset?' Mrs O'Reilly held the skirt up while Ellen donned the bodice, and having lost so much weight, her ribs could be counted.

'No. I had to sell it, too.' The bodice swamped her like a coat more than a fitted bodice, but Ellen didn't care.

'Dear God. Take that bodice off and you can have my old corset. You're positively indecent.' Mrs O'Reilly shook her head and burrowing down into a drawer in the wardrobe pulled out a cream boned corset. The lace was ripped, and a hole had appeared where one of the bones poked through.

'Thank you.' Ellen wrapped it around her and offered her back to Mrs O'Reilly to pull at the stays until her body gained some shape. With the black bodice worn over it, she looked half decent. The clothes, although worn and old, were better than anything Ellen had owned in years. She instantly felt stronger in mind and spirit, though a part of her was deeply ashamed of her reduced state. Widowed, homeless, wearing borrowed clothes and on the run . . . Could her life become any worse?

'Now, let us get breakfast finished with and then you'll be able to speak to Mr Wilton.' Mrs O'Reilly sailed from the bedroom.

Ellen hurried after her. 'I'll make a start in the dining room.'

'No, Kathleen can do that. After the night you've had, you need a rest. Your mammy looks as white as a corpse.'

'We'll be fine.'

Two hours later, Ellen had done her main duties in

106

the dining room, study, and parlour. Riona had helped in the kitchen while the children had sat at the table with their grandma, as if sensing she needed them near her. Mammy hadn't spoken a word all morning.

The study bell rang on the kitchen wall. Mr Israel, having just sorted out the mail, glanced at Ellen. 'That's for you. Follow me.'

Taking off her apron, Ellen glanced at Riona and then at Mrs O'Reilly before heading to the study.

Mr Wilton sat behind his desk, accepted the mail Mr Israel handed him on a silver platter and then dismissed him. 'Please sit down, Mrs Kittrick.'

Ellen lowered herself onto the edge of the brown leather chair opposite the desk.

'Now, Mr Israel informs me that misfortune has befallen you overnight? That you and your family are in the manor's kitchen?'

'Yes. Our cottage burned down.'

'Shocking. Shocking. Your family are unharmed?'

'They escaped unhurt.' She couldn't mention Father Kilcoyne. It had to be kept a secret for her own safety.

'Now you are homeless.'

'Yes, sir, which is why I wanted to speak with you. We need to leave, today, to make our way to Dublin and from there to Liverpool to Mr Hamilton.'

'It would take you a week to walk to Dublin, especially with children.' Mr Wilton rose and paced the room. 'You have been a good worker for me and suffered greatly through some difficult times. You have managed to keep your family alive through the crop failures. You have had tragedies such as losing your father, son and husband. Naturally as a Christian and a gentleman I would help you as you are a member of

107

my staff.'

Ellen sat, hands folded in her lap, holding her breath as he spoke.

'Mr Hamilton and I discussed your predicament before he left. Therefore, you will be pleased to know that there is a small fund here for you, provided by Mr Hamilton and myself, to see you safely to Liverpool.'

Relief made her light-headed. 'Thank you, sir.'

'Now, I have letters to write for you, references and so forth. What is your sister's name?'

'Riona O'Mara.'

'And she is a hard worker and of good character such as you, for I do not know her and yet I'm writing her a reference.'

'She is, sir. You have my word on that.'

'Very well. I shall make a start.'

'Thank you, Mr Wilton.' Excitement coursed through Ellen mixing with the grief over Father Kilcoyne and the fear of Major Sturgess until she felt faint.

'Mrs Kittrick?' Mr Wilton hurried around to her side as she swayed.

'Goodness, Mrs Kittrick.' He flapped a letter to fan her face. 'Stay with me, Mrs Kittrick. I know this is all a shock for you after your ordeal last night.'

A few moments later, the dizziness cleared, and Ellen had control of herself again. Mr Wilton poured her a brandy.

'You are too kind, Mr Wilton.'

'I was raised as a gentleman by my father, who was a minister of the church. His good deeds were legendary through his parish back in England and I can only hold myself up to his standards.' He walked back around to his desk. 'Now I suggest you go back to

the kitchen and speak with your family while I make arrangements. I will have my carriage take you all to Westport, where you'll take the stagecoach to Dublin. I shall pay for it, naturally. I will give you money to purchase tickets for a boat to take you to Liverpool. I will also write to Mr Hamilton, who will guide and help you from there. Is that satisfactory to you?'

Emotion rendered Ellen unable to speak. She fought the tears burning hot behind her eyes and nodded. 'Thank you,' she croaked.

'Good. Run along now.'

Back in the kitchen, Ellen told the astonishing news to Riona and Mammy with the others listening in awe.

Mammy said nothing, but Riona smiled tearfully. 'What a good and decent man Mr Wilton is and Mr Hamilton.'

'Come and have some tea, Ellen,' Mrs O'Reilly said. 'What a morning it has been.'

By three in the afternoon, Ellen and her family stood in the manor's stable yard saying their farewells to the staff.

'Right, here we are,' Mrs O'Reilly said, lifting a large basket into the Wilton carriage. 'There's enough food in there to keep you until you get to Dublin to save paying the prices at the staging inns. They'll rob you blind with what they charge.'

'You are too good.' Ellen embraced Mrs O'Reilly. 'You've been a true friend to me.'

Mrs O'Reilly wiped away her tears. 'Write when you can.

We'll all be interested to hear how you get on, so we will.'

Ellen nodded, and she embraced Kathleen and Patsy. Mr Israel had not joined them.

With the children talking excitedly and Riona helping Mammy into the carriage, Ellen turned to Mr Wilton as he walked through the arch and into the yard.

'All ready?' he asked, handing Ellen a leather wallet.

'Yes, sir.'

'Good. Your letters of reference are in the wallet and also the money I promised for the journey to Dublin and the boat to Liverpool. Haggle the price of the tickets if you can, be wise about it and keep that wallet on you at all times.'

'I will, sir.'

'Give my regards to Mr Hamilton, and may God keep you safe, Mrs Kittrick.'

Ellen held out her hand and after a moment's hesitation, Mr Wilton shook it. 'Thank you for everything, sir. You've done your father's memory proud, for over the last few years you have saved me and my family from the workhouse and likely death. You'll always be in our prayers, so you will.'

Embarrassed, Mr Wilton coughed a little. 'Make good the new life you've been given, Mrs Kittrick that's all I ask.' He bowed and walked away.

9

Shutting the door to his office, Rafe Hamilton strode to the window that overlooked the murky, bustling River Mersey, a river that was never empty of ships and boats that docked at the busiest port in the world — Liverpool.

Amongst the tall masks dominating the clear blue October morning skyline, somewhere to the west anchored his clipper, the *Blue Maid*. It was ridiculous to be so proud of a ship that he only part-owned, but he was, he couldn't deny it. The *Blue Maid* was the start of his empire, and he was determined to create such wealth that he'd never flinch again when members of his family caused gossip and whispers in the drawing rooms of noble homes.

Rafe turned as the door opened and his younger brother, Drew, entered without knocking. Swallowing his irritation at his brother's lack of manners, Rafe sat behind his desk. He'd skipped breakfast and left the house early to avoid meeting his brother or father. 'Yes?'

Grinning, Drew took Rafe's place by the window and stared out. 'Father is on his way up. He is none too pleased with you.'

Rafe's stomach clenched, and his hands gripped the arms of his leather chair. He glared at Drew, a slighter-framed younger version of himself, but that was where the similarities ended. Drew had no moral compass, no ethics, or consideration for how the family wealth was made, and worse of all, he had

no intention of finding out. All he wanted to do was spend the money, just as their father did.

Drew went to the cabinet on the far wall and poured himself a glass of Rafe's expensive Scottish whisky, despite it only being ten o'clock in the morning. 'He is threatening to return to London. He loathes Liverpool.'

'He doesn't loathe the city's inns and gambling dens though,' Rafe murmured, trying to concentrate on the invoices in front of him.

They heard Barnabas Hamilton thumping up the stairs, huffing and puffing and generally swearing at the world for no apparent reason. He stood in the doorway, a man who once claimed to be as handsome as his sons but who, now through overindulging in food and alcohol, had grown fat and flabby. Sweating from walking up the stairs, he leaned against the door-jamb and dabbed his forehead with a handkerchief. His overcoat was slick with rain, not having bothered to take it off in the foyer where, no doubt, Rafe's clerks would still be in shock at the abuse his father doled out to anyone in his way.

'It cannot be borne!' Barnabas declared, glaring at Rafe. 'To be treated this way by my own son. You are making me a laughingstock. I will not have it, do you hear?'

Rafe shuffled the papers in his hands, knowing his father's outburst would continue for some minutes.

Barnabas stomped over to a chair. 'Pour me one, Drew, for God's sake. At this rate it will be the last drink I ever have.' Again, he glared at Rafe. 'Cut me off, will you? Who do you think you are?'

Rafe slowly looked at his father, a man he no longer respected or liked. 'I am the one trying to keep this

family from ending up in debtor's prison, that is who I am.'

'Oh, hear that, Drew? We have a bloody saint in the family. Saint Rafferty Hamilton, what do you think of that, hey?' his father sneered, taking the glass from Drew, and throwing the drink down his throat in one gulp despite it not being long since breakfast. 'You have money and do not say the opposite, for I know you do.'

'Whatever money I have is for my business, Father, and to keep a roof over my head and that of my mother and sister since you seem unable to do so.'

'Think yourself so clever, do you?'

'One of us has to be. You cannot be relied on, sir, nor can Drew, so as the eldest son I must provide.'

'And who paid for your education, your lifestyle through the years you attended Oxford? *Me.*' Barnabas handed the empty glass to Drew for him to refill.

'You did not pay for any of that, Father. Grandfather paid for my education. You lied and schemed and borrowed heavily to keep up appearances. Forever chasing after some quick money scheme to save your reputation. Oh, there were times when you won a substantial amount at the card tables and for a while the family was free from creditors knocking on the door, but it never lasted long, did it? Grandfather died clutching bills you had accumulated. What is worse is that you encourage Drew to be just like you. A wasteful drunk and a gambler with no thought to anyone but yourselves. Furthermore, I paid off all your debts by working all the hours to build an import business, a business which I lost two years ago because you and Drew lived beyond your means.' Rafe stood, anger flowing through his veins like molten steel. 'I have had to start again, spend all my days building up my reputation again, desperately constructing the finances to once more create a business I can be proud of.'

'I said I would pay you back, did I not?' his father scoffed, swilling down another glass of whisky.

'You have no means to pay me back.' Revulsion for his sire seeped out of every pore. Rafe grimaced at the state of the man whose position in society had fallen so low that he was no longer welcome in any of the London homes of the upper class where he once belonged. Where they all had belonged.

Escaping the south and the rumours had been the only course open to them. Rafe had taken his ailing mother, Olive, and sister, Iris, and fled north to Liverpool to start again. He had used his wit and intellect, and the last of his grandfather's money, to create an import and export business and called on his contacts and close friends to believe in him to make it a success.

For the last year, the business had grown enough to make him expand and think the future might be brighter than before. Unfortunately, his mother begged him to consider his father and brother. Finally, last month he had sent for them, once more paying their debts to free them from threat of prison and embarrassment in London. However, now they were here and driving him insane with their laziness and selfish ability to consider no one but themselves as they spent his money without thought or consideration.

His father burped. 'I want money, Rafe. How do you expect me to live without it?'

'Go and earn it.' Rafe flung an arm towards the window. 'Out there, men work all day to provide for their families. Join them.'

'How dare you?'

'Oh, I dare all right. I will see to my mother and my sister, both who are innocents in this mess you have made, but not a penny more will you or Drew receive from me.'

'What have I done?' Drew stood straight from where he leant against the cabinet. 'I have been on my best behaviour since coming to this godawful town.'

'Do not lie to my face.' Rafe wanted to throttle his brother. 'Do you honestly believe that I do not know about your nightly jaunts to the White Ship inn and their gambling tables in the cellar?'

Drew paled and glanced at his father. 'I only had an ale.'

Rafe laughed mockingly. 'Lying is not one of your greatest talents, brother, which is why you lose so badly at the card tables. However, I am informed that lately, at least in the last couple of nights, you have been winning, which is why you are in high spirits and not grovelling and whining as our father is at present.'

Barnabas strove to his feet. 'You jumped up pup!' He wagged his fat finger at his eldest son. 'You lord it over me, your father, and Andrew as though we are nothing but slaves to do your bidding. Well, let me tell you, son, that I have had enough of it. Do you hear?'

'And what is the alternative, Father?' Rafe jeered him on. 'Do tell me, for I am curious to know.'

'I . . . I . . . You . . .'

'You shall flounder once more, Father. You have no capital to start again, and whatever income that remains trickling into your coffers is not enough to survive on, is it? But I do not care in the slightest. Go and take Drew with you. I'll support Mother and Iris without your help.'

A timid knock on the door disturbed them.

'Yes?' Rafe barked, annoyed with himself for letting his emotions get the better of him as they always did regarding his family.

Pollard, his senior clerk, took a step into the room. 'Mr Hamilton, sir, there's a woman by the name of Mrs Kittrick here for you.'

Surprised, Rafe swore under his breath. Of all the days for her to arrive, it had to be at this moment when he was arguing with his father. 'I shall come out and see her.'

'Who is Mrs Kittrick?' Drew grinned.

Rafe simply glared at him as he left the room.

Pollard opened the door opposite, which was his own small office. 'Mrs Kittrick, Mr Hamilton.' He then left them alone.

Rafe held out his hand and smiled with genuine warmth at the woman he had met at Wilton's home and who he had thought about far too much since leaving Ireland. 'I'm delighted you came, Mrs Kittrick, though shocked it is so soon.'

She took his hand briefly, her sweet face full of worry. 'Forgive me, Mr Hamilton. My situation has changed. We are homeless.'

'That is indeed a tragedy.' His heart broke for her. This poor woman had suffered so much.

'Mr Wilton gave me the money to come to Liverpool and said I should meet with you the minute I arrived. He's says you have a ship ready, and we can sail on it to New South Wales.'

'Yes, that is correct, but it is not sailing for a couple of weeks.' Her directness made him smile. She was so refreshing from the women he had known all his life.

Rafe gazed at her, wondering why this woman's presence absorbed him as much as it did. She was a poor Irish widow in ragged clothes too large for her and looked as though a strong wind would blow her over, but there was a strength about her that he admired.

He was about to speak when he heard raised voices coming from his office. He focused on the woman before him, who was still so thin, her blue eyes haunted, yet her chin was lifted in readiness for the next challenge in life. 'Are you and your family well?'

'Yes, though Mammy is not herself... Leaving home has been a wrench, so it has.'

'Indeed, it must be difficult. However, you must think of the future. You shall sail on the *Blue Maid* for New South Wales in roughly twelve days' time if the fit out is completed on time.'

She looked stricken. 'Twelve days?'

'Yes, is that a problem?'

'I thought it would be sooner than that...' She blinked rapidly. 'Sure, and we'll find somewhere to stay until then.'

He heard the forced brightness she put into her voice, but she couldn't hide the panic in her expression. No doubt she was terrified of being in a new country without a home or means to live. 'It is all taken care of, Mrs Kittrick. I have an arrangement with the Golden Lion inn. Other passengers will be staying there as well until the ship sails. Just give the landlord your name and tell him you have come from my office. The Golden Lion is just down the street about three hundred yards away, next to Renkin and Smith's Ship Building.'

She visibly sagged. 'Thank you. That is a relief knowing we have somewhere to sleep tonight.'

He realised too late that she would have no money but what Mr Wilton gave her. Was it all gone? He was desperate to help her.

Mrs Kittrick straightened her shoulders. 'May I ask a question, Mr Hamilton?'

'Of course.'

'I've brought my family over here and I must know what is expected. I understand the passage is free, but I'm ignorant of all other details.'

'I have a business partner in New South Wales, Mr Emmerson. I believe I mentioned him to you. He has contacts with the government over there who are eager for skilled immigrants. They pay him and me and now Mr Wilton to find such people. The colony is in desperate need of respectable people with trades. They want to build the population there. Mr Emmerson asked me to send people like yourself to the colony, people who are willing to start again and work hard in a new land.'

'So, you work for the Australian Government?'

'We are paid by them, but we don't work for them as such. Aside from passengers, my ship will take cargo that Mr Emmerson will sell. I own an import and export company. Mr Wilton has bought shares in it. Everything is above board, madam, I assure you.'

'I see.' She looked thoughtful, and he liked that she was clever. No other passenger had asked him such questions. The people he had met so far seemed listless and dull, but perhaps that wasn't fair to them. No doubt they had experienced horrors during the famine and were barely alive themselves. Was it any wonder they weren't excited and inquisitive? They had endured enough.

118

He wanted to take her hand and hold it in reassurance, but refrained. 'This arrangement is all very legal, Mrs Kittrick. You are in no danger. Mr Emmerson will help you once you reach the colony.'

'He will?' Hope brightened her pretty face.

'Yes. He has secured a place for the passengers to stay until they find work and homes of their own.'

'It sounds too good to be true.'

Rafe turned his head, hearing his brother and father arguing. 'Will you wait here one moment, please?'

She nodded, and he left her to cross back into his office. His father stood by the desk and Drew behind him. They both looked guilty.

Rafe fumed. 'Is it impossible for you both to show some respect when I have company? I could hear you fighting in the other office.'

'How dare you leave us to attend to someone less important than your own family?' his father shouted, stomping his way to the door. 'Drew and I do not need you. What is more I can care for my own wife and daughter.'

Puzzled, Rafe glanced at Drew, who shrugged his shoulders and followed their father down the stairs.

Sighing, Rafe returned to Mrs Kittrick. 'Forgive me.'

'I should be leaving. I've taken up enough of your time and my family are waiting.'

He gazed down at her, for she was a foot shorter than him. 'Yes, of course. I will come and visit you this evening to make sure you are settled.'

'That is kind of you, so it is.'

When the lovely Mrs Kittrick had left, Rafe walked back into his office and sat behind his desk. Both the argument with his father and the visit by Mrs Kittrick had alarmed him. The Irish widow had grabbed his attention weeks ago in Ireland, and it confused him as to why. Ellen Kittrick was nothing like any woman he had ever been attracted to. Why her? Why now when he had so much else to concentrate on?

Shaking the morning's events from his head, he opened the top drawer in his desk. He had much to do today and pondering on his father or Mrs Kittrick would not help him accomplish anything.

Frowning, he noticed the contents of the drawer were shuffled and his leather wallet gone. A dozen thoughts whirled through his head at the same time. There was a hundred pounds in that wallet. Money he was to pay the merchants he had accounts with for the passengers to buy what they needed before sailing.

His father must have it. He was sitting near his desk earlier.

The blow hit Rafe in the chest. His father had stolen from him, worse than that he had stolen from poor people in a desperate situation. What kind of man was he? How could he forgive him for this?

Rising, Rafe knew he would have to go home and face his father. He would also have to ask him to leave. He refused to have a thief under his own roof, even if it was his father.

Within the hour, he had traversed the sprawling city streets and entered the semi-detached house he had bought cheaply because of its location on the edge of Liverpool's slum area. It was all he could afford at the time, and an elegant house was not high on his list of priorities as he grew the business. His mother hated it, but Iris, when not caring for their mother, tried to make it a home. Iris was doing her best to settle here in a life far different to anything she had before. The

120

embarrassments suffered in London had hindered her chances of finding a suitable man to marry. She hoped Liverpool would give her another opportunity, but Rafe worried she now lacked confidence and self-worth.

No one was in the front parlour. A quick glance in the small dining room showed it too was empty. Cursing, he took the stairs two at a time, thinking his mother must be lying down with Iris attending her, but the master bedroom held no sign of life. He was about to leave the room when he noticed a wardrobe door hanging open. Before he opened it fully, he knew it would be empty.

He crossed the landing and went into his own room that he shared with Drew. The drawers were open and empty. Iris's bedroom showed the same result.

Downstairs, he entered the narrow kitchen. His cook, Mrs Flannery, and the maid, Susan, were busy washing fish in a bucket.

'Oh, Mr Hamilton, sir, you fair gave me a fright.'

'Forgive me. My family. Have they gone?' he asked the question already knowing the answer.

'Yes, sir.' Mrs Flannery dried her hands and from the Welsh dresser took a letter and gave it to him. 'Miss Hamilton asked me to give you this.'

He opened it and read.

Darling brother, forgive the hurried note, but Father is insisting we leave right away, and I am writing this as I pack. I do not know where we are going, but Drew let slip something about France. You know Father has a cousin in Paris. I suspect we go there. Father was in a terrible rage when he came home, and no persuasion from Mother or I could sway him to stay. He says you are dead to him, but you are not to me, or Mother. I will do my best to care for her in these uncertain times and write to you when I can.

Fondly,

Your sister, Iris.

Opening the drawer in the dresser, Mrs Flannery pointed to the empty tin. 'Your father took the house-keeping money, sir. I couldn't stop him. I had several pounds in there to pay the butcher and the baker this afternoon. He also took the silver tea service you bought last month for your mother and the silver candlesticks.'

'It is not your fault, Mrs Flannery.' From the breast pocket of his coat, Rafe gave her some money to cover the bills.

'Miss Iris and your dear mother seemed most upset.'

'They go to France, I believe.' Rafe forced a smile. 'To visit family in Paris. Mother is not keen on the boat crossing.'

'I don't blame her, sir. It can be rough.'

Rafe left the kitchen and walked out of the front door unable to speak decently to Mrs Flannery another minute such was the rage coursing through him. He wanted to hit something hard, preferably his father.

10

Closing the window on the rain and the noise from the docks and street below, Ellen smiled at Bridget who sat next to her on the window seat.

'Is it raining at home, too, Mammy?' her daughter asked, watching the boats on the river.

'Sure, and isn't it always?' Ellen tucked a lank piece of hair behind her daughter's ear. She needed a good wash. They all did.

Riona finished making the bed on the floor. The double bed held Mammy, who lay sleeping, exhausted from her constant praying. She'd not spoken to anyone since leaving Wilton Manor and refused to look at Ellen. She didn't have to speak for Ellen to know that she blamed her for Father Kilcoyne's death and the undignified burial would never be forgiven, nor would the leaving of Ireland.

Austin and Patrick were on the landing talking to three boys from the other Irish family staying in the room opposite. The inn seemed to be heaving with Irish and Scottish families waiting to board the *Blue Maid*.

'What are we to do for twelve days?' Riona asked, coming to sit with Ellen and Bridget.

'I was thinking of asking for work somewhere close by for a week or so.' Ellen had thought of the idea on the way back from Mr Hamilton's office. She'd been expecting to board the ship within a day or two, not twelve. 'If you and me can get some work, it'll help us buy what we need or have some money for when we arrive in Australia.'

'I thought you said Mr Hamilton will help with buying what we'll need on the ship?'

'He will. But you can never have enough money, Riona. I never want to be poor again and I'll make sure that we won't be.' Ellen stood and shook out her skirts, checking them for stains. 'I'll go down and ask the landlord if there's some work I can do at this inn, and if not, I'll continue down the street and ask in every place I see. I can't sit idle in this room for twelve days.'

'I know, but did you see the signs on some of the buildings as we walked here? 'No Irish' the signs said for those looking for work or lodgings. *No Irish*, Ellen. They don't want us here.'

'Will you calm yourself? We aren't staying here forever. Let us try and find some work for a week, that's all. I'll do anything that'll earn a shilling or two, cleaning, washing pots, anything.'

Riona nodded. 'Then I'll go along the dock and ask at inns, too.'

'Take Austin and Patrick with you. They might find work, too, and you're best staying together. A woman walking alone is easy prey in an area such as this.' Ellen took Bridget's hand. 'Stay with Gran. She's not feeling well and sure won't you be her little helper if she needs anything?'

Bridget straightened her shoulders. 'I'll watch over her, Mammy.'

'Good girl.'

Downstairs, Ellen parted from Riona and the boys and went along the dark narrow hallway towards the back of the inn. She could hear banging and shouting.

At the kitchen door she stopped and stared at the

active room full of industry. Several people were working, some at the large table preparing food, others washing the pots, a boy fed coal into the range while a young girl plucked a chicken, which by the pile of carcasses beside her wasn't the first one she'd done that day.

'Can I help you?' A man with grey whiskers, wearing an old threadbare suit asked as he came past carrying a basket of fish.

'I've come to ask for work for a week or so. We're lodging upstairs.'

'Oi, Edith,' the man shouted over his shoulder.

From a cupboard being used as an office, a large fat woman squeezed her bulk out and waddled into the kitchen.

Ellen stared. She'd never seen anyone so large in her life. The woman was munching on a pork pie; the pastry flaking onto her straining brown bodice. Ellen thought that the buttons on it would pop any moment and take someone's eye out.

'She wants work. She's from upstairs,' the man said, heading back to the bar.

'Well, this is the first time one of the guests has asked for work,' the woman said. 'Normally they're too weak to climb the stairs, never mind wanting to work.'

'I leave on the *Blue Maid* in twelve days. My family could use extra money.'

'Mr Hamilton's lot, are you?'

'Yes.'

'Nice man. Where are you from?'

'Ireland.'

'Aye, I know that. I've eyes and ears. *Where* in Ireland?'

125

'County Mayo.'

'Mayo?' The woman's small eyes widened in her chubby face. 'Louisburgh.'

'You must know of Westport then.'

'Yes, I left there a few days ago on the stagecoach.'

The woman's face creased into a full grin. 'That's my old home.' She wiped her hands on her skirt and stuck out her hand. 'Edith O'Brian.'

'Ellen Kittrick.' She shook her hand.

'Can you serve food?'

'I can.'

'Grab that tray over there and take it out to the guests seated at the window table in the taproom.'

Lifting an apron from the hook behind the door, Ellen collected the tray laden with plates of food and headed out to find the taproom.

She worked solidly for two hours, harder than she'd ever had at the manor. Soon the exhausting days since leaving home and lack of decent food had her energy flagging, but she was determined to keep going.

'Mrs Kittrick?'

Ellen glanced up from cleaning a table. Her heart did a little flip on seeing the handsome Mr Hamilton cross the bar room towards her. His appearance caused a few heads to turn, for not many in the inn were of his league. No one matched him in looks or stature or class.

'You are working?' He didn't hide the surprise on his face.

'Yes, Mr Hamilton.'

'You have only just arrived,' he said incredulously.

'Every penny helps.'

'I told you that your expenses were taken care of.'

126

'I understand that, but we still need money, especially when we get to the colony.'

'Of course, however, you have things to organise for the journey. You must purchase your supplies and be checked by the medical officer. How can you do that when you are working?'

'Between me and my sister, we'll sort it out, so we will.'

'You have been through a traumatic time. You should be resting.'

She gave him a quizzical look. 'Resting?'

'Taking it easy . . . rebuilding your strength for the voyage.'

'Sure, and we can do that on the ship.'

From under his arm, he gave her a slim booklet. 'This is for you to read. It is an account from previous travellers about what to pack for the journey and what you need to take with you to make life on the ship more comfortable. I thought it might help you when you are choosing items from the shops.'

'Thank you.'

'Perhaps you could share the information with those staying here at the inn who can't read?'

'Yes, I will.'

He glanced around the dim smoky bar room. 'I would rather you did not work, Mrs Kittrick. You have been through enough and should be focusing your energy on your family and the long journey you are about to make.'

She stiffened at the rebuke. 'My family don't need me sitting around a room all day when I can be down here earning.'

'For a shilling or two? Hardly worth the effort.'

'Believe me, sir, when you have nothing, everything

127

is worth the effort.'

'Forgive me.' He looked contrite. 'I do not mean to tell you what to do. I am simply worried about my passengers. I want them all to be in the best of health before they board. Australia needs strong people.'

'I will make sure my family eats well, Mr Hamilton. Thanks to you, they will have a warm bed to sleep in tonight and food in their bellies. You're giving us a start. We won't let you down.'

'I never doubted you would, Mrs Kittrick.' Again, he gave her that winning smile he had, which did strange things to her. 'On the back of the booklet is a list of nearby shops where you can purchase on account what you need. They will send the bill to me. They know what is required and will aid you in your selections.'

She nodded.

'Well, I should be going . . . ' He hesitated as though leaving was the last thing he wanted to do.

'Perhaps you will call again?' she asked hopefully, which was silly really, for why would he?

'I will, yes, in a few days, but if you need me before then, please don't hesitate to come to my office.'

'Thank you, Mr Hamilton, for everything.'

When he'd gone, Ellen finished her work with her mind on the handsome Mr Hamilton until Patrick entered the bar.

'Aunty Riona and Austin got work at a cigar factory,' he told her. 'The man didn't want me. He said I was too small.' Patrick pouted at the injustice of it. 'I told him I was ten, but he didn't believe me. He said he only had two places.'

Ellen hugged Patrick to her side. 'Sure, and it doesn't matter, my heart. You can help me if you want?'

128

Sullen, Patrick shrugged. 'Can I go out to the stables instead?

They are changing the coach horses.'

'Aye, but don't get in anyone's way.' Ellen followed him down the hallway and, as he walked out into the back yard of the inn, she turned and went into the steamy kitchen. The staff were seated at a narrow table, eating. The smell of food made her stomach rumble so loud the others stopped and stared at her.

'You've not eaten all day, have you?' Edith asked, heaving herself up and going to the range. 'You've missed the midday meal.'

'I'm not here to eat but to earn money for my family.'

'Tosh, how can you do that if you don't eat, woman?' Edith tutted and ladled a thick stew into bowls. 'How many are there of you?'

'Six, but my eldest son and sister are out working.'

Edith paused. 'You're not like any of the others who've come through here, and that's the truth.' She placed four full bowls onto a tray with thick slices of buttered bread. 'Take it up. Eat it and then you'll be ready for the evening rush.'

'Thank you.' Ellen couldn't believe the kindness. After years of struggling to have enough food to feed her children, years of eating whatever they could scrounge from the land or the shore, or scrapings from Mrs O'Reilly at the manor, here she was given bowls of thick stew as though it was nothing special. Yet to Ellen it was precious as gold. Tonight, her children would be warm, fed, and comfortable. Her eyes smarted, but she blinked back the emotion. She couldn't weaken with tears. If she started crying, she'd not stop for the memory of burying Thomas,

Malachy, and now Father Kilcoyne was hard to over-come.

Upstairs, she gave Bridget her bowl, and then Mammy, but Mammy turned away from it. Ellen opened the window and called Patrick to come up.

As they ate, Ellen kept glancing at Mammy, who lay on the bed, face turned away from them, quietly pray-ing. The clicking of her rosary beads matched that of the spoons in bowls. Perhaps Mammy would eat later with Riona and Austin.

Ellen worked late into the evening as the inn filled with men from the docks, seeking a bowl of hot food and a pint of ale. When she finally went up to bed, Riona and Austin were back and as grimy as if they'd worked down a coal mine.

'How was it?' Ellen whispered, taking off her worn boots and rubbing her aching feet. She shared the bed with Riona and Mammy, while the children slept on the mattress on the floor.

'Fine.' Riona finished praying and yawned, before scooting over into the middle of the bed. 'Sure, and I've not worked that hard in a long time. I can barely think straight I'm so tired.'

'Do they want you back tomorrow?' Ellen per-formed the quickest of prayers and climbed in beside her.

'Aye, me and Austin. Though no one talked to us. They hate the Irish and especially Catholic Irish. One woman spat at my feet when she found out. Another man called us bog Irish who takes all the work from the English. I thought Austin would punch him one.'

Ellen tensed. 'We can't have Austin getting into trouble. I'll speak to him.'

'It's not his fault. It's hard being surrounded by

130

people glaring at you with hatred in their eyes.'

'Have you eaten?'

'We were given a thin gruel. It was disgusting, but we ate it. We've eaten worse in the past.'

'Tomorrow I'll save you some food for when you get back.'

Riona nestled against Ellen. 'How's Mammy?' she whispered.

'She's not moved off this bed all day, nor eaten, so Bridget told me.'

'I'm worried.'

'Me, too, but soon we'll be sailing to a new life.'

'Thank Jesus for it. Only I hope Australia likes Irish people. I prayed to the Holy Virgin for it to be so.' Riona made a sign of the cross and then glared at Ellen when she didn't do the same.

Ellen quickly made the sign of the cross, but her heart wasn't in it. Lately she'd been finding her faith waning, not that she'd tell that to a living soul, but with each tragedy set upon her, she wondered if there really was a God watching over her. At times it didn't feel like it. She couldn't believe so blindly as Mammy, Riona and Father Kilcoyne did. Being Catholic could go against them in New South Wales. She'd have to warn the family to not be so religious in public to save them from ridicule.

'I hate the factory,' Riona murmured, half asleep.

'Just last a week or so, that's all. We'll have a few shillings to take on board the ship then.' The pleasant thought sent Ellen into a deep sleep within minutes.

★ ★ ★

Before dawn, Ellen was in the kitchen ready to work before some of the other staff had arrived. Edith poured her a cup of tea and told her to take a tray up to her family before she started helping with the breakfast rush of travellers arriving and leaving.

Like a queen offering gifts, Ellen took up bowls of porridge and a pot of tea. Riona and Austin ate quickly before they had to leave for the factory. Mammy refused the food and went back to sleep.

'Is Granny sick?' Bridget asked.

'She's just tired,' Ellen answered, stacking the empty bowls on the tray. 'Now I'll be downstairs working all day. Patrick tell the other families travelling on the *Blue Maid* that they can come to me for a list of what to take on board.'

'I can read it to them, Mam.' Patrick picked up the booklet and studied it. He read a few lines. 'The reg . . . regulation regarding passengers' luggage is, that only one box or bag be allowed in each sleeping berth, suff . . . suff . . . icient to contain a fortnight's clothing, at the end of which time they have access to their chests in the hold, replacing the clothes used by clean. Every em . . . emigrant should be provided with two chests, one large and one small, or one canvas bag, their names dis . . . distinctly marked on them. A carpet bag is far more useful than a box.' He grinned at her in success of his reading. 'I'm as good as Austin at reading now.'

She ruffled his hair. 'You are, my darling. Father Kilcoyne would be so proud. All those hours he spent with you reading have paid off.'

As she hurried downstairs, she thought of the booklet and the list of things she needed to buy and organise for the ship. Was she doing the right thing to keep

132

working when there was so much to do? She wished her mammy would return to her normal self, for she needed her. Mammy, with Patrick and Bridget's help, could easily start organising the things they needed from the shops Mr Hamilton mentioned.

For a fleeting moment she wondered if she'd see Mr Hamilton again soon, but then thrust him from her mind. She had no time to ponder on Mr Hamilton. A gentleman such as him wouldn't give her a second look and, besides, what good would it do if he did? She'd be gone by the beginning of November.

The smell of stale beer made her wrinkle her nose as she cleaned the tables and swept away the debris from the night before.

As the hours passed the inn became busier with patrons, dockmen out of work, sailors on shore leave or foreigners waiting to board their ships. More people, mainly Irish, arrived to wait their time until the *Blue Maid* sailed, and Ellen spoke to them, quickly earning their trust as she spoke to them in the Irish language and not English, which eased their nerves somewhat.

For the rest of the week, Edith gave small jobs to Patrick, mostly carrying trays of food up to the rooms, where he took great responsibility of reading from the booklet to those who couldn't read themselves.

On the evening of her fifth day working, Ellen was released from her duties and she gratefully went upstairs with a tray of food for Riona and Austin to eat later. Patrick and Bridget sat on the landing talking with other children, but Mammy still lay on the bed, eyes closed, rosary beads clutched in her hands.

'Will I get you something to eat, Mammy, or a drink?' Ellen asked, standing beside the bed, gazing down at her parent who was wasting away.

Mammy refused to acknowledge Ellen.

In secret, Bridget told Ellen that Grandma drank cold tea when they were alone and chewed some bread but didn't eat more than that and barely spoke a word that wasn't a prayer.

'Mammy, we've food. You must eat.' Ellen tried again to encourage her.

Mammy turned away from her and faced the wall. 'I don't have to do anything but die and be welcomed into the arms of the Holy Mother.'

'Don't say such a thing!' Sighing with frustration and worry, Ellen poured water from the jug into the basin and washed her face. 'Perhaps you'll feel up to going downstairs tomorrow, Mammy?' She spoke over her shoulder. 'We can start buying what we need for the voyage, so we will. A new dress for you?'

When she received no response, she dried her face and stared out of the dirty little window over the roof-tops. The sun had set an hour ago. She'd have to speak to Riona and have her persuade Mammy to get out of bed.

Austin came in looking tired and his clothes filthy. 'Aunty Riona has been made to stay back.'

'Why?'

'Mr Lester said her boxes weren't to his standards.'

'Have a wash and then eat.'

Austin did as he was told. 'Mr Lester is strange, Mam, so he is.'

'Well, he's not Irish, is he? He's bound to be strange.' She smiled.

Ellen watched him eat his pork chop and bread, while listening to his stories of the people who worked at the factory.

'I'm glad tomorrow is our last day,' Austin finished. 'I don't like it there and they hate us.'

'Your last day? I didn't know that. Riona never told me. You've only worked five days.' Ellen stared at him.

'We only found out today and I'm glad I ain't going back. Why do they hate Irish Catholics, Mam?'

'I don't know, darling.' Being Irish and a Catholic was proving to be something to be ashamed of and Ellen didn't like them being singled out. Would the prejudice be the same in the colony?

Austin handed Ellen some coins from his pocket. 'I've been paid. Will we be able to buy me some new boots?' He held up one foot that showed the sole of his boot had peeled away exposing his bare foot.

'Mr Hamilton said we were to buy what we needed, within reason. You'll have some new boots.' She kissed his head as he stretched out on the mattress. He was soon asleep.

Ellen called in Patrick and Bridget and as they said their prayers, Ellen kept glancing out of the window at the darkening night. Mammy didn't move from the bed or open her eyes, but Ellen detected that she was aware of the talk going on around her.

Not having a clock in the room, Ellen listened to the church bells sound eight times. She didn't like Riona being out so late. With the children and Mammy asleep, Ellen donned her shawl and slipped out of the room.

Downstairs the inn was crowded with men and so she let herself out of the back door and dashed up the dim dank alley beside the inn. A mist had rolled in off the river and the chilly night air made her shiver.

She scanned the street, picking out the shapes in the muted gaslights. A man was relieving himself behind a low wall, a dog was rummaging through rubbish in the gutter, a hansom cab rumbled past, a ship's horn echoed down the river and the smell of the sea drifted on the cold breeze.

Ellen had a vague idea of where the cigar factory was from Austin's descriptions, but she wasn't keen to go wandering about unknown streets in the dark, especially not near the docks where women of the night roamed, and Ellen could be mistaken for one.

Pulling her shawl over her head, she ventured further down the street in the direction of where Riona should walk on her way to the inn. A baby cried from one dwelling as she passed. Shadows danced in the subdued lights spilling from windows. Two men walked past her, eyeing her curiously. Ellen kept her head down and walked faster. A cat jumped out from an alley and she jumped in surprise.

She hesitated to walk any further than the next street corner. Should she wait here or turn back? Cold and damp from the mist, she dithered for a second and then decided to wait a few minutes more. Riona would be pleased to see her after such a long day.

As the church bells rang once, denoting the half hour, Ellen grew annoyed at Mr Lester for keeping Riona so late. Then, as she stood hugging herself to keep warm, she noticed the bent over shape stumbling towards her from out of the shadows. Fear trickled down Ellen's spine. What was it?

Torn between running away and going for a closer look, Ellen hesitated until the shape uttered a low moan.

Ellen rushed forward to the person. 'Can I help you? Are you hurt?'

'Ellen . . .' The woman's shawl slipped from her

head.

'Riona!' Ellen embraced her sister as she collapsed into her arms. 'Good God, what's happened?'

'Get me . . . inside,' Riona mumbled.

Taking Riona's weight, Ellen half carried her along the street to the inn.

Riona made no sound as Ellen guided her up the alley, past a couple kissing in the yard and into the back entrance.

'Not upstairs. Not yet,' Riona cried. 'Holy Mother, I can't go up there to Mammy.'

'The kitchen, then.' Ellen entered the darkened kitchen, for the staff had gone home and the food locked away for the night.

Lighting a lamp, Ellen placed it in the middle of the table to assess her sister's injuries. 'Who did this to you?'

Gently, Ellen took off the shawl Riona clung to, exposing her torn bodice. One of Riona's eyes was swelling, nearly closed, and dried blood caked her split lip. She had bruising around her throat and neck.

'Were they after money?' Ellen asked, pouring water from the kettle into a bowl she found on a shelf.

'No . . . '

A door opened and more light spilled from a lamp being held head high. 'What's going on here?' Edith shouted, her other hand held an iron poker.

'It's me, Ellen.'

'What in hell's name are you doing?' Edith edged further into the kitchen.

'My sister has been attacked.'

'God saves us.' Edith placed her lamp on a dresser and propped the poker against the wall. 'Do you need a doctor?'

'No!' Riona barked from where she sat at the table, her head turned away.

'I've an ointment in the top cupboard by the door, Ellen, grab it and I'll put the kettle on.' Edith, dressed in her nightgown, bustled about the kitchen, stirring the fire's embers to bring up some heat to boil the kettle.

Ellen sat opposite Riona and, dabbing a cloth into the water, she gently wiped away the blood on Riona's lip, making her wince. 'Who did this?'

'Sure, and it doesn't matter,' Riona whispered, tears in her voice.

'Of course, it matters, so it does!' Ellen fought back the rage at the unknown assailant. 'He needs reporting.'

'She's right,' Edith said from the dresser where she took down three cups. 'We can't have men roaming the streets attacking women like this.'

'We sail next week,' Riona murmured. 'I'm not going to the police.'

'What's the place coming to when a decent woman can't walk the streets at night on her way home,' Edith muttered. 'It's a disgrace, so it is.'

Ellen concentrated on washing Riona's face and neck, noticing the scratches and welts covering her skin. Her torn bodice and the dead look in Riona's eyes made her fear the worst. 'Sweetness, did he ... did he ... ?'

'I'll not talk of it, Ellen.' Riona gazed over at Edith. 'Can I have a bath?'

'A bath?' Edith stared at her as though she'd asked for a gold sovereign. 'Well, aye ... I mean I have a hip bath hanging out in the shed by the stables.'

'I'll get it.' Ellen stood wanting to do anything to

ease Riona's pain. 'Go to bed, Edith. I'll fill the bath.'

'I'll put some more pots of water on before I go. The buckets are full. I asked your young Patrick to fill them up for me this afternoon.' Edith banged and clattered about with pots and added more coal to the range.

An hour later, Riona sat in a few inches of warm water. Edith had gone to bed after making a pot of tea and cutting up slices of currant cake for them to have.

Gently, Ellen wiped the cloth over Riona's pale back, the knots of her spine stuck out like a ridge of a mountain. Ellen could easily count her sister's ribs, such as she could her own and her children's. Famine and starvation had rendered them walking skeletons, but still they lived, they worked, and they survived . . . just.

Riona's quiet sobbing broke Ellen's heart, but she knew her sister needed to cry and, as yet, she didn't want her comfort.

Ellen continued to wash her. Using the soap in the scullery she washed Riona's chestnut coloured hair, which was a shade darker than Ellen's and didn't have the touches of auburn that Ellen had.

Eventually, with the water turning cool, Ellen encouraged Riona to get out and dry herself on the small towel Edith had provided, while Ellen washed Riona's clothes. Her heart somersaulted as she washed the bloodstains from the thin chemise. She'd seen the blood between Riona's thighs when she'd stepped into the bath.

Her sister had been raped.

11

With a light rain falling, Rafe stood on the main deck of the *Blue Maid*, greeting passengers as they came aboard. He'd spent an hour with Captain Leonards, making sure everything was as the captain demanded it needed to be. The cargo, mainly fine furniture, English porcelain tea and dinner services packed in straw filled chests, crates of wine, Scotch and Irish Whisky, and port, as well as bolts of linen and wool made in Manchester's mills had been loaded throughout the week and secured in the hold. The colony was in desperate need of good quality products that the country had yet to start producing themselves, and Rafe was determined to have a slice of the colonial import and export business himself.

The numerous crates and barrels of provisions for the long voyage had been stowed away for there was to be no stopping at ports along the way.

Like monkeys climbing trees, a few of the crew scrambled high amongst the rigging, checking everything before departure as other seamen loaded luggage and provisions. Doctor Williams, the medical man Rafe had hired for the voyage, stood at the rail checking the last-minute documents given to him by the health officer on shore.

The *Blue Maid* was to sail on the evening tide and her passengers were encouraged to come aboard and be settled before sunset. As it was past noon, and the line waiting to board had grown longer on the dock, Rafe excused himself from the captain and Donaldson, the first mate, saying he'd try and hurry the passengers along.

At the bottom of the first gangway, two sailors were checking passes and medical clearance certificates. Rafe shook hands with the several first-class families boarding, asking them to make haste but to also enjoy the voyage and wished the best of luck to them in New South Wales.

The intermediate passengers were easy to spot, for they didn't wear the better-quality clothes of the higher class, but nor did they have the condemned haunted gaze of the steerage folk. He ushered them to line up behind the first-class passengers and wished them well.

Further down the dock, steerage passengers waited quietly for their papers to be checked before plodding up the other gangway to where they'd be shown down to the steerage deck. Some of the women were crying softly, while harassed fathers held onto the hands of small, excited children. Single women huddled together, scared to be the first to step foot on board. He gave them his regards as the drizzly rain stopped and after some encouragement, they quickly stepped up the gangway.

Rafe searched amongst the people for Mrs Kittrick and when he finally saw her, his eyes widened in surprise. Although terribly thin, she wore a dress of emerald and black stripe and an unadorned black bonnet. His heart skipped a beat. Although not of his class, in his eyes she was a woman like no other. Beside her stood two boys dressed in grey serge suits and shiny boots, and they held the hand of a little girl dressed in a dark blue dress with a red ribbon in her hair. Mrs Kittrick had obviously used the clothing allowance for the family.

As Rafe watched her, he frowned as Mrs Kittrick was clearly arguing with the older woman, all dressed in black, who he assumed was her mother. He walked closer to hear them and maybe offer some assistance.

'I tell you I'm not going and Riona isn't either!' the older woman shouted. 'You can't make us, so you can't.'

'Mammy, it's all arranged. We need to go to the colony and make a new life.'

'Holy Mother of God, I want my *old* life back.'

'It doesn't exist! It's gone, turned to dust like the cottage, like the people we loved and who are buried in graves!'

'Well, Ireland is still our home and we'll be better off there than anywhere else.'

'It's too late.'

'Jesus and his saints! I'll not hear it. We'll go back to Dublin and find work there, so we will.'

'It's impossible. We have no money to go back, Mammy.'

'Will you listen to yourself making all the rules?'

'I'm trying to do the best for us all, Mammy.'

'This is your fault, Ellen, and I'll never forgive you as the Virgin Mother is my witness, I won't. Sure, and aren't you to blame for everything?'

'Mammy, that's not fair,' the slightly built woman, Riona he presumed, her head covered by a black shawl, spoke from behind the boys.

'Whist, child. I'll have my say while there's still breath left in my body.' Mammy wagged a finger at Riona before turning back to Ellen. 'You pushed your husband into an early grave, you denied us the chance to live with Colm, your spat with the major killed my

142

brother, the only man who could have *saved* us, and now we're here in this godforsaken foreign land and Riona was attacked! *You did this!*' The older woman crumpled onto a large carpet bag, heaving for breath, her skin grey with exhaustion.

'Enough, Mammy,' Riona spoke between them. 'It's not Ellen's fault.'

'It is and I swear on all that's holy that I'll never forgive her.'

Rafe caught the eye of the sister before she ducked her head away, but not before he saw the bruised and battered face. He stepped forward. 'Mrs Kittrick.'

She turned and for a second he saw relief in her eyes as she gave him a brief smile. 'Mr Hamilton.'

His heart went out to her, for she was obviously struggling to convince her mother to make the journey. 'May I be of assistance?'

'No, thank you. We are waiting our turn to go on board, so we are.'

'May I have a word in private then?' He walked away a little, knowing she would follow.

'Yes, Mr Hamilton?'

He glanced back at her family. 'Your sister . . . She seems unwell?'

'She was attacked.' Anger flared in her blue eyes.

'You should have reported this to me. Where? At the inn?'

'No, not at the inn. She won't tell me where or who did it. She refuses to speak of the matter. She was working for Mr Lester at the cigar factory on some little lane near Waterloo Dock.'

'Working?'

'Yes, working. Every penny we earn is a penny to help us in New South Wales. It was only a few shifts.'

'Hardly worth it, I would have thought.' As her lips tightened in anger, he wished he'd kept his opinion to himself. He didn't need to add to her woes. 'Forgive me. I am not judging you.'

Her shoulders slumped. 'When you have no money, Mr Hamilton, *every* penny earned is worth it. I just didn't expect my sister to be attacked.'

'Of course, you wouldn't expect that. No one would. You believe Mr Lester is the culprit?'

'He kept her late the other night, and I found her beaten and . . . and . . .'

He rubbed a hand over his face, suddenly understanding what she was trying to say. He felt terrible. They were under his care. 'You should have come to me straight away.'

'She wouldn't allow me to tell anyone.' Mrs Kittrick smoothed down her skirt. 'Edith, who runs the inn, has been kind, so she has. Edith helped me get the things we needed for the voyage, as Riona wouldn't leave the room until this morning.'

'I wish I had known.' He shook his head, sorry that this decent woman and her family had been through so much.

Mrs Kittrick lifted her chin, determination clear in her eyes. 'Sure, and won't I make good all the bad things that have happened to us.'

'I have no doubt, Mrs Kittrick.' He smiled, liking her immensely.

'I'm pleased I've managed to see you before we sail, Mr Hamilton, as I wanted to thank you for the allowance to buy clothes. For the first time in years, we have new clothes and boots. Bridget has never had boots of her own before . . .'

Rafe gazed down at her beautiful face, which

despite being thin, still held an ethereal beauty that shone out amongst the crowd. With a healthy diet and beautiful clothes, she would be utterly stunning. He suddenly wanted to be the one to give her all that. Yet it was too late. She was leaving today, sailing away on his own ship to the other side of the world. What a fool he'd been to waste all this time with business when right under his nose was the woman who he'd grown attracted to, who he wanted to care for. 'Will you write to me, Mrs Kittrick?'

'Write to you?' Her eyes widened in shock.

'If it is not too much trouble? I would be interested, extremely interested, to know how you have endured the journey and what Sydney is like when you arrive.'

'Sure, and that is no hardship to write to you, Mr Hamilton, after everything you have done for me and my family.' She looked around anxiously. 'I'll have to buy some stationery when we arrive . . .'

He wanted to take her hand, but instead smiled. 'I shall go and purchase some right now.'

'Oh.' Mrs Kittrick stared at him. 'Now?'

'Mammy?'

Mrs Kittrick looked down at the small girl who came up beside her. 'I'm coming.'

'Who is this then?' Rafe asked. The little girl looked like her mother, except her hair was dark as a raven's wing and held none of her mother's auburn.

'This is my daughter, Bridget. Bridget, this is Mr Hamilton. We are sailing in his ship, so we are.'

Bridget stared up at him with blue-grey eyes, taking a moment to judge and scrutinise him.

Rafe crouched down in front of her. 'I am very pleased to meet you, Miss Bridget.'

'Are you coming on the ship?'

'No, but I wish I was now I have met you.'

She tilted her head and gazed at him. 'I'll be your friend if you want?'

'Will you? Then I am honoured indeed.'

'Do you have a horse?'

'No, not now, but I did a few years ago. He was called Phoenix.'

'When I grow tall, I'll have a horse, so I will, and I'll ride him every day.'

Rafe grinned up at Ellen. 'She has a sense of purpose your daughter.'

Ellen raised her eyebrows. 'She has a sense of her own importance, does that one.'

Straightening, Rafe noticed the line moving. 'I will be back soon.'

She nodded and taking Bridget's hand, walked back to her family.

Rafe watched her join the line and speak to her sister and then to her sons. Instinct told him she was a good mother. The eldest helped his grandmother to her feet while Ellen carried the bags as the rain started again.

Why had this woman come to mean so much to him? It was most inconvenient. He pulled his hat brim lower and headed down the docks.

★ ★ ★

Ellen didn't know what to expect on the ship. The small vessel that carried them from Dublin to Liverpool had been cramped and cold, with the passengers sitting on narrow benches in the dark as they crossed the Irish Sea. But as she edged down the steps from the upper deck to the bowels of the ship, dread began to creep up on her.

The steerage deck held three tier bunk beds down both sides of the hull, and in the middle ran a long wooden table. Single men were to sleep at the far end, families were in the middle and single women at the front.

The noise of a hundred people shuffling into a dim, cramped space echoed around the wooden hull. Babies cried and children fought while worried mothers tried to imagine months in such confinement.

Ellen and her family had been placed in a 'mess' with the Duffy family, another family from Mayo. Each mess was responsible for the cleaning and cooking of rations in their area. The Duffy family consisted of Seamus, his wife, Honor and their two daughters, Caroline and Aisling, aged ten and eight. The two families had met yesterday at the inn when the medical officer came to inspect them and give them clearance to board.

Situated in the family section, their bunks were double, and Austin and Patrick instantly climbed up to the top bunk, with Ellen and Bridget on the next, and the lower bunk would sleep Riona and Mammy. Three canvas bags were stuffed under the lower bunk and Ellen knew that within days everything they had bought new would soon smell of damp and the sea. The spare sets of clothes were in the hold and would only be brought up in two weeks' time when they were allowed to change their clothes.

Pulling out the sheets and blankets from the bags, she began to make the beds. Riona offered to help, but Ellen shook her head and Mammy simply ignored her. Little light filtered down from the hatch to steerage and there were no windows as they sat below the waterline. Ellen knew she'd be spending as much time on deck as possible. After her mammy's harsh words, maybe that wouldn't be such a bad thing. Mammy's accusations of blame replayed in Ellen's mind. The hurt speared deep.

Could she have done things differently? Was it her fault that Malachy and Father Kilcoyne were dead? In the space of weeks, she'd lost everything, but so had Mammy. The tragic deaths of Grandpa, Da, and Thomas had been the start. Without Da's fishing, which had kept them fed throughout the years of crop failures, the ending to their once happy lives had come quickly and without mercy. How much of the damage done by following events were her fault? To have her mammy hate her and Riona unwilling to discuss what happened to her, Ellen felt very alone despite being surrounded by a crowd.

She glanced at her sister and Mammy, but they didn't look up. Riona sat on the edge of the lower bunk next to Mammy, the pair of them praying with their rosary beads. That was another source of anger to Ellen. Mammy prayed constantly and glared at Ellen for not doing so, but Ellen couldn't. The God they had been brought up to believe in had turned His back on her, on them all.

How could such devastation as the crop failures that wreaked so much pain and misery and death be something He would allow? It didn't make any sense to her, and her disturbing questions often upset Father Kilcoyne.

Living as a Roman Catholic in Ireland seemed natural and true, but Ellen knew from listening to the talk at Wilton Manor and again at the inn that the wider world regarded the uneducated, poor Irish Roman Catholics as something of a scourge on society. She didn't know why, but she was determined not to be described in such a way any longer.

'Will you read to me the rules again, Mrs Kittrick?' Honor Duffy asked as she made the beds just as Ellen was doing.

Ellen fought back a sigh. Since meeting the Duffy family yesterday, she'd found Mrs Duffy to be a little annoying, yet kind enough.

Finding the booklet in her bag, Ellen once more read out the rules listed. 'Number one. Every passenger to rise at 7 a.m. unless otherwise permitted by the surgeon, or, if no surgeon, the master. Number two. Breakfast from 8 to 9 a.m., dinner at 1 p.m., supper at 6 p.m. Number three. The passengers to be in their beds at 10 p.m. Number four. Fires to be lighted by the passengers' cook at 6 a.m. and kept alight by him till 7 p.m., then to be extinguished, unless otherwise directed by the master or required for the use of the sick. Number five. The master to determine the order in which the passengers shall be entitled to the use of the fires for cooking. Number six. Three safety lamps to be lit at dusk, one to be kept burning all night in the main hatchway, the two others may be extinguished at 10 p.m. Number seven. No naked light to be allowed at any time or on any account . . .'

'I bought candles. What a waste of money,' Mrs Duffy muttered.

'Save them for when you get to New South Wales,' a woman said from the bunk opposite. 'I'm Mrs Moira O'Rourke, but just call me Moira since we're to be living together. Me husband is already in the colony. Went seven years ago in chains to Van Diemen's Land,

149

but has since been pardoned and is now in Sydney. Well, that's where his last letter was sent from.'

Some passengers standing close by gasped and then turned away from Moira, but Ellen knew that some convicts were sentenced for petty things such as stealing bread to feed their families. After her marriage to Malachy and his recent behaviour and being related to the secretive Colm, she could cast no stones.

Ellen waited for the timid introductions to finish in the married section and then continued to read from the booklet. 'Number eight. The passengers, when dressed, to roll up their beds, to sweep the decks, including the space under the bottom of the berths, and to throw the dirt overboard. Number nine. Breakfast not to commence till this is done.'

'Jesus, Mary and Joseph, are we in a prison?' Moira scoffed.

'Number ten. The sweepers for the day to be taken in rotation from the males above aged fourteen, in the proportion of five for every one hundred passengers.'

'So, us women aren't sweepers?' Mrs Duffy asked in confusion.

'Sure, and didn't she just say the men are?' Moira frowned.

Ellen glanced at Austin and they grinned. 'Number eleven. The beds to be well shaken and aired on deck and the bottom boards, if not fixtures, to be removed and dry-scrubbed and taken on deck at least twice a week.'

'What a load of old tosh,' Moira muttered, crossing her thin arms over her equally thin body. 'Sure, and who's doing all that when we are at sea being tossed about like corks in a barrel?'

'Mrs O'Rourke, you'll scare the children.' Mrs

150

Duffy looked pale at the thought.

'This ain't going to be no easy ride, Mrs Duffy. I've had three letters off me husband in seven years and in his first letter he said the journey over was hell on earth. Men died like flies.'

'Mrs O'Rourke!' Mrs Duffy covered Aisling's ears.

Ellen hurried on. 'Number fourteen. Two days in the week to be appointed by the master as washing days, but no clothes to be washed or dried between decks . . .'

Mrs Duffy scowled. 'Does that mean we have to wash our clothes up on deck, in front of everyone?'

'It seems that way, Mrs Duffy.' Ellen looked up and was amazed that a small gathering hovered close by to hear her read. Too many probably couldn't read, and she silently thanked Father Kilcoyne for his teachings when she was a child.

Mrs Duffy lowered her voice. 'What about that time of the month? How are we to keep that from the men's eyes?'

'Sure, and we'll make it work somehow, Mrs Duffy.' Moira laughed. 'They've seen it all before, so they have.'

'Mrs Kittrick.' Mr Hamilton weaved through the large number of people towards her.

Moira's eyes widened. 'Oh aye, what you done now, Ellen, to have the Master call on you down here?'

'Austin, finish reading this to Mrs Duffy.' Ellen gratefully passed the booklet over to him and gave her attention to Mr Hamilton, who carried a large box. 'You found us then.'

He wasn't smiling. In fact, he looked angry. 'Will you manage down here? I didn't realise it would be such a confined space. When I toured the ship before, it was empty and looked large enough to be comfortable.'

She sensed his unease. A gentleman such as he had probably never seen steerage before or even considered what it entailed, and she could see it was causing him some inner discomfort. She wanted to make him feel better if she could. 'We have survived worse things, Mr Hamilton, believe me. At least here we have a roof over our heads and daily food rations, something we were not always fortunate to have back home.'

He frowned. 'I did not want this for you.'

'We'll be grand.' She gave him a wide smile to ease his worry, secretly delighted that he was so concerned about her.

'I brought you some things,' he said as the boys scrambled down from the top bunk. Riona, too, looked up at him, though Mammy kept her head down, prayers rolling off her tongue like the murmuring sound of water tumbling over rocks.

Mr Hamilton placed the box on the table. 'Stationery, Mrs Kittrick. Paper, ink, pens and envelopes. I look forward to your accounts of the voyage,' he said it loud enough for Moira and the Duffy family to hear him. 'Personal accounts will be of great benefit to those that follow you.' He looked at the other passengers. 'If any of you wish to write to me and tell me of the voyage, I'd be most pleased to hear it.'

'Thank you.' She understood what he was doing. He was treating this as a business to save her from questions later. He had singled her out and it would cause gossip within the ship, not that she cared.

He gave the stationery to her, and she noted the quality of the paper and instantly thought she'd have to be careful to not blotch it with ink stains as she

152

wrote to him.

Turning his back on the others, he took out more items. 'And for the boys, I thought perhaps they might like these?' He handed to Austin and Patrick a small brown leather bag each, and inside were six tin soldiers with a small set of paints and a little paintbrush. 'To keep them occupied.'

'Thank you, sir.' Austin nodded to him while Patrick stared in wonder.

Ellen's throat constricted. They'd never had such a present in their lives.

'And for Miss Bridget.' He brought out a doll, about a foot long wearing a pink dress and with yellow ribbons in its hair.

Bridget's mouth gaped open. She cradled the doll gently to her as though it was as fragile as a newborn baby, then instantly hugged Mr Hamilton's legs. 'I knew you'd be my friend.'

Mr Hamilton squeezed her shoulder. 'I am honoured to be your friend.'

'This is too much, Mr Hamilton,' Ellen whispered, aware of their audience of fellow passengers who were wondering why he was showering gifts on the family.

As if sensing the ripple of talk, Mr Hamilton closed the box. 'There are a few other things in there for you, your sister and mother.'

Ellen pushed the box under the lower bunk. 'I'll walk up to the deck with you.' She didn't wait for his response and made her way through the single women, some of whom eyed Rafe Hamilton with open admiration.

Once on deck, the chilly winter wind and the smattering of raindrops cooled Ellen's hot cheeks. She didn't understand why Mr Hamilton had bought them gifts, and she didn't like how her silly heart had thumped in her chest in response to his kindness.

Amidst the hustling of the seamen getting the ship ready for being piloted down the river, and the rush of last-minute passengers coming on board, Ellen strolled to the rail and looked down at the dock heaving with cargo, people, and horse transports.

'Forgive me if I have embarrassed you, Mrs Kittrick,' Rafe Hamilton said, standing beside her and watching the scene below.

'You didn't. I'm not embarrassed. Your kindness is very welcome.' She found it hard to breathe. She was aware of his tallness, his lean strength, the expensive cut and quality of his clothes. Such a handsome man, with good teeth and clear skin, his jaw closely shaven.

'I simply wanted to give you some comforts after all you and your family have suffered.'

'I'm not alone in the suffering. We are surrounded by folk who have suffered and continue to do so. Not many of us on board are leaving their homes because they want to. Most of us have no choice, it's either sail to a new land or die in the old one.'

'As tragic as that may be, I believe you will do well in the colony. I sense in you a strength of spirit and determination. You survived such ordeals already, which proves my point.'

'I *will* make a success of the chance we've been given. I owe it to my family, to Mr Wilton and to you.'

'And to yourself,' he added, looking at her. 'I shall eagerly await each letter you send me. You must tell me everything, the good and the bad, for that information is invaluable in advising the people following you out there.' He searched in his jacket pocket and brought out an envelope. 'I wrote this reference letter

154

for you. To give to future employers. I assume Mr Wilton wrote one for you, too?'

Ellen nodded.

He smiled. 'Then you should have little worry about securing a position then.'

She held the envelope tightly, knowing the power reference letters held. Without one, finding a position could be nigh on impossible. 'Thank you, though those words seem too little for all you have done for me and my family.'

A whistle blew, and the seamen doubled their efforts as once again the rain began to pour from grey skies.

'Sadly, I think it is time for me to go.' Mr Hamilton still didn't make a move to leave.

'I wish you were coming with us,' she whispered boldly.

'I do, too, with all my heart,' he murmured.

She stared up into his blue eyes, her stomach clenching with emotion and fear. 'I'm frightened suddenly.'

'You will be fine.' He took both her bare hands in his gloved ones, his handsome face downcast. 'I wish you all the luck in the world, Mrs Kittrick. Safe journey to you.'

She squeezed his hands, wishing she had pulled her new gloves on to present herself as a lady, but the leather gloves she bought were put away so they wouldn't spoil before they reached the colony.

Detecting a bond between them, Ellen felt pleased and sad. To have such a gentleman as him as a friend was a true blessing, and yet the bittersweet feeling of knowing she'd never see him again pained her.

'Thank you for everything,' she said softly, unable to look away.

He hesitated a moment longer. 'If you ever need me, write to me.' He lifted one of her hands to his lips.

The tingle of his touch soared straight to her heart. She gripped his hands, not wanting to let go.

Another whistle broke them apart.

Despite the rain, Ellen stood on deck and watched him shake hands with the captain and first mate before descending the gangplank. On the dock, he turned and waved to her and she waved back. She watched him until he was out of sight.

12

Wiping the sweat off her brow, Ellen watched Bridget play chase around the deck with Aisling and Caroline and Patrick. To the side, Austin sat with a group of boys his own age, one of whom had lost his little sister to fever the day before and they'd all witnessed the captain say a few words as the canvas-shrouded body was tipped over the side of the ship.

The scene caused grave upset amongst the steerage passengers. The first death on the ship had come unexpectedly. The first two weeks of the journey were days of misery for most of the passengers. Seasickness had rendered a great number of them ill and unable to leave their bunks.

For days on end in the dimly lit steerage deck filled with groaning and crying people, Ellen and Riona helped to ease the suffering of the Duffy family and Moira and anyone who needed aid. Having lived by the sea all their lives and grown-up sailing in their da's small boat, seasickness didn't affect Ellen or her family, and so they spent their time taking care of others.

Those first two weeks kept Ellen so busy she wasn't able to pine for home or grieve for those she'd lost. Emptying buckets of vomit, washing soiled bedsheets and clothes, and trying to persuade their patients to drink sips of water kept her active around the clock, giving her little sleep or time with the children.

Doctor Williams had praised Ellen and Riona soundly. To their relief when the seasickness abated everyone was still alive, though weak. Moira returned to her old self the quickest, and as she had worked in a kitchen of a large house in Ireland, she volunteered to take charge of the cooking of their rations while Riona and Ellen rested.

Now in the sweltering heat, Ellen sat on one of the crates near the galley, which provided a small spot of shade and with pen and paper began a letter to Mr Hamilton.

Dear Mr Hamilton,

Today the Blue Maid's *crew and its passengers celebrated a month at sea. For four weeks we've been sailing down the Atlantic Ocean, skimming past rocky islands with the curious names of Tenerife and Cape Verde. I wished we'd been able to stop and visit, but I know how keen the captain is for us to make good time.*

In a few days we reach the equator and the sailors have mentioned how a ceremony would take place in honour of crossing it, which is something for us all to look forward to.

Yesterday at noon we passed a ship, but Mr Donaldson, the First Mate, told us we were making good speed and they were travelling too fast to send a boat to them. Instead, he wrote on a board telling the other ship our details. After reading the other ship's board, Captain Leonards said the ship, Ira Grey, was seventy-nine days out from Melbourne. If we'd been able to stop, I'd have scribbled a quick note to you to give to them.

I should have written earlier than this, but the first two weeks saw my sister and I busy below decks helping many who were afflicted with seasickness. Doctor Williams was grateful for our help.

You asked me to write and tell you about the journey. So far, we have had good winds and made good time, or so I'm told by Mr Donaldson, who I can reveal is a most

158

pleasant man, as are the captain and Doctor Williams. The crew are helpful with only a few being less eager to be kind to us who have never done this voyage before. They must get tired of all the questions we ask.

I would say this about the lower decks, especially steerage. There is a great need for light and fresh air. If some sort of system could be made to push air down the hatches for us, that would make life below more acceptable.

She paused as the children ran past. Watching Bridget squeal as Patrick caught her, made Ellen smile. The regular helpings of food on board had already given her children inches to their height and flesh under their skin. They were still too thin, but Ellen could see the difference in them. Gone were the pale sickly sheen to their faces, the dull eyes and lank hair. Ship life had transformed them. Days playing in the sun and sleeping without cramping, empty stomachs lifted their spirits.

Ellen's heart swelled with love for her three darling babies and she knew, no matter what happened in New South Wales, that she had done the right thing in getting them away from Mayo, from the hunger, the threat of the workhouse and the ghosts of the dead.

'There you are,' Riona said quietly, coming to stand beside her. She held onto the rail, though the ship's sails hung limp in the heat without a breath of air to fill them.

'Everything all right?' Ellen pulled at her damp collar, longing to swim in the ocean below her. She placed the pieces of paper, pen, and ink back into the small canvas bag she'd stitched together a few days ago.

Beads of sweat dotted Riona's forehead, her gaze

distant as she stared out to sea. 'I've started my monthly curse.'

'I did, too. Three days ago. Altogether the first one in years. Doctor Williams spoke to some of the single Irish women about it. Not eating enough, or starving, for a long time stops the body from having its monthly curse, so it does. Now we are eating regularly again our bodies will return to normal.'

'Thank the Lord.' Riona glanced at Ellen and crossed herself. 'One good thing to come from the crop failures and years of starvation and only eating whatever scraps we could gather from the land and sea saved me from carrying Lester's child.'

Ellen's head whipped around in surprise. 'What?'

'Isn't it possible that I could have been carrying Lester's child if my body had been normal and not starved?'

'Sweet Jesus,' Ellen whispered.

Riona stared back out to sea. 'God or the fates, whatever, decided that there is some justice after all.' Her tone was flat, and Ellen wished she could wipe the sadness from her sister's face. She wanted to see Riona smile and laugh again. When had they last laughed?

'Then there is something to be grateful for, so there is.'

Breathing in deeply, Riona raised her face to the sun high overhead. 'Now I know there is to be no child I feel I can breathe again.'

Ellen took Riona's hand. 'Sure, and isn't your whole life ahead of you?'

'I've been given a second chance, so I have.'

'We've all been given a second chance, thanks to Mr Hamilton.'

160

'Even without him I think you would have found a way for us to continue to survive just as you have done for the last few years. I'm thankful to have you as my sister.'

Ellen swallowed back the tickle of emotion her sister's words brought. 'I don't plan on just *surviving* in the colony. Oh no. I plan on us *thriving*. I won't rest until we do.' A steel band of determination straightened Ellen's spine.

'If anyone can do it, you can.'

They spoke no more as Bridget ran to Ellen to show her a graze on her knee where she'd fallen. Riona cuddled Bridget to her and said they'd go down below and clean up the wound.

Ellen watched them go before searching the deck for her boys. Austin still sat with his circle of friends while Patrick lay on his stomach playing with his tin soldiers. Every time she saw the tin soldiers, she thought of Mr Hamilton. Not that the soldiers were the only thing to remind her of him.

The box he'd given them had also held scented soaps, something that Ellen had never washed with in her life and so precious were they that she refused to use them and instead used the small cubes of soap provided in their rations.

Aside from the soap, there was a small sewing kit and six white handkerchiefs that Riona had started to embroider on the initials of each family member. At the bottom of the box had been three books, again something that Ellen had never owned. Books were items of wonder, things only the wealthy possessed. Even Father Kilcoyne had only owned a few, besides the Bible.

In the weak light on her first night in the ship, she'd

161

gently, reverently, almost afraid to touch the flimsy sheets, turned the pages of *A Christmas Carol* by Charles Dickens, *Pride and Prejudice* by Jane Austen and *Wuthering Heights* by Emily Bronte. Ellen treasured the books like gold. Having asked a seaman for a square of canvas, she'd wrapped them up to protect them against the damp and the water that seeped through the hull's timbers.

The box of items from Mr Hamilton gave her a sense of security. Those precious gifts, the small amount of money they'd earned, and the family's new clothes meant she was no longer a woman in rags and desperate.

In New South Wales, she could sell those items for food, should the need arise, but she hoped it wouldn't. She had Mr Emmerson's support and lodgings so that was a grand start, and every day she would walk the streets until she found work. Nothing would stop her. Her children would never see another hungry day.

★ ★ ★

Three days later, despite the suffocating heat, the ceremony when they sailed over the equator was one of hilarity and fun. A high-ranking sailor was dressed as King Neptune, and he preceded over the event seated on top of a barrel. Since all the passengers were first time sailors to cross the equator, it would take too long to douse each one with seawater and so it was decided a few passengers would be selected from each class.

To his delight, Austin was selected, and Ellen clapped as he was paraded around with the others to the cheers and laughter of the crowd. Austin grinned

162

as the bucket of seawater was tipped over his head. The head cook in the galley made fresh coarse-grained bread for the occasion as extra rations, and the captain allowed the sailors to hand around a small tot of rum for everyone.

As the ship's sails lengthened in a slight breeze, passengers danced on the deck to the tin whistles and fiddlers who played jaunty tunes.

Ellen stayed on deck all day, enjoying the games and chatting with fellow passengers. To watch the children laughing and playing with other children gave her great joy. With each passing day, the boys grew stronger, their thin limbs filling out and Bridget grew bonnier, with a cheeky grin, which she used on everyone and they fell under her spell.

'Mammy refuses to come up,' Riona said, coming to stand next to Ellen, who stood talking to Moira and Mrs Duffy.

Annoyed, Ellen tried not to let it show. 'Let her stay down there then.' She was tired of her mammy's stubbornness and her refusal to join in with anything happening. The children had lost interest in their grandma, who barely glanced in their direction.

'She's lost to her miseries, so she is,' Riona mumbled. 'Nothing will cheer her.'

'Maybe she'll be happier on dry land,' Mrs Duffy said pleasantly. 'We are all eager to be off this ship.'

'Aye, that's true,' Moira agreed, 'but to stay down there in a hot and airless deck is foolish.'

'Should I try and speak to her?' Mrs Duffy asked. 'She did speak to me yesterday.'

Moira chuckled. 'She told you to leave her alone, Honor.'

Mrs Duffy raised her eyebrows. 'She still spoke. It's

the most she's said to me since we left Liverpool.'

Ellen hid a smile. Poor Mrs Duffy tried to be everyone's friend, whether they wanted her to be or not. She chatted to anyone within earshot, which were many in the cramped conditions below. Although she meant no harm, her incessant chatter did try the nerves when all you wanted was some quiet, a rare commodity in steerage.

'Look how happy they are,' Riona said, nodding towards the children running about the deck, squealing as they played a game.

'Getting under everyone's feet, so they are,' Ellen replied, but it pleased her to see them have the energy to simply play. No longer did they have to fight for life. Austin could relax and enjoy just being a boy without shouldering the responsibility to hunt for food to feed his family.

'Leaving Ireland was the best thing we ever did,' Moira said.

'Truer words were never spoken,' Ellen said, believing it wholeheartedly.

'What will await us in Australia, I wonder?' Mrs Duffy murmured. 'I'm frightened we'll suffer the same fate as back home and not be able to find work.'

The thought had never entered Ellen's mind, such were her convictions that the colony was the promised land full of bounty. 'We make it what we want it to be, Mrs Duffy. Work hard and you'll succeed, so you will.'

'I wish I had your confidence.'

Riona patted Mrs Duffy's arm. 'Stick with us, Mrs Duffy, for my sister has enough confidence for us all, so she has.'

Ellen nudged Riona playfully. 'Sure, and isn't it

better to be positive?'

'Oh look, there's a sailor with another bottle of rum.' Moira disappeared into the crowd, intent on reaching him.

Shocked, Mrs Duffy stared after her. 'We've had our share.'

'After living with Moira for a month, you must realise she is one for taking opportunities when she can.' Ellen liked that about Moira. The woman was a law unto herself.

Doctor Williams strolled by with a couple from the first class, he paused next Ellen. 'Ah, Mrs Kittrick, how is your mother?'

'Fine, Doctor, thank you.'

'I tried to talk to her this morning during my inspection of your deck, but she refused to acknowledge me.'

'Forgive her, sir. She has taken the leaving of home badly.'

He nodded wisely. 'Melancholy is a great affliction. She is terribly thin. Her strength must be regained, or she will likely suffer from illnesses.'

'We do try to make her eat, but she takes very little.'

'I'll visit her again in the morning and speak with her.' With a doff of his hat, he moved on.

Ellen clenched her jaw. Melancholy. Mammy would be furious to hear herself described in such a way. She turned to Riona. 'I'll be back shortly.'

She hurried down the deck, patting Bridget's head as she passed her before descending the hatch to the intermediate deck before going down another hatch into the dim, damp recess of steerage.

A few passengers were taking advantage of nearly everyone being on the upper deck to sleep or sort out their bunks without fear of falling over luggage and bodies.

Ellen made her way to her own area and knelt beside her mammy lying on the bottom bunk. 'Mammy.'

No response.

'Mammy. Will you not come up and be with us all? The kiddies are having a grand day, so they are. Austin was doused with water by King Neptune. You should've seen the performance.'

Mammy's eyelids twitched in her thin, gaunt face.

'Mammy, sure, and aren't you fed up being down here? Come on deck and breathe the fresh air. It's hot as hell, but anything is better than the stuffiness of this dark pit. Bridget would be falling over herself to show you around. Will you not shift yourself for an hour at least?'

Mammy opened her eyes and stared at Ellen. 'Go away,' she croaked.

'Are you ill?'

'I wish I were dead.'

'Mammy!' Ellen rocked back on her heels in alarm. 'Have we not lost enough family?'

'You, *you* did this to me. I want to go home.'

'There's no one to take care of you at home, Mammy. New South Wales will be better for us, I promise you. I'll work hard and you'll never go without again.'

'It's too late.' She closed her eyes and shakily pulled her shawl over her head.

Striving for patience, Ellen stood. 'I never took you for a coward, Mammy. Ashamed I am of you.'

Sighing, she marched back towards the hatch and made her way up to the decks above.

Riona sat in the shade of a canvas awning the crew had erected for the comfort of the passengers. Bridget sat beside her with Aisling and as the two little girls chatted, Riona glanced at Ellen as she ducked under the awning and joined them. 'What were you doing?'

'Trying to coax Mammy into coming up here.' The sun was lowering in the sky, giving them some respite from the blazing heat.

'I worry, Ellen. Sure, and isn't she too weak to survive the voyage?'

'Don't speak so. She's eating a little each day.'

Riona turned her body away from the girls. 'She's even stopped praying. What will we do?'

'I don't know and that's the truth.' Ellen kept her eyes on the orange horizon, thinking of ways to improve Mammy's mood and despondency.

'Moira says we should just carry her up here. Ask some of the men to carry her up the hatch, for she weighs next to nothing and being up here might give her reason to believe it's not so bad.'

'Mammy would hate me even more.' Ellen lifted her skirts a little to cool her legs as the slight breeze grew a little stronger and the sails flapped above their heads. A few of the crew were high up in the riggings, taking advantage of the breeze to unfurl sails.

'I wish we could sleep up here tonight,' Ellen said quietly, closing her eyes and longing to swim in the cool sea like she'd done on hot summer days when she was a girl.

'I heard some sailors talking earlier,' Riona spoke as she braided Bridget's hair. 'They say if the winds are favourable when we go further south, then Australia could be within reach in eight or nine weeks.'

'Three months in total then?' Ellen mused. 'We'd be arriving at the beginning of February.' She thought of Mr Wilton's globe. 'All that way in a little over three months.'

167

'It's not been as bad as I thought,' said Riona, letting Bridget go and play with Aisling.

'No. We've managed well so far. Our quarters are damp and cramped, but we have food and are healthy.'

Riona made the sign of the cross. 'And we're together.'

13

Shaking on her shoulder woke Ellen from a dreamless sleep. She turned over in the narrow bunk, trying not to disturb Bridget, who snuggled against her.

'Ellen!' The harsh whisper came again.

Squinting in the murky light provided by the single whale lamp near the hatch, Ellen rubbed her eyes and awoke fully. 'Riona?'

'Get up. Mammy's not in her bunk,' Riona's fierce whisper filled her ear. 'I woke up and Mammy was gone.'

'She's probably relieving herself,' Ellen whispered back.

'I've been awake for a while and she's not returned. She uses the pot under our bunk in the night when everyone is asleep.'

Ellen dropped down out of her bunk and wrapped her shawl around her nightgown.

Riona gripped Ellen's arm. 'Would she have gone to see Doctor Williams?'

'Don't be soft in the head.'

'Then where can she be?'

'Let us get dressed and we'll go up and look around. Happen she's getting some air when no one is about.'

Holding her shawl out wide, Riona protected Ellen's privacy as she dressed, and when she'd finished, she did the same for Riona, though no one was awake at this early hour.

Quietly, they slipped between the decks, making little noise as they climbed the stairs to the upper

169

deck where the navy sky sparkled with waning stars and the breeze was refreshing. A thin grey line on the horizon showed the beginning of dawn as Ellen and Riona searched the shadowed decks.

'Ho there,' a seaman, one Ellen knew to be called Dick Floyd, hailed them as he came out of the door leading to the galley. 'Why are ye up so early?'

'We're looking for our mammy,' Ellen explained. 'She's not been well and we're thinking she's come up for some air.'

'I've been on watch these last four hours an' I ain't seen nothing an' no one,' he told them, pushing his cap back to scratch his head. 'She ain't' up here.'

'Sure, and it won't hurt for us to have a look around?' Ellen asked, glancing about. The ship creaked and groaned, and the sails flapped in the wind.

He scratched his hairy chin, looking doubtful. 'Well, be careful as ye go. Ye can trip walking along a deck in the dark. I ain't responsible for ye.'

For an hour, Ellen and Riona searched every nook and cranny of the upper deck before deciding to search the intermediate deck.

Becoming more frantic, and as the rising sun heralded another brilliant sunny day, they climbed back down into steerage and searched through the single women and married quarters as passengers stirred and muttered.

Ellen woke Austin and Patrick and told them that Grandma was missing, and they must search for her. Sleepily, the boys went above and began their own search.

'You'll need to tell the captain, so you will,' Mrs Duffy said, brushing her brown hair. 'What if she's fallen overboard?'

'She wouldn't have jumped, would she?' Moira asked, pulling on her stockings that had holes in the toes. 'You said yourself she's not been behaving normally.'

Riona rounded on her. 'What a thing to say, so it is!'

Moira held up her hands in surrender. 'Forgive me. Just a thought.'

'Well, keep those kinds of thoughts to yourself!' But when she turned back to Ellen, Riona's eyes were filling with tears.

Ellen embraced her. 'We'll find her.' Yet in her heart she knew they were too late. Privately, Ellen's fears were growing, not that she'd let on to Riona. They had searched the boat for two hours. How could a woman weakened by refusing to eat properly not be found by now?

Ellen dragged Riona back up to the upper deck with Mrs Duffy offering to see to Bridget for her.

On the deck, Ellen gazed up at the full sails billowing out to catch the breeze. Crew were climbing up in the rigging and as the ship came awake the smells of breakfast wafted from the galley.

Moira's words lingered in Ellen's mind as she leaned against the rail and glanced over to the grey sea below. Oh, Mammy. How could you?

'She wouldn't have jumped. It's a sin to take your own life,' Riona mumbled tearily. 'She'd not leave us on purpose.'

'Mammy left us long ago in spirit.' Ellen gripped the rail, the truth dawning quicker than the sun rose in the pink-streaked sky. Mammy wouldn't have fallen. No, in her state of mind she'd have gone willingly.

While Riona continued to search, Ellen stayed at

the rail, looking down at the sea as though it would reveal the answers she needed. Had Mammy really jumped overboard in the night? Had she the strength to pull herself up through the hatches and walk to the rail and then actually lift one leg and then the other until she was balancing precariously on the top of the rail?

Did she cry out when she toppled forward?

Did she struggle when she slipped under the water?

Did she fight to stay alive, regretting her decision to leave her daughters and grandchildren?

Or did she go gladly, silently?

Was she calm and resigned to her fate as she slid beneath the water and to her death?

'We can't find her, Mam,' Austin panted, coming to stand at the rail beside her. 'Where else is left to search? I've gone everywhere. I even slipped into the first-class salon and looked around.'

'Thank you, sweetness. Go below and have your breakfast. Take Patrick with you.' 'But where is Gran?'

A lump came to her throat. She hugged him to her. 'She must have fallen over the side during the night.'

Tears filled his blue-grey eyes. 'She'd have been scared.'

'She's with Grandpa now, and Thomas and Father Kilcoyne. She'll be happy. You must only think of that.' She kissed his cheek.

'I'll miss her.'

'We all will, my heart.' She hugged him to her again. 'Go down. I'll be along soon.'

Alone again, Ellen stared down at the deep water. What would it have felt like to be swallowed up by the cold black water, sinking down to the depths below, gasping for air, drowning, darkness closing over you like a shroud?

'Oh, Mammy.' Ellen shivered, haunted by her thoughts. Pain shattered her heart yet again.

The breeze stiffened the sails and the ship gained pace, blowing Ellen's hair from the pins that held it. She tucked it behind her ears and glanced around the deck for Riona. Instead, Doctor Williams came out of the first-class salon and headed towards her.

'Mrs Kittrick, your son informs me that your mother is missing?'

Ellen nodded, not trusting herself to speak.

'The entire ship has to be searched. With your permission, I'll notify the captain on your behalf.' His eyes behind his spectacles softened in sympathy.

'Thank you.'

'The more people searching, the quicker she'll be found.' He nodded once and left her.

Ellen knew the search would be futile.

Long after the noon bell had rung, with all hands searching the ship, it became clear that Bridie had either fallen or jumped over the side during the night.

The captain offered his condolences to Ellen and Riona and declared it an accident. He'd write it in his logbook as such. The sails were hauled in and the ship slowed to a stop as a special service was given, led by the captain. Riona cried broken-heartedly, with Patrick and Bridget holding her around the waist, crying with her. Ellen stood straight, silently holding Austin's hand, her gaze on the golden horizon.

With the sun sinking in the west, the crew and all the passengers crowded onto the upper deck to hear the captain speak, to say words of comfort, and as one they bowed their heads and prayed for Bridie O'Mara's soul. Except Ellen.

A rage simmered in her heart, denying her tears to form. She knew Mammy had thrown herself overboard and not simply fallen as most believed. Sin or no sin, Mammy had wanted to join Da in death and not start again in a new country.

Mammy had given up the will to live. She didn't want to leave Ireland and certainly didn't want to voyage to the colony. Dying was her only salvation. Her life no longer held meaning to her. She didn't want to live for her daughters or grandchildren. Mammy's heart and mind remained in her cottage by the sea, a mile from Louisburgh and in her beloved country, Ireland. Mammy longed to be with Da, her dead children and Father Kilcoyne in heaven and no one had been able to stop her from achieving that.

Ellen prayed that Mammy was at peace. That God had turned a blind eye, and He too believed she'd fallen into the black ocean last night. But, with her heart already damaged by so much tragedy, Ellen knew she'd never forgive her Mammy for leaving them.

★ ★ ★

As the captain guided the ship further south, the temperature dropped, and the wind sharpened to a gale. For a faster journey, ship masters now sailed lower into the Southern Ocean than ever before to catch the Roaring 40s; the gale force winds which would catapult them across the bottom of the world towards the east coast of Australia.

Sailors spoke to the passengers of how important it was to catch these winds to lessen the time at sea, and after weeks of being in the cramped, damp steerage

174

deck, Ellen was eager for the ship to catch the gales that would shorten the voyage.

Holding onto the middle bunk as the ship rolled from side to side, Ellen tried to brush Bridget's hair single-handedly. The crew had brought up everyone's trunks to allow the passengers to change into fresh clothes in celebration of Christmas.

Gratefully, Ellen had changed into a woollen navy-blue dress and clean chemise and petticoats, while the boys changed into their trousers and flannel shirts before darting off to see their friends. Bridget danced around in her new dress of pink and white stripe that Ellen realised would be mucky within a day. When browsing the shops in Liverpool, she'd been so excited at the novelty of buying clothes that for a short time her practical nature had been overrun by the sheer joy of purchasing new things for her children.

'I feel like a princess, though we should be in black for mourning,' Riona said, smoothing down her deep rust-coloured skirt and bodice with black trimmings.

'I didn't buy black clothes.' Ellen quickly tied a pink ribbon in Bridget's ebony hair and sent her off to play with Caroline and Aisling. 'I was sick of wearing black clothes.'

'Sure, and isn't it grand to be wearing new clothes, even if they do smell of the sea and dampness.'

'The smell will go soon.'

'Back in Ireland we'd never wear anything so fine.'

Ellen gave her a wry smile. 'In Ireland we wore rags. Without Mr Hamilton's generosity we still would be.'

'I'll never take for granted the blessing bestowed on us.' Riona bent and rummaged through the trunk. 'Oh.' She pulled out a brown woollen skirt. 'Mammy's clothes.'

Ellen hardened her heart at the sight of them. 'We can reuse them when we're settled. You can take them in.'

Riona nodded and pushed the garments to the bottom of the trunk. 'I still can't believe she's gone.'

Ellen didn't reply. In the few weeks since the incident, she'd held her children and Riona as they cried out their grief, but she'd not been able to share it. Her comfort was reading the books Mr Hamilton gave her and writing letters to him. She had eight letters ready to post to him already.

She gathered all the dirty clothes and put them in a canvas bag and shoved it into the trunk before closing the lid. 'We've one more change for when we disembark. Such washing we'll have when we arrive.'

The ship rocked sharply to one side, sending everyone and everything tumbling to the left. Trunks careered into bunks and legs. A few people were sick with the seasickness returning after the smooth ride across the equator.

Riona grabbed for the table as some women cried out in alarm as the ship pitched the other way. 'I won't mind the washing, for it'll mean we're off this ship.'

'Where are the boys?' Ellen looked around the dimly lit deck. 'I don't want them up above with the ship rolling so much.'

Together she and Riona looked beyond their own area, seeing if the boys had gone to their friends' bunks to chat. The smell of vomit caught Ellen's nose as she asked around the single men's quarter.

'A few of the lads are up on deck,' Moira told them, coming into their tight space as Ellen returned. 'I saw them when I came out of the galley. Dinner is salt beef and rice today, my friends. But that's only if the captain allows for the fires to remain lit. A storm is brewing, so we're eating at twelve instead of one o'clock. I suggest you eat it all as we might not get supper this evening.'

Ellen hurried to the hatch and made her way up to the upper deck as the ship rocked.

On deck, the icy wind took her breath away and whipped her hair out of its pins and into her eyes, blinding her. 'Austin! Patrick!' she called, but her voice was carried away over the rolling sea.

Her boys had been at sea with her da many times, and knew the dangers of a storm, hadn't one taken their great-grandpa, grandda and little brother only months ago?

The ship tilted again and the loud crash of the waves hitting the hull drowned out the sailors' calls as they stowed the sails up in the riggings, which swung dangerously in the gale.

Rounding a pile of crates near the galley, Ellen spotted a small group of lads watching the crew climbing high up on the first mast. The ship pitched over a swell, and the boys cheered. Waves of frothy foam flooded the deck.

Frightened by the peril they were in, Ellen rushed to grab Austin and Patrick's arms. 'Get down below, you fools, before you're washed overboard. Haven't I enough to deal with, so I have?'

'But, Mam — ' Austin began to protest, but she roughly pulled them along as another wave crashed over the bow, spraying them all in seawater.

'You should know better, Austin Kittrick, than to place your brother in danger. Come on now!' She turned to the other boys and shouted into the wind. 'You, Hamish, get below, your mammy is looking for you. She's not feeling well enough to come up here.' Ellen gave the other two boys a glare that sent them dashing for the hatch as well.

'It's wild up there,' Ellen told the others as she came back down. 'I'd not venture up unless you really have to.'

The midday meal, when it arrived, was cold and not well cooked. The rice was still a little hard and the half cups of tea barely warm.

'Nay and 'tis not my best efforts, but by it were hard work cooking when the whole galley was tossed from one side to the next.' Moira laughed, prodding at her plate of beef and rice. 'I fair swear that most of the food is on the galley floor, and the cook is swearing and cursing fit to burst as his pots and pans are sliding all over the place.'

'You did a grand job of it, Moira,' Ellen said. 'We're thankful, so we are.'

The ship rolled again and all their plates and cups slid and crashed across the table, held up by the lip running along the edge. Many hands grabbed what they could, but not before a cup of black tea, thankfully cool, spilled over Bridget's lap.

'My dress!' she wailed as though she'd been scalded.

Ellen and Riona hurried to soothe her and sponge off the tea with a towel.

'We'll wash it, so we will, my pet,' Riona crooned.

'I want to wash it now!' Bridget sobbed, pushing away her plate in resentment.

Ellen slapped her legs. 'You'll stop that carry on right now, madam. Eat your food. I never want to see you waste food. Sure, and wasn't it only a few months ago we didn't have any? Eat it and stop going on about your dress. It'll be washed soon enough.'

'Don't be so harsh, Ellen,' Riona snapped. 'She's only a wee little thing, and she loves her new dress, so she does.'

Ellen didn't answer as the ship pitched sideways and cries filled the air. The woman on the other side to Moira, Mrs Mullen, brought up her meal into a bucket and the sour smell wafted over the table.

Thankful she'd finished eating, Ellen cleared away the plates and cups, placing them into the bucket to take above deck to clean once the storm had passed.

'I bet the waves are big now,' Austin declared to Patrick.

'Bigger than a house!' Patrick added.

'Just make sure you two don't leave this deck until the storm is over, understand me?' Ellen wagged her finger at them.

Sullen, the boys climbed up to the top bunk, talking of huge waves and their favourite sailors amongst the crew.

'What's wrong with you?' Riona asked.

'Nothing.'

'You're too quick to anger these days, so you are.'

Ellen rounded on her. 'And why wouldn't I be with all that's gone on? The boys were up on deck as a storm was brewing with no thought to their own necks! They could have been tossed over the side in a blink of an eye.'

'But they weren't,' Riona spoke calmly. 'You found them, and they are safe.'

'They're not to be allowed out of our sight. I can't lose them as well.' Ellen turned away and pulled out the box Mr Hamilton gave them. It was too difficult to finish her latest letter to him, but if she could read for an hour that might take her mind off the storm.

Climbing into the middle bunk, Ellen opened *Pride and Prejudice*, the book she'd started reading a few days ago on the upper deck. However, the dimness in steerage gave such poor reading light she could barely see the words.

She put the book away into the box just as the ship tilted alarmingly to one side. Screams were drowned out as the ship's timbers shook and groaned.

'We're going to die!' Mrs Duffy made a sign of the cross and fell to her knees to pray.

'Pull yourself together, Honor,' Moira snapped, hanging on tightly to her bunk as the ship rolled the other way.

Ellen scrambled out of her bunk and held out her hand to the boys above. 'Get down here with me in my bunk. You could easily be tossed out of that top one,' she told Austin and Patrick. 'Riona can you manage with Bridget?'

'Aye,' Riona replied, climbing into her bottom bunk with Bridget. 'We'll make up a story for your dolly, won't we, pet?'

'We need to get our things off the floor.' Ellen hurriedly threw their small number of valuables onto the middle bunk. 'Austin put all that into the box and don't let go of it!'

The ship shuddered into another wave. Anything not secured careened to the other side, including piss-spots not emptied. Urine and vomit sloshed along the timber floor, soaking into fallen blankets and pillows and clothes. Trunks recently brought up from the hold were sent smashing into bunks and anyone foolish enough to be still standing. Passengers not holding on tightly lost their balance and fell into the tables or opposite bunks, banging knees and heads.

Children cried and wailed as frightened parents tried to soothe them.

Seawater began to run down the walls and the stairs leading to the hatches. The single women huddled together, crying as the water pooled around their feet.

Suddenly, the deck tilted upright as though climbing. Belongings fell backwards, crashing down along the aisle between bunks and the long table. Seamus Duffy pulled Honor off her knees and into the bunk just in time before a small chest crashed into her. She sobbed into his chest as their girls huddled around them.

Then, as though suspended for a moment, the ship abruptly dropped. The jarring thud as it landed at the bottom of the swell shook the hull. The timbers screeched in protest. Screams rent the air, which joined the sounds of retching and praying.

'We'll be at the bottom of the sea at this rate,' Moira mumbled, grinning at Ellen.

Ellen stared at her; the woman seemed to be unfazed by anything.

A large bang made them jump and cry out.

'What the bloody hell was that?' Moira asked, eyes wide.

'The hatches! They're closing the hatches!' Seamus Duffy yelled as the hatches were closed, plunging them into darkness broken only by the weak haze given from three whale lamps, one for each section.

Yells of protests rang out. The crying grew more intense and louder.

'They close the hatches when a storm hits, Mam,' said Austin. 'It's all right. A sailor told me that it's to stop the water going into the ship.'

'Of course, we'll be fine, so we will.' Ellen eyed the

swirling water covering the floor, hoping for it to be true. 'This storm will pass over us soon enough.'

'I wish you could read to us, Mam.' Patrick held the book, *A Christmas Carol*.

'If I could see to read it I would, my heart.' Ellen kissed the top of his head.

Cries and screams grew louder as the ship pitched violently as though being tossed around by a giant's hand. Water swirled in through cracks in the hatches, and the smell of the sea was strong in Ellen's nose. She held on to the timber post of the bunk as the ship swayed aggressively.

The sound of something breaking above their heads added to the chaos of items being flung around the bunks. The hull groaned and shuddered, and more water poured down the stairs. A child was thrown from his bed and hit his head on the table. His mother wept and dragged him to her as blood poured from the wound.

Once more the ship climbed a wave, tilting them all backwards before it plunged down, sending them all flying forward.

Caroline fell off the bunk next to Ellen's. Seamus lunged for her, only to lose balance and fall headfirst onto the floor.

Ellen jumped up to help, slipping and sliding on the wet floor. She gathered Caroline to her and guided her back into her mother's arms while Seamus shook his head to clear his senses.

'Thank ye kindly, Mrs Kittrick.'

'We need to tie ourselves to the bunk posts, so we do,' Ellen joked, peering at the bump forming on his forehead.

'We'll not die, will we, Mam?' Patrick whispered.

182

'No, my love. I'll not let anything happen to you, I promise.' Ellen prayed she could keep that promise.

For twelve hours they were kept locked in steerage while the sea tossed them about like a pebble on a beach. Each time Ellen believed they were over the worse, another wave smashed into them. She encouraged the children to sleep, for there was no food or drink coming to them and it was too dark and risky to perform any activity.

Finally, as a new day dawned, the storm lessened gradually until it was calm enough for the hatches to be opened. A weak light and cold air filtered down into their quarters.

Ellen woke stiff and cramped, her legs tucked up to give more room to Austin and Patrick and the box she'd kept beside her all night.

Carefully, she sat up and swung her legs over the side. Water inches deep eddied over the floor. The violent pitching had eased enough to make standing less treacherous.

The freezing water shocked Ellen fully awake as her feet touched the floor. She shivered. Holding up her skirts, she bent to see that Riona and Bridget still slept.

'Gee God, what a bloody mess,' Moira mumbled, climbing out of her bunk.

Ellen stared around at the destruction. People slept in damp beds, clothes and belongings littered every surface. Trunks were overturned, their contents spilled into the murky water. The smell of urine and vomit seemed so thick she could taste it in her mouth.

'The ship will take some cleaning.' Ellen picked up a man's shirt that lay soaked by her feet.

Wearily, Ellen began to sort out the items closest

to her as Moira did the same. Mrs Mullen also woke, but was so weak from being sick, she could barely raise her head.

'I'll go up to the galley and fetch some jugs of fresh water, if there's any to be had.' Moira weaved through the mess to the hatch.

Ellen scooped up a bucket of slops and set it near the stairs. Several single women were waking and groaning at the state of their quarters.

While Ellen was picking up sodden bedding, Doctor Williams came down the stairs and over to her, a handkerchief covering his nose.

'Any injures, Mrs Kittrick?'

'Not everyone is awake yet, Doctor, but there's bound to be some bumps and bruises.' She nodded to his handkerchief. 'Do we smell that bad?'

'Horrendous, my dear woman. How did you manage it? It was bad enough up there.' He pointed to the upper deck.

'We had no choice but to get through it.'

The doctor stared around. 'A lesson is here to be learned. Everything must be battened down in readiness for the next storm.'

'Including us.'

'It is unfortunate but must be done.' He gingerly made his way through the married quarters to the single men, where he urged those that could to go above and help the crew right the damage done to the ship.

Ellen worked for another few minutes before the urge to breathe fresh air became too much. She picked up two full buckets of filthy water and climbed her way up to the upper deck. She met Moira at the top of the stairs.

'Cook has lit the fires. We'll have some warm food

soon enough,' Moira said. Planting her feet wide to brace herself, she held out a cup of tea for Ellen.

'Let me get rid of this.' Teetering out onto the deck, the icy wind surprised Ellen. The ship plunged through the waves, making it difficult to walk.

The temperature had dropped since yesterday. All around her was debris of the storm, broken crates, ripped canvas and dangling ropes from the rigging above. The sky still looked angry and mutinous and white-topped waves peaked on the grey untamed sea. The ship sailed faster than it had for the entire voyage. The sails were unfurled and billowed out, catching the gale and easily cutting through the water like one of the dolphins they'd seen weeks ago swimming gracefully beside the hull.

She staggered back to Moira and took the tea gratefully. Although so cold her teeth chattered, being on deck was a grand change to the fetid, damp deck below.

'So, within a few weeks we'll be in the new country,' Moira said, watching the crew dash about the deck tidying and fastening the crates that had come loose.

'What will you do when we arrive?' Ellen asked.

'Find my husband and see if we still like each other.' Moira grinned. 'It's been so long I'm not sure I'll remember what he looks like.'

'Are you excited?'

'Aye. Are you?'

Ellen tucked her hair behind her ear, thinking briefly of all she'd left behind in Ireland, but pushed it from her mind. 'Won't it be the finest thing to start again?'

'Aye. I hope I can find work. I don't fancy starving again, so I don't.'

'Mr Emmerson is bound to help us. Mr Hamilton said he would.'

'Think a lot of Mr Hamilton, don't you?' Moira smirked. 'I see how many letters you have written to him.'

Finishing the tea, Ellen handed the cup back to Moira. 'I would think highly of anyone who helps me to keep my children alive.' With that, she picked up the buckets and carefully went back down the hatch to continue the cleaning up.

Mr Hamilton lingered in her mind and she focused on his charming smile as she descended the stairs into steerage, but then the foul smell hit her and wiped away any nice thoughts. How much she had to tell him in her next letter!

14

For the next four weeks, the captain sailed the ship through more storms and gales. Icebergs were sighted, but no other ships. The crew spoke of them sailing lower and lower to at least fifty-five degrees south, taking advantage of the curve of the world to shorten the journey's distance. Despite ice coating on the ship like a fine white mantle, the captain kept full sail. The ship sailed faster, eating up the distance.

Ellen layered the clothes on the children as the temperature dropped to below freezing. Passengers fell ill with chest colds and fevers, and their clothes would barely be dried before the next storm descended and flooded steerage once more. Three passengers died during the last raging storm. A gentleman in first-class died of heart failure and in the married quarters a woman died in childbirth along with her baby. They were buried at sea without ceremony as the gales ravaged the ship.

The deaths brought the mood of the passengers to a new low. After two-and-a-half months at sea they were fed up with the dirty, crowded quarters of the deadly storms and lack of privacy, of the badly cooked food, the seasickness in the stormy seas and the wintery damp conditions.

Christmas and the dawn of the new year of eighteen fifty-two did little to cheer them as they battled to get along with each other with nowhere to escape.

Ellen barely acknowledged her twenty-ninth birthday, but Riona told Moira and Mrs Duffy and they wished her well. Riona managed to make a small present for her, which was a square piece of calico with a border of embroidered flowers and her birth date on it. The present touched Ellen deeply. That she had done that in such depressing conditions without Ellen being aware meant a lot.

They sailed east as fast as the winds carried them until at last and with great excitement to all passengers, Captain Leonards instructed for the course direction to be changed to north-east and back up into the Roaring 40s and at last they were heading for the southern coastline of Australia.

The closer she got to the voyage ending, the more nervous and excited Ellen became. The weather cleared finally, allowing Ellen to bring up the bedding and their clothes to air them in the sunshine on the upper deck.

Other passengers did the same, and every conceivable space on deck was draped with pillows, sheets, and washed clothes. Mattresses were dragged into the open air and for once were able to dry out. With the steerage deck empty of belongings, it was swept and scrubbed. Broken bunks were repaired by the ship's carpenters, the long dining table sanded, and personal items stored away.

Sewing a tear in Bridget's pink dress, Ellen sat on a crate on the upper deck, smiling as the children played chase around the deck. To see them playing again in the sunshine gave her much contentment after the terrifying stormy days when she fully expected the ship to go down to the sea bottom. Being brave in front of the children was exhausting, but she kept up her false confidence by telling them stories of when she was a girl.

'That's the last of the clothes hung up.' Riona joined her. 'My stockings are beyond repair, I feel, and one of Patrick's shirts has a stain I can't get out.'

'As soon as I find work, I'll replace our clothes.' Ellen held up the dress and inspected her work.

'You're confident work is to be had?'

'Aye. It was in the newspaper, remember? They wanted workers. They wouldn't print that if it wasn't true. Mr Hamilton told me the colony needs people of trade and good morals.'

'What if Mr Hamilton has got it wrong? After all, his business is cargo, not people.'

'The two go together.' Ellen glanced at her sister. 'Sure, and you're worrying is normal, so it is, but I won't let anything stop us from being happy.' Ellen grinned. 'Who knows, you might find a husband!'

Riona shook her head. 'No. Not after Lester. I don't want any man, nor will they want me. But you might marry again.'

Shaking her head, Ellen sighed. 'No, I'll not marry again. Once is more than enough for me. I want to be in control of my own life and the children's. I want to make the decisions.' She watched the children, but her mind wandered to the handsome Mr Hamilton. Marrying a gentleman would change her mind, for a wealthy gentleman would keep her and the children safe. But such an idea was never to be. Mr Hamilton was in the past. The future was all she cared about now. 'I just want them three to be happy and safe and to never know a moment's hunger again.'

'They won't know hunger again. Not like back home, and not if there is plenty of work as you think there is. We'll manage.' Riona looked up as a sailor shouted from the rigging. 'What did he say?'

189

Ellen stood and stared where the sailor pointed. 'There's something in the water.' She went to the rail and searched the ocean.

'He said it's a shark.' Riona joined her, eyes wide. 'Can you see it?'

'Look, Mam.' Austin came to stand beside her. 'See the sharks?'

In amazement, Ellen watched in fascination as several sharks tore into the bloated white shape of a large whale. She'd never seen such a thing.

'Magnificent, isn't it?' Mr Donaldson asked, coming alongside.

'I'm not sure . . .' Ellen couldn't take her eyes off the sharks tearing into the whale. 'Such big mouths and their teeth rip the flesh so easily.'

'Sharp as razors those teeth,' Mr Donaldson added. He glanced up at the sails, which deflated a little. 'The wind is dropping. We'll have to tack our way for a bit.' He rubbed his hands and smiled. 'But I'll have some men throw a few lines over the side. We might have fresh fish for supper!'

'As long as they don't catch a shark,' Riona uttered in fright.

'Nay, Miss O'Mara, shark tastes delightful.' He sauntered away.

Ellen nudged Riona. 'He'd make a nice husband for you, so he would.'

Riona blushed. 'Hush yourself.'

'He's a good decent man.'

The colour drained from Riona's face. 'Am I not soiled goods now? No man will want me.'

'Will you listen to yourself?' Ellen tutted. 'You were attacked. That wasn't your fault. Not every man is the devil like Lester. When you meet a good decent

190

fellow, he'll either understand or run a mile and if he runs, then he was never the right one for you.'

'You make it sound simple, so you do, and it's not. Besides, Mr Donaldson is a sailor, Ellen, living his life in the dangers of the oceans. I'll not ever marry a seaman. Hasn't the sea taken enough from me? I'll be glad enough to never lay eyes on a boat or the sea again!' Riona hurried away from the rail.

Ellen sighed and gazed down at the water. The sharks and the whale carcass had drifted behind in the wake of the ship. She couldn't fault Riona's emotions. Despite living beside the sea all her life, Ellen was keen to turn her back on it. After this voyage, she'd not board a ship again. She would make or break herself in the colony.

★ ★ ★

Two weeks later, the cry of 'Land' echoed around the ship.

Ellen, Riona, and the children joined the rest of the passengers rushing to the rail on the starboard side for their first sight of land.

In the distance, an emerald-green line smudged the horizon under heavy clouds.

'Is that Australia?' Austin asked.

A sailor walking by stopped and hitched up the coil of rope on his shoulder. 'Nay, lad, 'tis King Island. But on the stern side ye might see the mainland soon if the fog doesn't cover us, which I think it will.'

'So, we'll be in Sydney soon?' Austin asked him.

'Nay, we're still a couple weeks out from Sydney yet, lad.'

True to the sailor's prophecy, a thick fog descended

as they sailed slowly into Bass Straight. The temperature dropped slightly, shivering the passengers, but they still braved the upper deck hoping the fog would lift and they'd see the mainland. However, as the day grew older, the fog grew denser. The captain issued for a horn to be blown at intervals for Bass Strait was the main thoroughfare for shipping from Melbourne to Sydney and many ships sailed the choppy waters.

Night fell and wearily the passengers went below, disappointed not to have seen land close up.

For the next three days it rained heavily. The source of freshwater filling buckets and barrels lifted spirits slightly. They would have water to wash themselves and some of their clothes before they arrived in Sydney in a few days. The children created a game of catching water in cups to see who held the most, then they quickly drank it in a contest.

The passengers were inspired by the crew to start cleaning out their quarters and sort out their belongings. In turns, trunks were brought up and clothes arranged. Weighted bags full of rubbish and items no longer needed were sent overboard.

'Will you cut my hair, Riona?' Ellen asked one morning a few days out from Sydney. Ellen received their trunk that morning and was sorting out clothes. She was surprised how much the children had grown on the voyage. Austin and Patrick's trousers were inches shorter in the legs now, and it gave Ellen a sense of pride that her sons were growing with the supply of regular food after years of surviving on mere mouthfuls a day.

'Cut your hair. Is it mad you are?' Riona's eyes widened in shock.

'Not all of it,' Ellen scoffed. 'Just the ends. They are

ratty and untidy, and I want to make a good impression on Mr Emmerson.'

'Holy Virgin and the saints save us! Sure, and your hair will be under your bonnet? Mr Emmerson won't see it. Roll it up.'

'I will roll it up, but I need it trimming. Oh, fine. I'll ask someone else to do it!' Ellen snapped.

'Give me the scissors!' Riona grabbed the scissors from Ellen's hand. Tempers were short and fraying the closer they got to ending the voyage. For too long they'd been cooped up without the relief of any privacy.

'Just the ends mind,' Ellen warned. Her nerves were tight with tension.

In a few days she'd be facing Mr Emmerson and so much depended on him liking her enough to help her find a position somewhere. Would New South Wales be against Catholic Irish? Would she be reading signs saying, 'No Irish Apply?'

She knew from hearing the sailors talk that New York and Boston had seen similar signs in the streets. The Irish had emigrated there in their thousands, swamping the cities with people begging for work and housing. In some places they lived like rats in cellars, begging on the streets, or turning to illegal activities to make ends meet. Was that waiting for them in Sydney? Had she made a mistake? Should she have tried to find work in Dublin first? At least there it was her people. Or should she have stayed in Liverpool close to Mr Hamilton?

The thoughts and worries whirled in her mind the closer they sailed to Sydney.

When the following day, word spread that land was sighted again, Ellen rushed above to look. Overnight a steady southerly wind had hastened the journey up along the coast of New South Wales and now that dawn had broken, excitement filled the crew and passengers as the ship sailed close enough to land to see a hazy greenness of the shoreline.

Several white birds swooped over the masts; their cries not heard for months. Cheers filled the air and women wept in joy, men shook hands and children ran about whooping.

'Australia, Mammy.' Austin stared wide-eyed at the rugged cliffs. 'We did it. We sailed all the way here.'

Tears caught in Ellen's throat. 'We did, darling.'

He looked at Ellen, pride in his eyes. 'You saved us, Mammy.'

She hugged him to her side. 'There's nothing I wouldn't do for you and your brother and sister.'

Bridget gazed up at the birds in wonder. 'Look, Mammy, look at the birds.'

'I see them, sweetheart.' Watching the birds, Ellen noticed the crew busy up in the rigging. The sails flapped and snapped in the wind.

Riona stood beside Ellen, tears running down her cheeks. 'If only Mammy had lived . . .'

'She lives on in us,' Ellen murmured, not wanting to dwell on sadness, not today. She clapped her hands. 'Right, stir yourselves, we've much to do.'

By evening the captain had sailed the ship to the opening of the large harbour and there waited for the pilot to come aboard. The stiff breeze was against them, so it was decided they'd wait out at sea and make the journey into the harbour the following day.

The excitement on board gave the ship a carnival atmosphere, and the passengers sang and danced on the upper deck, knowing it to be their last night on board. The captain allowed the crew and passengers a double ration of rum and food for supper.

'You'll be happy to go ashore tomorrow, Mrs Kittrick?' Mr Donaldson asked.

'I will indeed.' She smiled, watching Patrick twirl Bridget to the music of a fiddler and someone playing a tin whistle.

Mr Donaldson sucked on a pipe. 'The medical officer will come on board in the morning and begin to examine everyone. Thankfully, we are in good health, thanks to the captain and his faster route. The deaths have been few. I've been on worst voyages, believe me.'

'We've been truly fortunate, but I will be glad to get off this ship and onto land. I'm eager to begin my new life.'

Moira came up to them. 'Will you not have a dance with me, Mr Donaldson?'

'How could I refuse, madam?' He laughed, taking her hand and joining the others who swung about on the deck.

Mrs Duffy took Donaldson's seat on the crate beside Ellen. 'Come tomorrow so begins our new lives, Mrs Kittrick.'

Ellen glanced at the other woman, who over the weeks had become a friend of sorts. 'So, it does.'

'Thanks to the Virgin Mother for her protection, so we are. I must say you've changed a lot in the last three months, I suppose we all have.'

'I've changed?' Ellen queried. 'How so?'

'You've grown prettier, Mrs Kittrick. Your body has filled out. Spending days in the sun and not always wearing your bonnet has brightened your hair to a copper colour.'

'I couldn't wear my bonnet in fear of the wind taking it.' Ellen grinned.

'You didn't suffer seasickness as many of us did, which coming on top of years of hunger nearly finished some of us off.'

'As I mentioned to you before, my da had a boat. Are you excited to leave the ship, Mrs Duffy?'

'Not really. Oh, I'll be happy to get off the ship, but I'm fearful of what happens next, so I am. Seamus has spoken to a few of the crew and a few of the single men passengers who have family here in this country. The knowledge is there's work in Sydney. The town is expanding, and Seamus can labour on the new buildings.'

'Then surely you must put your worries aside?'

'I hope I can. I'd like to have a cottage and tend to a few chickens.'

Ellen smiled. 'Chickens. What fine creatures they are and of such use to a family. I miss the ones I had.'

Mrs Duffy gave a nervous laugh. 'I know you've told me that you want to find work, but aren't you frightened, being a woman, of not finding any?'

'There's work if you look hard enough. It's not like back home. There's no famine here. This is a new country.'

'It's still run by the English. They still hate the Irish. How can any of us succeed with that over our heads?'

Pausing, Ellen's eyes grew misty with the dreams that swam in her head. 'I will thrive, Mrs Duffy. I'll never go another day with hunger pains, or an empty purse and my children will be happy and healthy.'

''Tis the dream we all share, Mrs Kittrick, but it's not always easy to achieve.'

Lifting her chin, Ellen frowned at Mrs Duffy. 'I'll

devote my life to achieving it.'

Mrs Duffy glanced away, as though uncomfortable with Ellen's passion. 'We must stay in touch, Mrs Kittrick, for the children have grown close, so they have. I'd wish for Caroline and Aisling to marry like-minded people as we are, and young men who belong to the true faith like Austin and Patrick.'

Ellen stiffened. She'd not have her sons married off to the Duffy girls whose parents had no ambition. She wanted better for Austin and Patrick and Bridget, too. 'The true faith may not bring us the comfort we would wish, Mrs Duffy.'

'How so?' The other woman scowled.

'I'll not start my new life shackled to the parts of the old country which may hinder my success in the colony.'

Mrs Duffy gasped. 'You'll give up the true religion?'

'If I have to, that and my family will no longer speak Irish.'

Mrs Duffy looked ready to faint. 'Holy Virgin Mother. To deny your children their church and their native tongue?'

Ellen stood, enjoying the cool breeze on her face as the sun set. The sky blazed orange, and the water glistened as though sprinkled with a thousand jewels. 'I'll do *whatever* it takes to give my children the best in life, Mrs Duffy.'

★   ★   ★

Leaning against the rail, Ellen breathed in the strange scent as the ship slowly made its way along the harbour. The sun blazed, burning them in its intensity. They'd been informed that it was summer on this side of the world. Summer in February! It seemed ridiculous. But the heat wasn't a lie and Ellen had changed from her woollen dress to a printed linen one, insisting Riona and the children change to lighter clothes as well.

She looked everywhere at once, trying to absorb the details of this new home. Sandstone rocks jutted out of tree covered cliffs edging the water. Gangly olive-green trees coated the dry land, running down to little bays and sandy beaches. Here and there small wooden huts appeared in a clearing before being swallowed up by more forest.

Large ships, like the one they sailed on, were anchored in various spots in the harbour or making their way out to open sea, likely back to England. Smaller boats kept to the shoreline and Ellen could see men fishing with nets just as her da had done. Overhead birds dipped and soared, filling the air with their cries.

'What is that smell?' Riona asked, holding Bridget's hand.

'It's eucalyptus, miss,' a sailor told her as he passed them. 'The native trees have an oil that is most useful. The blacks use it for medicinal purposes.'

'The blacks?' Riona blinked in confusion.

'The aborigines, the natives.'

'I didn't know there were natives, Ellen?' Riona squeaked.

'The city ones are harmless enough,' the sailor added. 'Not sure about those further inland. I doubt you'll see much of them.' He went about his work, leaving Ellen pondering on his information.

'Riona, I think we need to find out how to rent some land,' Ellen said.

'Sweet Jesus, Ellen, we've not yet arrived. We don't even know if we'll have a roof over our heads tonight, never mind renting land. We've no money to rent anything!'

'Not now, but once we've jobs and saved our wages, we will. I want a farm.'

'Let us settle in a bit first before you start making bigger plans.'

Ellen didn't reply. She would ask Mr Emmerson. He'd know how she could rent some land. Her stomach knotted with nerves. Soon she'd meet the man who hopefully would help them start again. What if he was an awful, unfriendly eejit of a man?

The pilot steered the ship further into the harbour and Ellen was pleasantly surprised by the buildings coming into view. Houses were now made of bricks with formal gardens. A carriage trundled along a dirt road leading into populated streets. Warehouses and buildings crowded the shoreline. Numerous boats and ships of differing sizes filled the cove, which seemed to be the hub of industry and commerce.

Ellen gazed at it all in excitement. They'd done it. They were safe on the other side of the world. She hadn't known what to expect, but her glimpse of the sprawling city of Sydney was better than she'd hoped.

For the rest of the day, they were kept waiting as the medical officer and his assistant came aboard to examine all the passengers and crew for fever and other illnesses. Ellen prided herself on her family being fit and healthy. The gauntness and grey skin of the years of hunger had left them, and days spent in the sunshine on the upper deck gave the children a healthy tan. Dressed in their best clothes, Ellen knew they'd never looked better in their lives.

Given the clean bill of health, the captain gave the order for the small rowing boat to be lowered and for the first-class passengers to be disembarked. The mail was called for and Ellen added ten letters to the mail-bag, parting with some of her hoarded coins to send them. She had nine letters to Mr Hamilton and one to Mr Wilton.

The process of getting passengers ashore was slow. Despite having days to be prepared, several passengers were tardy in getting themselves organised. The Duffy family being one, as Mrs Duffy was constantly packing and unpacking her trunk, looking for items.

Ellen took advantage of this and had her luggage and family ready on the upper deck.

'I see you're waiting to go ashore, Mrs Kittrick?' Doctor Williams said with a smile.

'We are, sir.'

He held out his hand and she shook it. 'I wish you all the best, Mrs Kittrick.'

'Thank you, Doctor, and to you, too.'

Half an hour later, as the burning sun slid slowly in the west, the captain gave the orders that the last boat was going ashore for the day. The rest of the passengers would be sent in the morning, for it was too dangerous to disembark in darkness.

Ellen strode up to Mr Donaldson. 'Can we go next, please?

We've been waiting all afternoon.'

Mr Donaldson, looking a little tired and stressed, checked his list and nodded. 'Are you entirely ready, Mrs Kittrick? Nothing left in the hold?'

'We are ready.'

He issued instructions to the sailors and within minutes, Ellen and her family were being helped down into the small boat. Once Moira and another family and all the luggage had been placed in the boat, the sailors rowed towards the shore.

Lit up by the orange glow of sunset, the whitewashed buildings grew closer until finally Ellen stepped onto the wooden wharf.

Land. Australia.

Her legs wobbled, and the children laughed as they all stumbled like drunkards as they walked towards the customs office building not used to having solid ground beneath them.

Once passed through customs, Ellen led the family out of the building to the roadside. She held one handle of the trunk and Riona held the other, while Austin carried the two carpet bags and Patrick was told not to let go of Bridget's hand. Numerous horse-drawn vehicles plied up and down the road, warehousemen pushed wheelbarrows while gentlemen hurried along, newspapers tucked under their arms.

It was noisy and the smell of the sea mingled with the stink of rubbish in the gutters and on the breeze, Ellen smelled something cooking from one of the inns.

'Where are we to go, Ellen?' Riona asked, worried. 'It's getting dark.'

'I expected Mr Emmerson to meet us.' Ellen turned around, looking back at the customs building. 'Did we miss him in there, do you think?'

'It was so busy we could have, aye.'

'Jesus, Mary and Joseph!' Ellen fumed. 'I'll have to go back in.

Stay here. I'll be as quick as I can.'

'Mrs Kittrick!' Moira waved to her as she exited the building. 'Moira, have you seen Mr Emmerson?'

'Aye, he's here.' Moira gestured over her shoulder

into the building. 'He's just fetching the last of the stragglers and then we're all going to the government building up the road which is our lodgings.'

Ellen sagged in relief. 'I was fearful we'd be sleeping on the road tonight.'

'Nay, he's lovely is Mr Emmerson. He'll look after us. There he is.'

Searching through the crowd of fellow passengers, Ellen craned her neck to see anyone new. 'Are the lodgings far?'

'No, I don't think so.' Moira heaved her small trunk up into her arms.

'We need a cart,' Ellen said, picking up Moira's canvas bag.

'Ladies, ladies, let me help you,' a voice behind them spoke.

'Oh, Mr Emmerson, what a gentleman you are,' Moira cooed. 'Ellen, this is Mr Emmerson. Mr Emmerson, Mrs Ellen Kittrick.'

Ellen stared at the face of a man much younger than she was expecting. In her mind Mr Emmerson had been in his late fifties with grey whiskers and a bit of a round belly.

'Alistair Emmerson at your service, madam.' He smiled widely, revealing a dimple in his left cheek. His green eyes shone happily and when he doffed his hat, she noticed dark blond hair the colour of wet straw.

'I'm pleased to meet you, Mr Emmerson.'

'I am sorry I did not find you in the building, Mrs Kittrick. It is rather crowded in there, is it not? Where are your family?'

'Over there.' She pointed to where they all stood by the road.

'Good, good. Shall we get you settled before we

lose all light?'

Following behind the group of people, Ellen shared the weight of the trunk with Riona, carefully keeping an eye on the children who were growing tired and hungry.

A few streets away Mr Emmerson stopped and indicated for them to enter a warehouse type of building made of sandstone blocks. Inside, the delightful smell of simmering stew made Ellen's mouth water.

Mr Emmerson stood on a raised platform at one end of the long room that held numerous tables and benches. 'Ladies and gentlemen, please listen up. Firstly, welcome to Sydney. I am most pleased that you have arrived. Mr and Mrs Weston, standing over there near the refreshments table, are in charge and they live next door should you need them in an emergency during the night. There are three levels in this building. Single men will stay on this level, married couples and families on the middle level and at the top, the single women. All bunks have clean bedding. Meals are provided three times a day, a lot like the routine of the ship you just disembarked from.' He smiled, one hand holding sheets of papers. 'Washing facilities are out the back through the door there.'

'He's easy on the eyes, isn't he?' Moira nudged Ellen.

Ellen shushed her and listened to Mr Emmerson.

'I shall be back in the morning to discuss with you all about work positions and other such important matters, but for now, it is late, and you must be tired and hungry. Mr and Mrs Weston will help and guide you through your first night. Please eat the meal that has been prepared. Good night.' He stepped down and walked through the crowd, who began dispersing into groups.

Ellen told the children to sit down at the nearest table and she'd get them some food.

'I'll help you,' Riona said.

Ellen pushed the trunk to the end of the table to get it out of the way. 'I think you should go up and find us some bunks. Take Austin with you. I'll send Patrick up once he's eaten to take over the minding of it.'

'Are you worried we'll not have a good position upstairs?' Riona glanced around. 'Everyone is only bothered about eating.'

'Good, then we can get the best bunks, which we don't want to be near the door.'

'I'll go up now.' Riona grabbed some of their bags. 'What do you think of Mr Emmerson? He wasn't what I was expecting.'

'I know,' Ellen declared. 'I thought he'd be old and fat and full of self-importance!' She grinned. 'Where are his whiskers and cane?'

'I do have a cane, but alas not whiskers,' an amused voice said behind Ellen.

She swung around, heat flaring to her cheeks. 'God and his saints! I didn't mean to be rude, sir. Forgive me.' Ellen wondered if she should fall to her knees and beg his forgiveness.

'I try not to run to fat either.' Emmerson winked.

'Mr Emmerson, I'm sorry, truly.'

'I see the joke, Mrs Kittrick.' His boyish smile brightened his eyes. 'What is life if we cannot laugh, especially at oneself?'

She nodded, hoping she'd not ruined her chances of getting his help.

'From my notes I thought there was to be six of you?' He glanced at the sheets of paper in his hand.

204

'But on the ship Doctor Williams informed me that your mother died on the journey.'

'She did, yes.'

He bowed. 'My deepest sympathies, Mrs Kittrick. That must have been extremely difficult for you.'

'Thank you, sir.'

'I hope you sleep well. I shall bid you goodnight.'

'What a lovely man,' Riona said, watching him shake hands with a few men by the door before leaving.

'Come on now, let us get sorted.' Ellen watched him, too, wondering what opportunities would come their way.

15

Rafe left the bank and headed along London Road towards the docks. The quick walk in the crisp February air would help clear his head after a morning of meetings.

With his loan secured from the bank, he had charted another ship and filled it with cargo. It made financial sense to have two ships operating at the same time. While one was heading to Australia, the other would be coming back. And now that gold had been found in the south of the colony, the government was crying out for more men to replace those that had gone bush to seek their fortunes digging in the ground. He could easily fill a dozen ships, but he must start slowly and build a solid business structure. To be fickle and greedy at this point would be too daring, too risky, something his father would have done.

He bounded up the stairs to his office, meeting Pollard at the top.

Pollard took his top hat and coat. 'Sir, you have a visitor, Mr Milford.'

Rafe paused, then opened the door. 'Milford? This is a pleasant surprise.'

'Rafe.' Milford shook Rafe's hand and clapped him on the back. 'Long time no see, my friend. You look well.'

'I am. How are you, and the family?' Rafe waved him to the chair opposite his desk, happy to see his long-time friend. 'It must have been a year since I saw you last at the club.'

'Yes, it must be. Mayfair is lost without you,' Milford joked.

Rafe grunted in amusement. 'Not likely. What brings you to Liverpool?'

'My father. I am to take control of the shipping business in New York, whether I want to or not. I sail in the morning.' Milford shrugged. 'I always knew I would have to go sometime, but leaving is difficult. My mistress is none too happy about it either.'

'No, I suppose not.'

Milford laughed. 'Well, I will soon be replaced, have no fear about that.'

Pollard knocked and brought in a tray of coffee and placed it on a small table before discreetly leaving again.

While Rafe poured the coffee, Milford stood by the window, gazing at the ships scene. 'How are you finding it living here and not in London?'

'I like the lack of gossip.' Rafe took his coffee and sat behind his desk. 'Here I can simply just get on with what I have to do. No fires to put out.'

'Speaking of fires . . . ' Milford sighed.

A tingle of anxiety trickled down Rafe's back. 'What is it?'

'I met your sister two days ago.'

'Iris? You saw her in Paris?'

'No, the family returned to London a month ago. I met Iris by chance walking along Oxford Street.' Milford sipped his coffee.

'They have been back in England a month and I did not know.'

'I think that was deliberate, my friend.'

'You might as well tell me it all,' Rafe said, bracing himself for whatever was to come.

'Iris married Edgar Porter-Denning two weeks ago.'

'No!' Rafe could not believe it. 'Porter-Denning is older than my father. They were at university together. Why would she marry *him* and so quickly? They only left here three months ago to go to Paris. Why did Iris not write to me? I could have done something.'

Milford held up his hands. 'Iris asked me to tell you that you must not be offended. The marriage is done and cannot be annulled . . . .'

Rafe took his meaning and swore under his breath. 'That bastard has taken advantage of her.'

'No, by all accounts I have heard Iris was willing, perhaps not swooning in delight, but she went willingly to the church.'

'But why?' Rafe could not understand it.

'There is more . . . '

'Naturally.' Rafe groaned and ran a hand through his hair.

'Drew got himself into trouble in Paris. He was arrested for cheating at a card game. They all fled back to London. It seems Porter-Denning helped them. All he asked in return for the aid was to marry Iris as he needs an heir. She agreed. Her new husband has them all living at his estate near Watford. Iris said she will write to you and explain.'

'I cannot believe it.' Rafe sagged against his chair. 'My family have once more become the gossip fodder for London's drawing rooms.'

Milford drank some more coffee. 'Unfortunately, your brother is wilful and selfish. He does as he pleases, with no thought to the shame he brings upon your family. Iris may have married well, and she is now secure, but your father and Drew will think this gives them free rein to do as they please once again. I am sorry, old chap.'

'I have no words.' Rafe shrugged despondently. 'When I believe that they can sink no lower, they manage to achieve it. For Drew to be arrested for cheating . . . and dear Iris must marry an old man to save the family . . . '

'It is not your fault, Rafe.'

'I tried so often to help. I brought them here thinking a new city would change them. Then when they left, I was glad of the peace and that is the honest truth of it.'

'Your father and brother cannot be tamed. You have tried to curb their excesses, and nothing has come of it. They are determined to ruin themselves, just be thankful Iris has made a good marriage and is safe.' Milford placed his cup on the tray. 'I must go, old chap, much to do before I board the ship.'

Rafe shook his hand. 'Take care of yourself. Enjoy New York and all it has to offer.'

'Huh, I'd rather be sailing to the colony and join in the gold rush there.'

'You? Digging in the dirt?' Rafe laughed. He had never seen Milford dirty, ever.

'Well, maybe not me personally, but I would pay someone to do it for me. I do like the thought of striding out over land no one has ventured on before.'

The idea gave Rafe pause for thought. Such a thing would be exciting.

'Though should I not go to New York, my father would easily disinherit me, and I enjoy my luxuries too much for that to happen.'

Rafe chuckled. 'Safe travels, my friend, and thank you for bringing me my family's news.'

Milford nodded gravely. 'Put them from your mind,

Rafe. Find yourself a lovely lady and get married, raise some sons. Life cannot be all about making money, or at least do both those things at the same time. Farewell.'

Rafe stepped to the window after Milford had left, his mind pondering on Iris but also on Mrs Kittrick. Had she arrived safely in Sydney? What was she doing right now? It would be another three months before he heard from Emmerson that the *Blue Maid* had arrived. Had Mrs Kittrick written to him? Did she think of him as he thought of her?

He stared out at the numerous ships' masts, the gulls flying against grey clouds that held rain. Below on the street a man walked past pushing a handcart holding a trunk and some carpet bags. The man was going on an adventure, likely boarding a ship today which would take him far across the oceans to experience new places and meet new people, to try different foods and cultures.

Suddenly Rafe felt confined, limited. He had travelled the British Isles and some parts of France, but for the last five years he had been so busy rescuing his family's wealth and rebuilding their financial status with new business ideas that he'd forgotten what it was to simply relax and enjoy his life. When had he last gone game shooting with friends, or seen a show at the theatre?

He was thirty-two years old and each night he left the office, went home, and worked in his study, eating meals at his desk from a tray. Since Iris and his mother left for Paris, he had forgone all entertainments. He did not have a mistress, and the few businessmen he knew in Liverpool did not entertain him socially, nor he them. They would meet in clubs during the day and discuss business before parting ways. He had been so focused on regaining the family's reputation and wealth that he'd forgotten to actually live.

At this rate, he would die a lonely old man.

He tapped his fingers together, deep in thought. Milford was right. He should find a lady and get married, raise some sons . . .

Mrs Kittrick sprang to mind. Her sweet face and those beautiful eyes which spoke to him when she was not even aware.

Yet she was on the other side of the world.

She was where *his* ship was sailing to . . .

★ ★ ★

'Do I look decent?' Ellen asked Riona.

'Will you listen to yourself? Aye, you're fine.'

Ellen wiped down her skirt one final time, primped the lace at her throat, and took a deep breath. 'Wish me good fortune.'

'I pray to the Holy Mother you'll find a position.'

'What have I said about speaking of religion so openly?'

'Whist, what is the harm in wishing you well?' Riona snapped.

Ellen closed her eyes in exasperation. No matter how often she said it, Riona refused to consider reducing her Irishness.

In the three days since they arrived, Ellen and her family had walked all over the city, getting familiar with the streets and way of life here. She had posted two more letters to Mr Hamilton telling him about their arrival and accommodation in Sydney. She hoped he would be pleased to receive so many letters from her, as she believed he would be.

What she also noticed when walking the streets were several signs stating Irish need not apply for work or lodging. Just as in Liverpool, the Irish had a reputation for drunkenness and laziness. It strengthened Ellen's resolve to play down their native speech and hide the obvious signs of their Catholicism.

'Behave for Aunt Riona,' she told Austin and Patrick. 'Watch over your sister.'

Giving the children a kiss, Ellen tied her bonnet over her newly washed hair and slipping on her gloves, headed for the stairs.

'Good luck, Ellen,' Moira called from her bunk.

'And you, Moira. I hope you receive word on your husband today.' Ellen smiled and descended the stairs just as Mrs Duffy came up. 'Good morning, Mrs Duffy.'

'Mrs Kittrick.' Mrs Duffy nodded stiffly. 'I see you're on your way out?'

'Aye, I'm going out to look for work again. When I spoke to Mr Emmerson yesterday, he said I should easily find a position at one of the hotels, especially those that serve food. If I have no luck there, he says to try some private homes along the harbour shore and apply for a housekeeping position.'

'May God deliver you such an opportunity.'

'I'd rather depend on my own skills than leave it up to God,' Ellen snapped, and the other woman stiffly turned away.

Outside, Ellen chastised herself for riling Mrs Duffy. The poor woman didn't deserve it. Mrs Duffy held onto her religion like a child held onto a favourite blanket. It was her security and Ellen had no right to patronise her about it. After all, Mammy had been just the same. If her own faith was waning, and it was, then she still had to be considerate of others.

Hurrying along Cumberland Street away from the harbour, Ellen turned a corner and bumped straight into a man, his newspaper flattening between them.

'Good gracious me, I do apologise, madam.'

'Forgive me!'

They both spoke at once.

Ellen smiled at Mr Emmerson. 'I wasn't looking where I was going.'

'Nor I, Mrs Kittrick. I was reading the newspaper, which I should be taken to task for. I can do such an activity in the comforts of my home. However, it is fortuitous that we have met, for I was on my way to visit you.'

'*Me?*'

'Indeed. You see, my housekeeper has left me, Mrs Kittrick. She has decided to marry a man, the butcher's delivery man to be precise, and they have taken themselves off to the gold fields beyond Melbourne. Tent cities are springing up all over the place down there, apparently. They stretch deep inland.'

'Oh.' Ellen didn't know how else to reply. She knew of the gold rush fever that was gripping the colony.

'So, I am without a housekeeper and I thought of you.'

Hope blossomed in her chest. 'Thank you.'

'Would you care to accompany me back to my abode? I can show you around and we can talk about whether it would be suitable for you?'

'Yes, thank you, sir.'

They fell into step together, heading back towards the harbour.

'My house is not too far, situated on Lower Fort

Street, close to the shore,' he told her as they turned left and walked west along Argyle Street. 'I bought my house when I arrived here three years ago. It is small but perfectly agreeable for my current lifestyle in Sydney. I do of course want to build a beautiful house on the farmland I have out in the country.'

'You have land as well?' Ellen asked him eagerly.

'Yes, five hundred acres was granted to me last year. I've a large herd of cattle roaming it with a man to watch over them.'

'How are you granted farmland, Mr Emmerson? It is my wish to have some myself.'

'Twenty years ago, or more, land grants were given to free settlers and some ex-convicts. Now, in most cases, you must have done something for the government or be a person of good standing to receive such land grants. The rest of the land must be bought.'

'I see.' Disappointment filled her. The land grants were not for the likes of her but if she could save and in time buy land herself . . .

'My import business has been successful, and through my contacts I was able to apply for a grant some time ago. With Mr Hamilton and I conducting the emigration scheme, I plan to extend my land holding. The government is rather pleased with me, as I have offered my services to many an expedition inland. By becoming useful to the government and having a great many friends of importance, one has the opportunity to advance here, and I intend to, Mrs Kittrick.'

Ellen glanced at him and realised that under the friendly, boyish exterior was a smart business brain.

Emmerson stopped before a picket fence in front of a red-bricked two-storey house. Shingle roof tiles,

214

small sash windows and a smoking chimney completed the picture. Vacant land with a horse grazing ran beside the house down to the water's edge.

'Millers Point is to our left, and Dawes Point is to our right. From the upstairs windows you can see over the harbour.' Emmerson opened the gate and led her to the front door, which he opened with a key.

The house was indeed simple. A square sitting room and dining room was on either side of the hallway. Beyond the staircase was the narrow kitchen and pantry with steps leading down to a cellar. A lean-to near the back door provided a scullery, and down the back garden was the lavatory and a small stable. Upstairs were three bedrooms and in the loft space, room for a few single beds.

'I thought your children could share the loft space, while you and your sister have one bedroom?' Emmerson said, opening the door to a spacious bedroom. 'The other bedroom is mine and the middle room is for storage, I am afraid.'

'It's lovely.' Ellen followed him downstairs. The house wasn't as grand as Wilton Manor, but it was three times the size of her cottage back home.

'As a live-in housekeeper, it would save you on renting lodgings. There is a good Roman Catholic school just up the road. I would not charge your sister to stay. She could either help you, and I would pay her, or she could find a position elsewhere?'

'It seems perfect, Mr Emmerson.'

'I am a remarkably busy man and am gone from morning until evening. Therefore, I would not be under your feet or need you at my beck and call every moment of the day.'

Ellen nodded, thinking quickly as she gazed about

the sitting room. 'I'd like to take the position, thank you.'

He smiled widely. 'Excellent. Now, I have an appointment in King Street, but here are the keys. You can bring your family here and get settled. I will be back this evening.'

'Shall I make you a meal?' Ellen asked, taking the key from him.

'That would be most agreeable. I shall be home for seven o'clock.'

Left alone, Ellen took her time to visit all the rooms again. In Emmerson's bedroom she noticed the neatly made double bed with its green and red patchwork quilt cover. The book of poems on the little table by his bed. The wardrobe held all his clothes and on top of a set of drawers was his shaving equipment and a basin and bowl. Everything was neat and tidy.

Downstairs, in the kitchen, the cupboards held plain white porcelain crockery. An earthenware tea-pot stood on the narrow table, pushed against one wall. The range, which needed a good black leading, smouldered with glowing embers and Ellen added pieces of wood to it. If she was to cook a meal later, she needed a good fire going.

Next, she unlocked the pantry, making note of the food stores, tea, sugar, oats, molasses, salt, and flour. Opening the door to the cellar, she went down a few steps and could see the shelves were dimly lit by the slatted vent in the far wall. A sack of potatoes was at the bottom of the steps and hanging on a hook above was a leg of ham.

That was supper sorted.

Another glance about the house gave Ellen a thrill of excitement. She had a paid position and home for her children and Riona. She would work her fingers to the bone to please Mr Emmerson for giving her this chance.

★ ★ ★

Rafe entered his house, shaking the rain off his hat and coat.

'Evening, sir,' his housemaid greeted him, taking his wet things. 'Dinner will be ready in half an hour, sir. The fire is lit in your study.'

'Thank you.' Rafe welcomed the heat in the room as he walked into the study. Outside, the rain was turning to ice and a freezing gale blew off the coast.

Retrieving the mail from his desk, he stood with his back to the fire and sorted through the envelopes until he recognised Iris's handwriting.

12th February 1852.

Dear darling brother,

I suspect that by now you would have met with your good friend Mr Milford and he in turn would have told you my news. Please do not be disheartened by it.

When I considered all the facts before me, I realised that my chances of marrying well had greatly diminished over recent years, and even more so lately with Drew's arrest in Paris. Marrying for love is unlikely to be my fate. I am nearly twenty-seven years old, Rafe. No longer a young girl with a head full of dreams.

Marrying Edgar made many people happy.

Also, I would like to be a mother and have a home of my own. By marrying Edgar, I am mistress of two houses, Cherrybank, the country estate and Edgar's London townhouse and soon I would hope, God willing, I shall be blessed with a dear baby to love and cherish. Most of all, I have security — a rare commodity in our family, do you not agree?

Edgar admires and respects me. In his own way he loves me, and I am content with that. He needs a wife and wishes for a son most passionately. If I give him that, then my life will be worth something. For his part, he has been a good friend to Father and Drew. Once again, they are debt free. Father promises to change. Time will tell.

Drew has been commissioned into the army. Edgar insisted upon it when he cleared his debts. Hopefully, it will be the making of him. Once Drew's training is complete, perhaps the army will send him far from London and the evil hold of the gambling dens. We can but pray for it.

Mama is as well as can be in her fragile state. Fleeing Paris brought her undone in many ways, and I feared we'd be burying her along the way. She rallied at Edgar's estate, but I feel her time is limited. Therefore, I wish to invite you to come to Cherrybank and visit us. Mama would be so delighted to see you as I would be, and I would like you to spend time with Edgar, who is kind and considerate. Perhaps then it would put your mind at rest that I have not made a terrible decision.

With love, your sister,
Iris.

Rafe folded the letter. His sister was not a foolish woman. She would have weighed up the situation and realised how much good she could do by marrying Porter-Denning. How could he blame her for wanting to be secure? Still, he harboured some guilt that he had not been able to keep her safe and happy,

Mother as well. He had tried hard to, but obviously not enough. Father had won.

His fists clenched at the thought of his smug father sitting in the drawing room of *Cherrybank* without a worry in the world, knowing he would forever have a home with his daughter and live in the luxury he had been born to.

And Mama . . . Dear sweet Mama. Frail and worn out with the anxiety of being married to a gambler and the mother to one. He must see her again before it was too late, and she was forever lost to him. He would leave tomorrow. Spend a day or two with Iris and Mama and then leave England as he planned.

16

Hanging out multiple white sheets and tablecloths, Ellen squinted in the glare of the sunlight that reflected off the water. She'd been up before dawn to beat the heat, for washing day was hard enough without doing it in soaring temperatures. Scrubbing and rinsing the pile of washing would take all morning, and she had so much to do afterwards.

Mr Emmerson entertained many people each week and with so much cooking and cleaning her time was never her own. But he paid her well, and she listened and learned from him. He was happy to share his knowledge of the city and living in the colony, which Ellen stored in her mind for future use.

The harbour shone in the March sunlight, dazzling and blue. Small vessels tacked across from bay to bay while slightly to her left larger boats unloaded their cargo into warehouses lining the shores.

The sudden blast from a cannon made her jump. The soldiers were firing at the battery to the east.

'That scared me!' Bridget laughed where she stood by the fence feeding Pepper, Mr Emmerson's horse.

'We should be used to it by now, shouldn't we?' Ellen grabbed the empty basket and went back to the washing tub.

Another ten minutes had the basket full of Mr Emmerson's clean wet shirts. 'Bridget, leave Pepper alone and come and help me.'

'When will I have riding lessons?' Her daughter's eyes shone with excitement.

'We'll see. Now put all those dark clothes in the tub and swish them about with the stick,' Ellen instructed, carrying the basket to the line strung between the stable and the lean-to.

As Ellen pegged out shirts, she thought about Emmerson's announcement last night as he came into the kitchen after dinner. He ate his meals alone in the dining room, yet the moment he finished he would come into the kitchen to talk to Ellen and the family.

At first Ellen had been surprised that he'd want to spend time with them, but she soon realised he was lonely. He enjoyed talking to the whole family, listening to the children as they spoke about their day at school, or how Riona lost her way going to buy supplies, or he'd praise Ellen on how she had made another tasty meal and the house had never been so clean.

Last night, he'd mentioned the horse riding lessons for Bridget. Her birthday was next week and when he made the announcement, Ellen thought her daughter would simply faint with shock. She loved horses and had become sweetly devoted to Pepper.

Yet, on reflection, Ellen couldn't help but wonder why Emmerson would spoil her daughter? Even now, he was with the boys, having taken them into the city to inspect some cargo recently arrived from India, which he wanted to sell on to various shops not only in Sydney but down south in Melbourne and perhaps even New Zealand.

That he wanted to involve the boys in his business gave her some concern. She was delighted that her children were getting special treatment, but such kindness also extended to her. She'd seen the way he looked at her, the eagerness to talk to her. What could it all mean? She was his housekeeper. Why was he being so friendly?

'I've seen an advertisement in a shop window this morning,' Riona said, coming out from the house. 'Evening sewing classes.'

'You already know how to sew. Mammy taught us at her knee as little girls.'

'This is more advanced, with emphasis on millinery.' Riona's enthusiastic tone couldn't be ignored.

'You want to join the classes?'

'I do. It's a small fee, but I hardly spend any of my wages Mr Emmerson gives me. The classes are in the early evening, so after my work is done for the day here.'

'If that's what you want to do.' Ellen smiled.

'It is and I'll meet new people. It would be nice to have a friend or two, so it would.'

'Aye, it would.'

'The first class is tonight.'

'Then enjoy yourself.'

'You'll not come?'

'No. I'm too tired in the evening.' Ellen started scrubbing the trousers. 'You could then teach Bridget?'

'Aye, I'll teach her what I know.'

'I want riding lessons!' Bridget glared mutinously.

'You, my girl, will also learn to sew.' Ellen glared back at her. 'By your age me and your aunt could sew very well.'

'Come, Bridget.' Riona held out her hand. 'You can help me unpack my baskets. We'll boil the kettle for some tea and get the irons hot, for in this heat those sheets and clothes will be dry before we know it.'

After another hour of scrubbing, rinsing, and

hanging out, Ellen's back felt ready to snap in two. Using her forearm to wipe the sweat from her brow, she tipped the tub over and let the water soak into the hard dry ground.

'Mrs Kittrick.' Emmerson strolled out from the house, frowning. 'You look positively done in. All this washing is too much for you. As of next week, we will hire someone to do it for us. What do you say?'

Tired, Ellen nodded. 'I say that's the best news I've heard all day, Mr Emmerson.'

He beamed. 'Excellent. Now, Austin and Patrick met some young fellows they know from school and are out the front with them.'

'Did they behave for you?'

'Indeed. Splendidly. A credit to you, madam. Austin is extremely interested in the business and asked lots of questions.'

'He may be an apprentice in time?' Ellen packed the tub in the corner of the stable.

Emmerson rubbed his hands together. 'Indeed. I am dining out for supper tonight with friends. So, no need to set a place for me this evening.'

'Understood, Mr Emmerson.'

He hesitated for a moment. 'I was wondering, Mrs Kittrick, if you'd be interested in accompanying me to visit my land in the south? I understand you are keenly interested in the holdings in the country.'

Ellen's eyes widened in surprise. 'You wish for me to go with you to visit your land?'

'Yes. I could show you what it is like if you are agreeable? We could take Austin, too, if you wish.' His expression was hopeful.

'I would enjoy nothing more, Mr Emmerson.'

His shoulders sagged in relief. 'Fabulous! Bridget's

223

birthday is on Tuesday. Therefore, we shall leave on Wednesday. I will start making the arrangements. I shall hire a carriage and driver for the duration. The weather has been dry for weeks so we shan't get bogged down in mud. The roads are mere tracks and notoriously uncomfortable. From experience, I suggest we sit on cushions. Good day, Mrs Kittrick!' He left whistling a happy tune.

Inside the kitchen, Ellen sat at the table stumped for words.

'Will you look at the state of you,' Riona said, cutting up vegetables for the midday meal. 'Your face is red and all sweaty. It's too hot out there for washing.'

'It's done now.'

'Bridget's gone outside to be with the boys.' Riona poured her a glass of water. 'What did Mr Emmerson want?'

'He said he's hiring a woman to come in to do the washing. I have enough to do.'

'What a good and kind gentleman he is.' Riona sighed. 'How is such a man not married?'

'He's asked me to accompany him to the country next Wednesday.'

'You?' Riona stared at her. 'Why?'

'He knows how interested I am in land.'

'We've no money for land.'

'No, but with Mr Emmerson's contacts we might be granted some located many days ride into the country. I read in the newspaper they want to open up the land in the far reaches of the country.'

'Nay, will you have some sense? They'd not give land to penniless Irish, so they won't.'

'But they *might*, Riona, *might*!' Ellen stood and paced the narrow kitchen. 'And if they do, I need to

224

know what to do. This isn't Ireland where you can stick potatoes in the ground and months later have a crop. No, this country is different. It so hot and dry and cattle and sheep make men money here.'

'Cattle and sheep. Have you lost your wits?' Riona scoffed. 'Sure, and we can't afford to buy one cow or sheep with the few shillings we have. So, what would we do with this land they give us?'

'Holy Mother of God, do you always have to argue with me over this?'

'Because you're living on dreams, Ellen.' Riona slammed the knife down. 'Why can't you be grateful for what you have? Look how lucky we've been ever since we left home. Mr Wilton, Mr Hamilton and now Mr Emmerson. No one gets that amount of luck.' She hastily crossed herself. 'You work for a good kind man. We have a roof over our heads and food in our bellies. You wanted to come to this country for a better life and we have it. Why go searching for something you'll never have?'

'Who says I mustn't dream? Why should I work for a man when I might be able to have my own place? Just think, we could have a home that's ours, Riona, ours. No landlord. No one to kick us out when the whim takes them. Our land. Our home. Why shouldn't I want that?' Angry, Ellen stormed from the kitchen. Not wanting the children to see her, she strode down the vacant land to the water's edge.

A walking track along the shoreline allowed people to walk between Millers Point and Dawes Point. Ellen turned left towards Millers Point, and once past the numerous warehouses, she found a spot on a grassy area between two wharves and stared out at the boats on the water.

225

Her temper calmed a little, though she still felt annoyed at Riona's comments. Was it so terrible that she wanted to have control over her own life?

'Mammy!'

Ellen turned and shading her eyes saw Austin running along the track. He flopped down on the grass next to her.

'Is something wrong?' She frowned at him, worried.

'No. I saw you walking and wanted to come with you.'

'I needed a minute of peace, darling.'

Austin laid on his back and closed his eyes. 'I like that Mr Emmerson took us with him this morning.'

She grinned as he didn't take the hint to leave. 'He's a good man.'

'The best.'

'He wants you and me to go with him to the country next week.'

Austin sat up quickly, eyes wide. 'Really? Into the country?'

'Aye.'

'That'll be something, won't it?' He sounded so grown up. He'll be thirteen on his next birthday. No longer a little boy.

Ellen gazed back at the water. 'One day we might have our own land.'

'I hope so, Mammy, as I know you want it, but I'd like a big house here in Sydney.'

'You would?' This surprised her. 'You'd stay in town?'

'Aye. I want to be a rich gentleman like Mr Emmerson with my own carriage and servants. You could live with me, Mammy. I'd look after you. We could eat cake and go to shows.'

She couldn't laugh at his dreams, for they were his, just as she had hers.

★ ★ ★

'Hold the reins gently, Bridget,' Mr Emmerson instructed. 'You don't need to jerk them.'

Heart in her mouth, Ellen watched Mr Emmerson give his first riding lesson to Bridget on the vacant ground next to the house.

He began by riding Pepper himself and explaining to Bridget all the parts of the tack used on a horse. Then he had lifted her up to sit before him and they gone around in circles with the family watching on.

Now, he had dismounted and allowed Bridget to stay on the saddle while he held a long lunge rope tied to Pepper's bridle.

Ellen had never seen Bridget so happy. Having a good diet now, her little girl was growing. Her ebony hair was thick and satiny down her back. Without prejudice, Ellen knew her daughter was incredibly pretty.

'I want to go faster!' Bridget shouted, not in the least frightened.

'No. You need to learn to ride properly.'

'I can ride properly.' A stubborn tilt to Bridget's chin annoyed Ellen.

'You'll listen to Mr Emmerson, my girl, or get off. Birthday or no birthday, you'll do as you're told.'

'Perhaps a cup of tea would be nice, Mrs Kittrick?' Mr Emmerson suggested from the middle of the field.

'Go. I'll watch her,' Riona said to Ellen, leaning on the fence beside her. 'Mr Emmerson will take it slowly with her, so he will.'

'She's too headstrong.'

227

Riona grinned. 'Aye, sure, and doesn't she get it from her mammy?'

'Can I learn to ride, Mammy?' Patrick asked.

'Of course, you can.' Ellen turned back to Mr Emmerson. 'Would Patrick and Austin be able to have a turn, Mr Emmerson?'

'Indeed. Certainly,' he answered happily.

'No. Not them, just me!' Bridget demanded.

Ellen clenched her jaw. 'She'll be getting a slap in a minute will that one.'

'Go make some tea, Ellen. Leave her alone.' Riona sighed. 'It's her birthday and sure, hasn't she never had a special day before? She's grown up only ever knowing hunger and being poor. Let her have today.'

Later, Mr Emmerson insisted they use the dining room table to eat the birthday treats Ellen and Riona had made. Salads, sliced meats, jellies, and cakes filled the table.

'It's too much food.' Riona frowned, looking at the spread as the children ate and laughed with Mr Emmerson.

'Aye, maybe it is,' Ellen agreed. 'But will you look at how pleased they are. This is what I promised myself I'd do for them. I want to erase the memories of our old damp dark cottage with its empty shelves. I want to make them forget they ever had to eat boiled nettles or seaweed.'

'Only six months ago we were homeless and without hope. Who would have thought we'd be standing here in another country feeding our faces until we nearly burst?' Riona shook her head in amazement.

'I thought it.' Ellen sipped her tea. 'And this is only the start. All our birthdays will be celebrations. Just you wait and see.'

The following day, dawn was barely breaking when Ellen gave her bag to the driver of the hired carriage, who secured it at the back with Mr Emmerson's small trunk. Austin full of excitement was patting the two horses.

With a quick breakfast made and eaten, Ellen kissed goodbye to Riona, Patrick and Bridget. 'Take care. Be good for your aunt,' she said, eager to be off.

Mr Emmerson came out of the house last and with a wide smile also said his farewells.

Bridget impulsively hugged his leg. 'I'll miss you, Mr Emmerson.'

Since her first riding lesson yesterday afternoon on Pepper, Bridget had been as happy as a dog with two tails.

'Take good care of Pepper for me, dear girl.' He patted her head. 'Are we ready, Mrs Kittrick?'

'We are, Mr Emmerson.'

'Let us go then.' He handed her into the carriage and then Austin, before climbing in himself.

They made steady pace out of the city heading southwest towards Ashfield. As the buildings and busy streets gave way to open fields, farming and dirt roads, Ellen sat back and relaxed. For a week she'd have no work to do. She liked the thought of that.

'If we make good time, we should sleep this evening at an inn on the road through Glenfield,' Mr Emmerson said. 'We have a long way to go, and I don't wish to overly tire the horses. My holding is up in mountainous country and some parts of the road getting there are decidedly steep. The horses have their work cut out for them.'

'Can you tell me some more about your land, Mr Emmerson?'

'My five hundred acres are in the south Camden District, close to the village of Berrima. I am most fortunate that I have a good water supply running through it and excellent grazing. The soil is rich, and my thoughts are that I should put some fields to plough.'

'But there is no house there yet?' Ellen queried.

'No. My reason for this visit is to stake out the house plan I commissioned to be drawn only a few weeks ago. I shall be engaging local builders, if I can, to begin construction as soon as possible. I am most excited about it.' Mr Emmerson glanced out of the window on his side and Ellen did the same on her side, gazing at the different farms they passed.

Austin asked Mr Emmerson questions about what they saw, and Ellen listened as eagerly to his answers as her son did.

They stayed the night in the Glenfield inn before setting off at dawn the next day, heading for the small town of Campbelltown. Here after a break to feed the horses and to have some food and drink themselves, they then turned west towards Camden where they stayed another night at an inn.

The next morning, they set off again, passing through Cawdor and climbing up the dangerously steep sides of the Razorback Range.

Two days in the carriage with Mr Emmerson gave Ellen a clearer understanding of the man. He was widely read and adventurous. He filled the hours of travel with stories of his expeditions of exploring unknown forests with members of the government's surveying parties.

Mr Emmerson kept Ellen and Austin entertained with descriptions of valleys and gorges, unique animals, and bird life. He spoke of his parents in England

230

with admiration and a touch of longing.

'Will they travel here to visit you?' Ellen asked him.

'No, my mother is too ill and my father, well he was an old man when I was born. He's in his seventies now and rather set in his ways. A trek to the other side of the world would be too much for them.'

'And you are an only child?'

'I am. A later in life child for my parents when they thought they would never have children,' he said wistfully. 'They adore me and I them.'

'They must be sad you're not with them?'

'Indeed. However, my father encouraged me to travel, to make something of myself. He is a fourth son and could never really offer me a financial legacy as my cousins have. I attended Harrow and then Oxford and thought to become a schoolmaster or join the military. Alas, I did none of that, for on my Tour after finishing at Oxford I met Rafe Hamilton in Paris and we travelled together for a few months. We parted in Lyon. I carried on to Athens, but Rafe returned home to England due to family problems, but we kept in touch and decided to go into business together. A cousin of mine, Robin, was travelling to the colony and asked me to join him. I did, and Rafe and I decided the import and export business would work between the colony and England.'

'Is Robin still in the colony?'

'Yes. He journeyed south to Melbourne last year. I am fortunate to have a contact there for the business.'

Austin squirmed in his seat. After two days in the carriage, he was becoming bored. 'Tell us more about your treks into the wilderness, Mr Emmerson.'

Emmerson grinned. 'Heavens, lad, I thought I had told them all.'

231

The carriage slowed and the driver, Higgins, called down to them.

Frowning, Emmerson leaned out of the window. 'What is it, Higgins?'

'A bullock dray has broken down in front of us, sir. I'm not sure we can go around.'

'Blast.' Emmerson climbed out of the carriage.

Ellen and Austin followed him, interested to see the commotion.

Ahead, halfway up the first incline of the range, an overturned bullock cart lay across the rutted dirt track. The bullock driver cursed as he unloaded his wagon of household goods.

'Can we help him?' Ellen walked with Emmerson and Higgins closer to the accident.

'It will delay us some hours.' Emmerson hailed the bullock driver. 'My good man, you are in a spot of bother.'

'Aye, sir. Axle broke in a rut and down she went.' He spoke between teeth clenched on a clay pipe. He scratched his head. 'Not sure what I'll be able to do. I can't leave this cargo on the side of the track and go for help. It'll be taken by thieves before I get back.'

'If we can get around you, we will go ahead to the next village and send help back to you,' Emmerson said, walking around the strewn furniture, trunks and crates.

'Let's help him move everything to one side,' Ellen suggested. 'Austin, grab that bag over there.'

'Thank you, missus,' the bullocky said.

They set to clearing the road as the heat rose. Ellen noted the fine goods that were being transported and wondered about the family who owned them.

Below them another cart came up the track, and the

232

driver stopped and came to help them. With the men working together, they were able to shift the back end of the cart over to allow traffic to pass. The bullocky unharnessed his team of bullocks and once shackled, he allowed them to roam the grassy plain at the bottom of the hill.

'Thank ye kindly.' The bullocky shook hands all round. When he came to Ellen, he also doffed his hat. 'Most kind of ye, missus.'

'Good luck. We'll send someone back to you.'

'Sir,' Higgins came up to Emmerson. 'I think it best if we lighten the load for the horses going up the pass. It's mighty steep and the heat could distress them.'

'Indeed. We shall walk.' Emmerson looked at Ellen. 'Unless you want to be in the carriage?'

'No. The horses are important. We can walk.' Lifting her skirts, Ellen started up the winding track.

With the hot sun blazing down on them, they walked single file at the edge of the track, trying to stay beneath the overhanging trees. The horses laboured up the steep incline, which had sheer drops on one side. Through breaks in the trees, Ellen could look back on the view of the small village of Cawdor and the farms cutting into the forests.

At the top of the range, they stopped to rest. Ellen wearing a light dress of sprigged cotton sat under an eucalyptus tree as Emmerson brought her a flask of cold tea. A lizard darted into the long grass making her jump. She laughed in embarrassment.

'You've done marvellously well, Mrs Kittrick,' Emmerson said.

She gave him an exhausted smile and fanned her face with a small leafy branch Austin gave her. 'I'm pleased it's over.'

'Look, Mammy, kangaroos!' Austin pointed to the next hill where a group of five or so kangaroos laid in the shade of a tree.

'Aren't they wonderful?' Ellen peered at the native animals. 'They don't seem to be frightened of us.'

'Not from this distance, but any closer and they'd bound away,' Emmerson told them.

'Mammy, can I ride up top with Higgins, please?' Austin asked.

'I'm not sure.'

'He'll be fine, Mrs Kittrick, as long as he holds on.' Higgins grinned.

Once on their way again, Emmerson looked at Ellen. 'You must not worry about Austin. Higgins will watch him.'

'Sure, and I'm not worried about Austin. He's sensible enough to hold on tight. No doubt he'll enjoy every minute of it, so he will.' She cursed herself for slipping back into her accent. Since arriving, she'd been doing her very best to speak less with an accent if she could.

As if picking up on it, Emmerson smiled. 'Are you missing home?'

'No. Not really. I miss the people who were there. My son, Thomas, Mammy, Da and Father Kilcoyne and all the others who left this earth.'

'Not your husband?'

She thought for a moment, realising she'd not thought about him for some time. 'No. Malachy changed a lot when the blight hit us. Not that it was his fault. He felt burdened by not being able to provide for his family. He turned to drink . . . '

'Ah. An evil curse that afflicts many.'

As the carriage picked up speed going downhill,

234

Ellen was tossed about on the seat. She held onto the wall of the carriage but was still violently shaken about.

'Holy Virgin!' she cried at one point when the carriage wheels lifted over a rut, nearly tipping them over.

Outside the windows, the view of gullies and trees flashed by. She heard Higgins steadying the horses, and the brake squeaked harshly when he applied it. Ellen prayed that Austin was holding on tightly.

Finally, at the bottom of the range, she let out a breath.

'We made it, Mrs Kittrick.' Emmerson seemed a little shaken, too. 'We shall stop at Picton and rest for an hour before going on to Myrtle Creek.'

In the sleepy town of Picton, they stopped in the main thoroughfare. Emmerson reported to a police constable about the bullocky's accident while Ellen and Austin refreshed themselves at the George IV inn and had a basic meal of mutton stew.

'Myrtle Creek is not far, eight miles or so. We shall stay there this evening,' Emmerson said, drinking an ale. 'Tomorrow, we continue south and we should make it all the way to near the border of the Argyle country, and Berrima itself.'

'Can I ride up with Higgins again?' Austin asked, eating his stew hungrily.

'If Higgins agrees,' Ellen answered.

'You are not regretting the decision to accompany me, Mrs Kittrick?'

Ellen gave him a warm smile. 'No, Mr Emmerson. I'm more than happy to be here.'

His green eyes darkened a little. 'I am most pleased you are, too.'

Her smile faded, and she turned back to her meal.

She'd seen desire in his eyes. The thought shocked her a little. Would Emmerson want her? He couldn't, surely? Not his housekeeper. Not when he was one of Sydney's most popular bachelors? Unless he wanted a mistress? They'd become friends, true, but was her interest too confusing to him. Did he want more? Or was she overthinking it?

Her head throbbed with a headache as they climbed into the carriage. She closed her eyes and was thankful Emmerson didn't speak for the journey to the next inn.

Ominous clouds greeted them the next morning. The temperature had dropped from the heat of the previous day and Ellen was thankful for it. Her headache had persisted all evening, and she'd gone to bed early and had a restless night.

'You look pale, Mrs Kittrick,' Emmerson remarked as they left Myrtle Creek.

'My headache didn't ease all night. I think it was walking up the range in the sun yesterday.'

'I am most sorry. I should not have asked you to.' Emmerson looked stricken. 'I would not want you made uncomfortable in any way. Forgive me.'

'I'm fine, Mr Emmerson. Breakfast has fortified me.'

'Tomorrow we shall rest all day, I promise.'

'I'm stronger than I look, Mr Emmerson. I've been through worse, believe me.'

'Indeed, you are the strongest woman I know.' Again, the admiration filled his eyes.

Ellen watched the bush and scrubland go past, not knowing what to think.

The settlement of Bargo was nothing more than mere slab huts and some farms. They did not stop.

236

Thick forests soon replaced the open farmland, and the dirt track became narrow in parts. The denseness of the forest, or *the bush*, as the locals called it, shaded the track that with clouds overhead gave them a dimly lit trail broken only by rough timber bridges or stone-bed creeks which they forded easily.

With the monotonous trees and shrubs to look at and the rocking of the carriage, Ellen was soon napping. The restless night took its toll, and she gave into the welcoming sleep.

Suddenly, she was wrenched forward so abruptly she landed on Mr Emmerson's lap. 'Mother of God!'

'Mrs Kittrick, are you all right?'

'Mr Emmerson, I'm so sorry.' She scrambled back off him and onto her own seat.

'Higgins! What in hell's name are you playing at!' Emmerson barked out the window. 'Forgive my language, Mrs Kittrick.'

Rubbing her banged knees, Ellen peered out of the window at the trees and scrub.

A horse rider came into view, his face covered with a red handkerchief. 'Out of the carriage!'

Stifling a scream, Ellen clapped her hands over her mouth.

'Stay here,' Emmerson whispered, before opening the door and stepping down. 'What is the meaning of this?'

'It's a holdup, my good fellow.' The rider waved a pistol at Emmerson. 'Who else is in there? Everyone is to get out. Now.'

'What do you want? Money? I have money.' Emmerson reached inside his waistcoat pocket.

'Wait. Stop!' The rider nudged his horse closer to Emmerson. 'Get your hands where I can see them.'

He also noticed Ellen. 'You, woman, out!'

Slowly, legs shaking, Ellen descended the step, her hands raised. She'd heard stories from Emmerson about bushrangers and how terrifying the bandits were, but she hadn't taken it seriously, at least not thinking she'd ever see one.

Once clear of the carriage she counted three other men, all on horseback, all with pistols or rifles pointing at them. Each man wore a long beard and had handkerchiefs over their faces.

She glanced at Austin, who looked terrified seated up beside Higgins. She had to be brave for Austin. Nothing could happen to Austin.

'Rightio, Danny lad, let's see what these people have that we can relieve them of.' The leader spoke to the rider at the back of the carriage, who quickly dismounted and opened the luggage.

Ellen gazed at each man in turn, taking in details she hoped to remember later for the police constable. She had nothing of value in her carpetbag, simply a change of clothes and toiletries. They could search all day and find nothing. But she had a small purse tucked into her sleeve that held a few shillings from her last wages.

Emmerson smiled reassuringly at her; his expression anxious but not overly worried. 'Stay calm.'

'Stop talking!' The leader raised his pistol straight at Emmerson's head.

Her legs shaking, Ellen kept her focus on Austin, willing him not to do anything stupid.

'Not much here, Eddie.' The other bushranger, Dan, walked over to Emmerson and took his pocket watch and leather wallet. 'Some pound notes in the wallet.' He passed it up to Eddie, then stood in front of Ellen. 'Give me what you have, missus.'

'I have nothing.' She looked into his eyes, noting his Irish accent. She glanced up at the leader, Eddie, trying not to show her nervousness. 'Sure, and I'm just a housekeeper, so I am.' She spoke in her accent that she'd been doing her best to be rid of so as not to be labelled by society.

'Ahh, a gal from the old country, so you are.' Eddie rested his pistol on his thigh. 'Where you from, missis?'

'Mayo and you?'

'Connemara. Where in Mayo?'

'Louisburgh.'

'Ah ye never are! I've been to Louisburgh.' He sat back in his saddle. 'Sure, and I'm from Tully. Dan's from Galway, so he is. We came out in chains twenty years ago as lads and been serving a sentence one way or another ever since.'

'May the Holy Mother protect you.' Ellen made a quick sign of the cross.

Eddie watched her and pointed to Emmerson. 'Is he your master?'

'Aye.'

'Does he treat you well?'

'Aye, he does. He's taken me and my family in. Given us work and pays us decently.' Ellen swallowed. 'He's a good man.'

'For an Englishman?' Eddie snorted.

'Aye. I'll not lie to you.'

'You could join us. Be my woman?'

A tingle of fear shivered down her back. 'That's my son up there, and I've two more back in Sydney. They need me.'

Eddie seemed to weigh up the situation, and Ellen

239

wondered if he'd simply just take her. She could be abducted easily by the four men. Emmerson and Higgins didn't carry weapons and couldn't stop them. No one would find her again.

'I'd treat you fair.'

Her mouth went dry. 'I'd rather you let us go. I'm a mother, so I am, and they suffered enough back home without losing me now that we've managed to make it alive to this country. Will you let us go?'

He paused. 'Sure, I will, but we need money, lass. We're starving, so we are.'

From her sleeve, Ellen took the little canvas pouch and threw it up to him. 'There's three shillings and sixpence in there altogether. Not a lot, I know, but it's yours. You have the wallet, too. Go to the inn we've not long passed in Bargo and buy some food.'

'Well, will ye look at that? Someone treating us decently, so they are. It's a rare thing for us.' Eddie pocketed the pouch. 'We're ye headed?'

'South to the border of the Argyle country.'

'What's your name?'

'Ellen.'

He touched the tip of his pistol to the rim of his hat. 'Safe journey, sweet Ellen.'

In seconds they'd cantered off down the track, leaving only a cloud of dust behind.

Stumbling a little, Ellen reached the carriage before her legs gave way.

'Mammy!' Austin jumped down from the high seat and wrapped his arms around her waist.

'Whist, child. I'm fine.' She held him to her.

'Mrs Kittrick, your courage is astounding.' Emmerson helped her up into the carriage, holding onto her hand longer than was necessary. It looked as though he wanted to say more but refrained as Austin sat next to her holding her arm.

'Bushrangers, Mammy,' Austin said in awe. 'Patrick won't believe me.'

She kissed the top of his head. 'No, he won't. I'm just pleased Bridget wasn't with us or she'd have had something to say to them, no doubt.' She tried to jest, to lighten the tense atmosphere and to ease her son's anxious expression.

With their luggage re-secured, they carried on, not speaking, still in shock at being held up.

Ellen stared at her clenched hands, breathing deeply. The incident replayed in her mind. How easily that could have gone differently. Would those men have shot them, left them for dead in the road?

Travelling in the heat and dust with only the bushland to look at, Austin nodded off to sleep against Ellen's shoulder.

'You are the bravest woman I know, Mrs Kittrick,' Mr Emmerson said softly, respect in his tone. 'I do not know what would have happened if you had not been able to talk to them sensibly.'

'I had my son to protect, sir. Mothers will do almost anything to protect their young.'

'What a fine mother you are, Mrs Kittrick. I am honoured to know you. Moreover, to consider you as a friend is something that I treasure.'

'Thank you, Mr Emmerson. That's kind of you.' His words touched her.

'What news I have to tell Rafe and my parents. Such daring to befriend the bushrangers. How fortunate it was that they and you were from Ireland. It is astonishing.'

Ellen turned away and closed her eyes. In her

mind's eye, she thought of Rafe and wondered how he would have reacted to the bushrangers. She somehow thought he'd put up more of a fight than Emmerson did.

17

Rain kept them indoors the next day, for which Ellen was thankful. Being Irish, the rain never bothered her, but she had listened with half a smile to the inn's residents as they complained of being bogged in the road or not able to dry out their clothes.

However, she did need an excuse to have some time from Emmerson and the rain provided the perfect opportunity to stay in her room for hours, keeping occupied by writing a letter to Riona and washing hers and Austin's underwear in the bowl on the table. The kind landlady had happily provided homemade soap and lit the fire. Ellen had hung up their washing to dry on the rack in front of the flames. Austin came and went, flitting between Higgins in the stables and chatting to Emmerson downstairs in the public room.

From what she'd seen so far, Ellen admired the small village of Berrima, which sat in the mountains much higher than Sydney. The greater rainfall and cooler winters in this area were likened to British counties than the harbour city and its coasts.

From her open bedroom window Ellen looked out over the spacious green situated in the middle of the village and watched people rushing about, trying not to step in the mud left behind from the rain showers. The main street was wide, and much traffic plied through the village.

A bullock team plodded by, its wagon burdened. Ellen hoped the one they'd come across on the range had been rescued. She thought fleetingly of the bushrangers but quickly dismissed them.

A soft breeze lifted the curtains, and the sun poked out between fluffy clouds as though enticing her to leave her room.

Instead, she sat at the table by the window and began a letter to Mr Hamilton.

Dear Mr Hamilton.

I hope this letter finds you in good health.

I am writing from the Victoria Inn in Berrima — a pretty little village several days' travel from Sydney. Mr Emmerson invited me and Austin to journey with him as he wanted to visit his property in this part of the country. He is aware of my interest in land.

A few miles to the north of here, in Mittagong, is the iron works, which I think would be beneficial for you to mention to future passengers regarding work.

The countryside here is very productive and farms prosper with good soil and rainfall. This I was told about last night over supper by a local man living nearby and who had come to the inn to have an ale. He and Mr Emmerson spoke of many things that would aid a new arrival. This area is becoming more settled each year and would be another area you can mention to your passengers. No doubt Mr Emmerson will mention this to you in his letters, and you do not need me to repeat it when I am not as wise in these matters as Mr Emmerson.

I hope it won't be long before my previous letters are delivered to you. How surprised you will be when you receive a letter stating I am working for Mr Emmerson as his housekeeper. I shall post this letter tomorrow, as the mail coach leaves this area twice a week and the next departure is in the morning.

The children and my sister are all in good health. Bridget

*started her riding lessons with Mr Emmerson, and she has
a natural ability, so Mr Emmerson says.*

I believe you would like this country . . .

The door opened and Austin came in full of energy
and high spirits. 'Mammy, we're to go to Mr Emmerson's land.'

'When?'

'Now. He's having Higgins get the horses ready. He
said for me to see if you wished to go or are you still
resting?'

'I do want to go, aye.' Ellen put on her bonnet and
tied the ribbons. 'Resting!' Ellen snorted in contempt.
'Am I great lady needing to rest, am I?'

Austin laughed. 'I did tell Mr Emmerson you were
sorting out your clothes and writing a letter to Aunt
Riona.'

Downstairs, Ellen smiled at Mr Emmerson. 'I'm
eager to see your land, Mr Emmerson.'

'I have ordered the carriage, though I fear we may
have to venture some way on foot, Mrs Kittrick. It is
a shame you cannot ride, for in the country it is a skill
most appreciated and useful.'

'I've walked everywhere all my life, Mr Emmerson.
I'm sure I'll manage.'

They took the road north out of Berrima, the
same way they'd come in two days ago, but once at
the summit of the hill at the beginning of the village,
Emmerson instructed Higgins to turn right onto a
barely conceived track.

'Head east, Higgins, if you please,' Emmerson
called to him, his head out of the window so he could
see the boundary markings.

'Are natives a problem here, Mr Emmerson?' Ellen

245

asked.

'No. Those that were in the area were pushed back years ago, further west, once settlers came and started farming. The few that are seen are friendly enough but they keep to themselves and cause no bother to anyone.'

A few farms were situated along the track but petered out as the track soon stopped in a belt of native trees.

'We must walk from here, Mrs Kittrick, Austin.' Emmerson took a leather bag with him and led the way through the trees. 'Further to the east and down the hill is the area called Bong Bong belonging to a Mr Oxley. To reach it, you must go down a rather steep hill. My land's eastern border stops short of that, though.'

On a slight rise, Emmerson turned right at a marked tree. Stepping through some thick scrub and trees, he stopped and stared straight ahead.

Ellen stood next to him and sucked in a breath. Before her was undulating grazing land with grasses knee high. In pockets, trees grew, but the land was excellent for grazing.

'This is just the beginning of my land, Mrs Kittrick.'

'It's beautiful . . . '

'And this is not the best bit either. Come.' He strode south through the grass and they followed, eager to see where he was taking them.

After several hundred yards, the view came into sight.

Ellen thought her heart would stop. Before her stretched a valley and at the bottom a wide river wound through the grazing land like a grey ribbon. Down near the banks a large herd of long-horned cattle meandered. A white canvas tent was pitched nearby.

'That is the Wingecarribee River. It is the southern border of my land. I own from the track to the river. The man I hire to watch my cattle lives in the tent you see down there, but I feel the best position for my house would be right here on the edge of this bluff. What do you think, Mrs Kittrick?'

Ellen gave it some thought and walked a few paces, judging the view and the location. 'I think, Mr Emmerson, that this is the most perfect spot for a magnificent house.'

He beamed in response. 'Excellent. Would you care to see a drawing of the house plan?'

Austin and Ellen crowded around him as he took a rolled sheet of paper from the bag. When spread out, it revealed a house of square design, with a small courtyard in the middle and verandas going all the way around the outside. Ellen noted the six bedrooms — three on either side, complete with dressing rooms, the dining room and formal drawing room were at the rear of the house which would get the views of the valley. At the front was a morning room, the wide entrance hall and a study. To the side of the house through a walkway between two of the bedrooms was an extension for the service rooms, including the kitchen, pantry and a small staff dining room. Every room had a fireplace and large windows.

Ellen knew she'd enjoy working in such a fine house. 'It will be a glorious house, Mr Emmerson.'

'I am thrilled you admire it, Mrs Kittrick.' He turned to Austin. 'Shall we peg it out?'

While Austin and Emmerson were pacing and hammering pegs into the ground, Ellen sat on the grass and

247

appreciated the view. To own such a glorious piece of land was what dreams were made of, at least to her. Granted, she'd never own such a prestigious site, but if she could one day own a few acres somewhere, it would still be her most crowning achievement — that and bringing up her children through a famine-ravished countryside.

She soon saw the overseer saddle his horse and ride up to join them and alerted Mr Emmerson.

'Ah, Thwaite. Yes, he is a good man, Mrs Kittrick. Ex-convict, but clever and sensible. Wasted as a herdsman, really. He can read and write. I'd like to make him my manager one day if he stays.' Mr Emmerson shook Thwaite's hand after the man dismounted. 'Mrs Kittrick, please allow me to introduce you to Mr Thwaite, my overseer.' Mr Emmerson made the introductions.

'Do you find cattle do better here than sheep, Mr Thwaite?' Ellen asked.

'Both run just fine, Mrs Kittrick, but cattle are easier to care for when the master of the run is not here.'

'The run?' she inquired.

'A run, or station, is what they call a large property out in the country,' Mr Emmerson explained.

'Oh, I see.' She glanced over at the herd in the distance. 'In Ireland we didn't have such huge horned cattle. They look fine beasts.'

Mr Thwaite swelled with pride. 'I take great care of them. The grazing is second to none here.'

'Any lost since your last letter?' Mr Emmerson asked.

'No, sir. We lost one of the calves a month or so ago, as you know, but the others are growing well.'

'The builders will be here within days, Mr Thwaite,

to start on the house.' Mr Emmerson showed him the plans. 'I will pay you extra if you can keep an eye on them.'

'Certainly, sir.' Thwaite nodded. 'I'll come up each evening and check on the progress. Any problems I shall send word to you.'

'Excellent. I will have someone managing the build until I can return but having another man I can trust is wise. I have heard that a few of the stonemason teams can be lazy. I have ordered stone to be delivered from the quarry in Joadja. It should arrive within a week or so.'

'I'll keep an eye on everything, sir.'

'If you do a good job of seeing to the place, Thwaite, I will make you my manager.'

'Very good, sir. You can rely on me.'

Ellen left them alone to talk more about the cattle and future plans, and she strolled to where Austin sat on the edge of the bluff overlooking the valley.

'It's nice here, Mammy.' Austin chewed a grass stem.

She sat down beside him. 'Aye, I can't disagree. It's beautiful.'

'It's not home, but it's nearly as good.'

'Ireland is in the past, darling. We must think of the future.'

'I like it here, so I do.' Austin plucked another tall grass stem. 'I want to be like Mr Emmerson one day and build a house on a hill and have herds of animals and a carriage and a house in Sydney. Then I'd be rich.'

'And you will. I know it.'

'You think so?'

'Aye, if you work hard and are sensible. A stupid

249

man cannot make a fortune, Austin, only intelligent men can do that.'

'Like Mr Emmerson.'

'Yes, and Mr Hamilton, and others.'

'But not my da.'

Ellen sighed. 'Sure he was, in his own way. Your da was a simple man with simple needs. The cottage and our plot of land was all he ever wanted.'

Austin squinted against the sun. 'If I ever have land, I'll not let it be taken from me.'

She reached for his hand and squeezed it. 'Nor will I, son, nor will I.'

★ ★ ★

Returning to Sydney, Ellen felt a little restless. She worked hard, caring for Mr Emmerson and his house, but she believed something was different. Mr Emmerson spent a great deal of his time when at home talking to her about the country estate.

Often in the evenings, he would invite her to sit with him in the front room with Riona in the corner knitting or sewing. He wanted Ellen's opinions on nearly everything he planned. Although pleased to be invited to such discussions about the estate, it gave Ellen a sense of dissatisfaction. She wanted to be planning her own future, her own land. She asked Emmerson if he would investigate for her about obtaining a land grant. He said he would, however, so far, nothing had come of it.

As March slipped into April and then into May, the heat of summer gave way to cool autumn days. The changing seasons made Ellen feel a little despondent. She had received no letters from Mr Hamilton and decided to stop writing to him. Had she been foolish to think a gentleman such as he wanted to keep receiving letters from her? She'd sent him so many letters explaining her thoughts on the passage, the arrival and living in Sydney. Had she done too many? After all, he had Mr Emmerson's letters. Maybe when he had asked her to write, he'd expected her to only write about the voyage in his ship. Beyond that, he would have no need to hear her thoughts or share her experiences. She meant nothing to him. Had she made up the feelings she thought he held for her?

Her attraction to him needed to die, and it would in time, she was sure of it.

She went up to her room and put away the remaining stationery he had bought her the day she left Liverpool. In the box, she also placed the books, which were a little tattered and weathered from the constant reading on the ship.

Closing the lid, she slid the box under her bed. A deep sense of loss filled her. She had liked Mr Hamilton too much. It had been a daydream to think he could ever be anything to her.

Downstairs, she heard the children come home from school. Riona greeted them in the kitchen.

Ellen stood and took a breath. The children were the only ones she needed to think about. As long as they were happy, she'd be happy.

Joining the others in the kitchen, she began preparing the evening meal, listening to Austin speak of the mathematics he was learning, while Patrick described the drawing he'd given his teacher of the harbour before Bridget demanded to be heard as she had a story about how she was pushed over by a bigger girl and scraped her knees.

251

Such was the noise and distraction that Ellen didn't hear Mr Emmerson enter the kitchen until she turned from the stove and saw him standing in the doorway. 'Oh, Mr Emmerson.'

'Sorry to interrupt, Mrs Kittrick, but may I have a word, please?' He looked tense, holding himself stiffly.

'Yes, of course.' Ellen took off her apron and glanced at Riona. 'Keep them quiet. He looks angry,' she whispered.

Stricken, Riona nodded, holding Bridget to her as the girl kept talking about how she had pushed the bigger girl back.

Apprehensive she may have done something wrong, Ellen entered the front room, hands behind her back, praying silently they weren't about to be dismissed and sent packing.

He stood staring at a painting on the wall. 'Close the door, please.'

She did as he bid and faced him, stomach churning.

He turned and seeing the worried expression she wore, he instantly softened. 'Mrs Kittrick, please do not look so concerned.'

'Have I done something wrong?'

'No —'

'Or the children? Are they too loud? I will keep them quiet. I promise! You'll not hear them again.'

He took a step towards her. 'It is not the children. Sit down.'

She groaned. 'Sit down?' It was bad news, she knew it.

'Please?' He waved to the sofa.

Ellen perched herself on the edge of it, bracing herself.

252

'Now,' Emmerson scratched his forehead as if not knowing how to begin. 'You see, I have come to realise something most important . . .' He sat on the chair near the fireplace and gave her a quick look before standing up again. 'The thing is . . .'

Ellen clenched her hands in her lap.

'Mrs Kittrick, I have decided I would very much like to marry.' His tight smile matched his jerky movements. 'I have come to the conclusion that without a wife and children, my life is rather incomplete, especially with the plans I have. What is the point of building a grand estate only for myself to live in it?'

She let out a breath. He wanted her to know she'd have to soon be working for his new wife. Unless the new wife wouldn't want her and her family? Of course, she wouldn't. What young wife would want to start her married life living under the same roof as a large Irish family? Panic filled her. She'd have to find another position.

'What are your thoughts, Mrs Kittrick?'

Startled, she realised he'd been talking, and she'd not been listening. 'On what, sir?'

'On marriage.'

'Oh, well, sure, it can be wonderful, so it can. A true blessing.' In her distress, her accent sounded thick and provincial.

He beamed. 'My thoughts exactly.'

Suddenly he was before her on one knee.

She stared at him as he took her hands in his.

'Will you do me the greatest honour of marrying me, Mrs Kittrick?'

'*Me?*' Ellen squawked like a trapped chicken.

Emmerson blinked. 'Yes, you. It is you I wish to marry.'

'Me?' She couldn't believe she was hearing correctly. 'Me?'

'Yes, my dear. You. The finest woman I know.' He sounded sincere.

Yet, Ellen couldn't believe it. 'I'm your housekeeper, sir.'

'Indeed, but does that matter?'

'Not to me, but it might to you and your family and friends. I'm Irish, beneath your class.'

'You are more intelligent than many women of my class that I am acquainted with. That is no lie.'

'But they'll never accept me.' Her mind whirled.

'They will as long as you behave as a lady and a trustworthy wife, which I have every confidence in that you will.'

Ellen stared into his green eyes, seeing him for the first time as a man and not her employer. Alistair Emmerson. One of the prominent men in Sydney. A successful businessman. A man who attended Oxford and who had friends in the government. He wanted her as his wife — not as his mistress — *his wife!*

'Are you sure?' she blurted.

He smiled, the dimple appearing. 'I am absolutely certain. It has been on my mind since I first met you. A strong, clever woman, one who knows what she wants from life is a rare thing in my society. I was instantly attracted to the flame that burns in you. The drive, the eagerness to succeed. How can a man ignore such a woman as that?'

'But I have children . . .'

'Yes. Children I genuinely enjoy the company of and who I believe like me in return.'

'They do.'

'And you? Do you like me?' he implored.

254

She put her hands to her face, feeling hot and bothered.

'You do not feel the same,' he spoke quietly.

She glanced up. 'No, it's not that . . . I . . .'

'I have surprised you greatly.'

'Yes, you have. I never expected such a proposal.'

'But it is not wholly unwelcome?'

She smiled shakily, getting her thoughts in order. This fine man wanted to marry her. 'No, Mr Emmerson, it is not unwelcome.'

He brought her hands to his lips and kissed them. 'I understand you do not love me. However, perhaps in time, you will come to have feelings for me?'

'You are a kind and decent gentleman. Someone I know I could rely on to treat me and my children well.'

'Oh, I would,' he interrupted. 'Your children will become my children and will be treated accordingly.' He frowned. 'I understand this is an enormous decision for you to consider. Yet I believe it is entirely advantageous for you to be my wife. You will be mistress of all my properties. Your children will be brought up in a lifestyle far exceeding anything you might have thought possible. To gain all that, all I ask is that you be a true and generous wife to me. Am I asking too much?'

Ellen took many moments to consider all that he said. She would be his wife and all that entailed, such as the activities in the bedroom. Could she lie with this man? Have his hands touch her and more? She did not love him. Would she in time?

As Mrs Emmerson she will be in charge of this house and the country estate in Berrima and have a position within society. Austin and Patrick will be brought up as gentlemen, Bridget a lady. Never again will they know the danger of being thrown out onto the roads without a roof over their heads. They will never be without boots and their clothes will always fit them and not be too short or full of holes.

By doing this, agreeing to be this man's wife, her children will never go hungry again.

She would be the wife of a landowner . . .

She gazed at him, studying his face. He was kind, she knew, and in his own way handsome. She thought briefly of Mr Hamilton, but shook him from her mind. He was never hers to consider and belonged in the past, just the same as Malachy.

'Mr Emmerson . . .' She sucked in air, for the room seemed awfully close. 'Mr Emmerson, I'd be honoured to be your wife.'

His shout of joy startled her. He crushed her to him and then kissed her on the mouth. 'I will make you happy, Ellen, I promise until my dying day.'

She grinned at his dramatics. 'I hope to make you happy as well, Mr Emmerson.'

'You must call me Alistair. I shall go to see the reverend straight away.' He paused. 'You can marry in an Anglican church?'

Ellen stiffened. She was Catholic. Did it matter which church married them? She wanted his security and religion didn't play a part of it in her head. She may end in hell for it, but while on earth she'd do anything to protect her children and give them the best life she possibly could.

'I'd be pleased to marry you in any church, Alistair. I'm sure God will not judge me too harshly. Maybe we can have Father Joyce from the children's school attend the wedding to give us his blessing as well?'

256

Would that be enough to ease the guilt she would feel on the day?

'I shall see to it, dearest. I will go there directly and ask for an audience with him and explain the situation.' He kissed her again, pausing to stare into her eyes. 'You have made me incredibly happy, Ellen. I am a lucky man.'

When he'd gone from the house, she walked back into the kitchen. The children had gone out to play.

Riona sat peeling potatoes. 'Well? Is it bad news? You were gone for a time, for sure. I've sent the children out to tend to Pepper.'

Ellen sat down at the table, still shocked by the turn of events. But now she knew breaking the news to Riona would be far more difficult than saying yes to Mr Emmerson. 'It was an unexpected conversation.'

'He's not throwing us out, is he?'

'No . . . Instead, Mr Emmerson has asked me to marry him.'

Riona's mouth gaped open. 'You're jesting.'

'No.'

'Holy Mother of God!' Riona gasped. 'It's not possible.'

'He wants me as his wife and will take on the children as his own.'

'He's a Protestant! You *can't* marry him. The idea is ridiculous!'

Restless, Ellen jerked up from the chair and attended to the stove. 'Do you remember the second winter of the blight? How we all suffered when in the village was a soup kitchen giving out food if you became a Protestant? Do you remember Mammy and Father Kilcoyne herding us away?'

'Yes . . .'

'Mammy and you told me not to go to the Protestant soup kitchens when my children were hungry. I didn't go. I didn't give up my faith then, and I saw my children suffer. What mother denies their children bread and soup? I swore I would never do that again. I would never put religion before my children's well-being. So, I went to work for Mr Wilton, a Protestant Englishman, and as the blight worsened and the hunger continued suddenly accepting Mr Wilton's food scraps weren't so bad, were they?'

'We could still be Catholics when eating Mr Wilton's food. He wasn't asking us to convert,' Riona defended.

'The principle is the same.' Frustrated, she wished her sister would understand her feelings about this.

'This is important, Ellen. We are Catholic.'

'You think I don't know that! Yet, how did our religion save us when our people were dying in the thousands through no fault of their own? Why did God take so many innocents, answer me that?'

'You can't speak like this, it's sacrilege!' Riona glared at her.

'I'll speak as I find, sister.'

'You need to go to church right now and pray for forgiveness. You must confess!' Riona took off her apron. 'We will go to Father Joyce. He'll know what to do. We must pray with him.'

Ellen folded her arms across her chest. 'Pray? *Pray*? What good is praying? I've prayed all my life and still my siblings were taken, then my darling Thomas, Da and Grandpa, my home and the man I married. My prayers have never been answered. So, I shan't waste my breath with prayers.'

Riona quickly crossed herself. 'The Lord brought

258

us through the blight, the hunger. *He* saved us through his blessed child, Jesus.'

'*I* saved us.'

'No . . . Oh Holy Virgin Mother, protect us from my sister's sins.' Riona searched in her apron pocket and brought out her rosary beads.

Ellen hardened her heart to her sister's upset. 'I will convert to a Protestant, and so will the children.'

'You can't!' Riona looked ready to faint.

'It's still the same God.'

'You're turning your back on everything we believe in for what, a man?'

'No, not just a man, but for the price of living a good life. If becoming a Protestant means my children will never go hungry again, then I'll do it.'

'You don't have to marry him for that. We have a good place here and earn wages. The children are fine.'

'Are you asking me to deny them the chance to live a life without struggle? As Emmerson's children they will want for nothing.'

'Except the true faith.'

'If they want that when they are older, they can, but for now, they'll appreciate an education and a fine home more.'

'You're selling your soul!' Crying, Riona ran from the house.

Sighing, Ellen sat back down and hung her head. She felt ashamed for arguing with Riona and saying such things to her. She was a terrible Catholic, but circumstances had led her to it. Once she'd been as devoted as the rest of her family, but not now. Too much heartache had turned her away from her church, from God, from everything but the belief in herself.

18

The cool autumn days of May confused Ellen and the family. In Ireland May was spring, when the weather became warmer, the days longer and the land opened in rebirth. In Sydney, May meant shorter days, chillier evenings and frequent rain showers, which were a relief from the heat of summer.

Ellen took Alistair's arm after they finished signing the register and walked back down the aisle to the smiles of Alistair's friends who filled the pretty sandstone Garrison Church on the corner of Argyle Street.

Emerging from the church, sunshine greeted them and more well-wishers threw rose petals over the newlyweds. As people filed from the church, shaking the reverend's hand and then Alistair's' and Ellen's, she smiled and chatted, relieved it was over.

The last month had given her many moments of anxiety as she considered her decision to marry Alistair. The children had accepted the idea of marriage with Alistair well. They liked him and he liked them, and she knew the children would adapt to their new life quickly. Riona on the other hand was proving a thorn in her side. For a week Riona didn't speak to her after she told her she would marry Alistair and she remained quiet all through the weeks of wedding preparations.

Alistair provided Ellen with a generous allowance to purchase anything she needed. The children and herself were all fitted for new clothes. Riona declined, refusing to accept Alistair's generosity.

In her new position as Alistair's fiancée, Ellen began a round of social events meeting Alistair's friends in the city. A task that frightened her at first, wondering how well they would accept her into their elite society, but it soon became apparent that most of Alistair's male friends admired her and they encouraged their wives to be civil to her, especially those that needed Alistair's business.

Her worry about being accepted still bothered her a little. She wasn't flooded with invitations to tea parties from the wives in the city, but Alistair said they'd soon come around to having her in their circle. After-all, there were more than a few of the colony's first class who had skeletons in their closets. Bloodlines were not all pure bred and many could name ancestors who came out in chains, not that they spoke about such things in public.

Hearing this, Ellen calmed a little. She may have been working-class poor, but at least she hadn't arrived in chains. Still, she knew it was going to be a long road for her to be accepted into the bosom of the people Alistair mixed with and although those people accepted the wedding invitations, Ellen felt most came out of curiosity than a genuine concern to see them happily wed.

Ellen employed a cook and a housemaid, giving her more time to prepare herself for the enormous leap into being a woman married to a successful business-man. Dress fittings for new clothes, acquiring new boots, bonnets, gloves and undergarments for herself and the children took hours each week. Then Alistair insisted they attended dinners and garden parties, theatre nights and music recitals. On Sundays after church, he would take them all on cruises on the harbour or walks in the park around Government House. He wanted society to see them as a family and accept them.

The children thrived under their new life of being well fed, well dressed, and treated to various entertainments. They blossomed and laughed, and Ellen knew she had made the right decision to marry Alistair when she saw them gasp with joy at receiving the gifts Alistair bestowed on them at regular intervals.

'Are you all right, my dear?' Alistair asked her as their guests made their way to their carriages.

'Yes, I'm perfectly content.' She could answer his question honestly. As his wife, she and the children were safe from poverty.

'The wedding breakfast is held at Houghton's Tea House,' Alistair said to one of his friends whose name Ellen had forgotten. 'We'll meet you there.'

Ellen searched the departing crowd for Riona and couldn't see her. She hoped she'd come to the wedding breakfast, but Riona's mood fluctuated so much Ellen could never be sure what she was thinking.

'Shall we go?' Alistair took Ellen's arm and Bridget's hand, who looked so grown up in her flouncy white dress with a blue satin sash.

'I'm not sure where Riona is.' Ellen glanced around.

Alistair sighed unhappily. 'I wish she'd be happy for you on this our special day.'

'I know, but it is difficult for her. I've married a Protestant and she'll never forgive me.' Ellen thought she spotted her walking down the hill towards their house. 'There she is. I'll go and talk to her.'

'Dearest, we have guests waiting for us at the tea house.'

'Take the children and go on ahead. Send the carriage back for us. I must talk to her, Alistair, or I'll not enjoy the day.'

He kissed her cheek. 'Be as quick as you can, please. I want to show off my beautiful bride.'

'I will.' She smiled, appreciating the compliments that he gave her every day.

He called for the children and they entered the carriage. Ellen waved to them and then started down the hill towards home. How she would convince Riona to come to the breakfast she didn't know. They could both be so stubborn.

In front of the house a carriage stood; the horse tossing its head as flies pestered it. Beside it, Riona talked to a tall man dressed in a pewter grey suit and top hat.

Ellen frowned. Was a guest lost? Did they think the wedding breakfast was held at the house? She hurried a little, lifting the hem of her pale blue skirt. Her wedding dress was the finest she'd ever owned. Never had she worn such a delicate pale shade of blue, or the flimsy delicate lace that edged the collar and sleeves. Her hair was worn with several blue ribbons to match and arranged in soft waves. She'd forgone a bonnet, something which no doubt the many wives would comment on, but today she wanted to feel young again and not twenty-nine and a mother of three and having her hair in a loose wavy style studded with rosebuds and ribbons gave her that feeling.

Ellen walked closer to her sister and the gentleman and shaded her eyes from the sun as she neared.

'Ellen . . . ' Riona's voice called to her, but Ellen was staring at the man.

It couldn't be.

263

She blinked again. Was she imagining it?

Another step confirmed it. Rafe Hamilton stood talking to Riona.

He watched her approach, his eyes staring at her as she stared at him. In that one look, she felt stripped of all emotion and thought. In a suspended breath she was weightless, unanchored. The one person who she never expected to see again was standing right before her, as handsome as ever.

He had journeyed here!

She had never imagined he would do such a thing.

'I believe congratulations are in order?' he said simply. His face closed, unreadable.

'Yes . . . ' Her heart banged in her chest at his nearness. So many times, she'd thought of him, dreamed of his charming smile, hoping he would write to her. Yet no letters had arrived. Not once had she heard from him. And would it have mattered if he had? He was a businessman. Someone who helped her family. She wasn't anything to him but a passenger on his ship.

Straightening her shoulders, Ellen summoned her strength. 'It is a surprise to see you here, Mr Hamilton.'

'It was an impulsive decision, Mrs Kitt . . . Emmerson . . . ' A pulse throbbed in his jaw.

He was the first person to call her Mrs Emmerson, and it sounded strange to her ears.

'Alistair will be incredibly happy that you have arrived.' Her words sounded flat.

'I hope so. It is a long way to travel.'

Riona glanced between them. 'Why aren't you at the tea house, Ellen?'

'I came to see why you weren't in the carriage,'

Ellen answered stiffly.

'I tore the seam in one of my gloves. I've come back to find my other pair.'

'You should have let me buy you a new pair.' Ellen couldn't look at Mr Hamilton. She concentrated on Riona, silently begging her sister to help her in some way. How she could, Ellen didn't know. All she knew was that her heart felt laden with some unthinkable regret that she was no longer free.

'I can take you both in my carriage.' Mr Hamilton waved towards the hired carriage.

Ellen summoned her manners. 'You must join us, Mr Hamilton. It will please Alistair.'

At that moment, the Emmerson carriage came trundling down the road. 'Oh, here is the carriage.' Ellen turned, anxious to climb in. 'You are welcome to pay off your hired one, Mr Hamilton, and travel with us.' She climbed in and sat down, not looking at anything other than her hands and the shining wedding band on her left hand.

Riona and Mr Hamilton soon joined her, and they headed for the city and the tea house in silence.

Somehow, Ellen managed through the day. Alistair monopolised Mr Hamilton, introducing him to all his friends while Ellen chatted to their wives and fussed over the children until Bridget grew tired.

'I'll take her home,' Riona said, clutching Bridget's hand.

'I'll come with you.' Ellen glanced around for Austin and Patrick.

'No. You stay with your new husband,' Riona's clipped tone told Ellen she still wasn't forgiven.

All Ellen wanted to do was go home and lie down. She was exhausted with smiling and being sociable when the whole time she would notice Mr Hamilton's gaze on her.

'Dearest,' Alistair came to her side, 'I think it is time we went home. Guests are leaving. I have invited Rafe to supper, and he has agreed.'

Surprised, Ellen looked at Mr Hamilton over Alistair's shoulder. 'How lovely,' she lied.

'He would not take no for an answer,' Mr Hamilton added. 'I told Alistair it can wait until tomorrow.'

'Nonsense!' Alistair beamed. 'I have not seen you for some years and we have much to discuss.'

'It can wait, my friend.' Mr Hamilton forced a laugh.

They were prevented from talking about it as more guests came to say farewell.

When Ellen had finished saying goodbye, she noticed Bridget standing next to Mr Hamilton.

'You gave me my dolly,' Bridget said, smiling up at Mr Hamilton.

'Do you still have it?'

'Yes. She sleeps on my bed.'

'I am pleased she gives you comfort.'

'I'm learning to ride.'

'Are you just? Well, that is a worthwhile skill to learn. Every young lady should know how to ride.'

'Will you ride with me one day?'

'Nothing would give me more pleasure, Miss Bridget.'

Bridget placed her hand in Mr Hamilton's as Ellen came beside her. 'Mr Hamilton and me are going riding.'

'I don't think you have enough experience yet, my sweetness.' Ellen brushed away a dark strand of hair from her daughter's face.

'I do!' Bridget glowered.

'Quiet now. Behave.' Ellen's eyes met Mr Hamilton's. 'She gets ahead of herself.'

'She knows what she wants, like her mother.'

Bridget ran off to join her brothers by the door.

'I am happy you have settled well in the colony,' Mr Hamilton said.

'We have been fortunate. Mr Emmerson has been a true friend.'

'And now your husband.'

Ellen blinked rapidly. 'You disapprove?'

'It's none of my business.'

'True.'

'But I do hope your decision was not made in haste for both your sakes.' He gave a small bow and turned on his heel.

Left alone, Ellen's chest tightened. She didn't know whether to be angry or give in to the tears hot behind her eyes.

Once they left the tea house situated in a reputable hotel, Ellen's thoughts swirled wildly through her head of the night to come.

At the house she encouraged Alistair to take Mr Hamilton for a walk along the harbour shore, while she informed the cook that a guest was staying for supper.

Austin and Patrick visited their friends in the nearby street, while Bridget sat at the table in the kitchen and quietly played with her doll.

In the front room, Ellen paced, her thoughts in a whirl until Riona came in. She watched her sister sit by the window and pick up her sewing. 'Can we not be at war, Riona, please?'

Silence stretched between them before Riona put

down her sewing. 'I don't know if I can ever forgive you, Ellen. You have gone against the true religion. How do I live with that?'

'That's for you to decide, isn't it? You can either accept it or no longer have a family.'

'Sure, and I don't have a choice,' she whispered painfully. 'I can't live without you all, so I can't.'

'I'm sorry I've hurt you.'

'It's yours and the children's souls I worry about, not my own feelings. I've prayed morning and night to the Holy Mother for you to see sense, but my prayers haven't been answered.' Riona sighed and then faced Ellen. 'But today I realised that even if you hadn't married Mr Emmerson, you'd have married Mr Hamilton, another Protestant, if he'd asked.'

Ellen gaped. 'What?'

'I'm your sister. I know you better than you think. I know how much you care for Rafe Hamilton. Oh, sure, and you've hidden it well enough even from yourself, no doubt. But seeing your face when you recognised him after the wedding, well . . . You looked stricken and so did he.'

'I . . . I . . .'

'Christ and all his Angels don't try to deny it. You've been sweet on him since the day you met him at Wilton Manor and he you.'

'That's not true.'

'Sure, it is. A blind man can see it. Mr Hamilton thinks a great deal about you. Why else would a gentleman offer his time and carriage to take a friend's housemaid to visit her dead husband in a morgue? Answer me that? Why would he buy us a box of lovely things for the voyage and no one else?' Riona shook her head. 'I may not be wise in the ways of love, but I know it when I see it.'

Ellen sat down abruptly; her legs too weak to stand.

Riona gazed at her sadly. 'You do love him, don't you?'

'I think I do, yes.'

'Then you should never have married Mr Emmerson.'

'Alistair knows I don't love him. I never thought Mr Hamilton would come here. He's never answered my letters . . .'

'How could he have when he's been three months on a ship? He must have left Liverpool only weeks after we did.'

'I didn't know that, did I?' Ellen shot up and paced the room, her mind and heart in turmoil.

'When I told him that you had married this morning, his face lost all colour. Poor man. He's come all this way to find you only to be told you and Mr Emmerson are married.'

'We don't know for certain he has any attachment towards me.' Ellen felt sick. Did Mr Hamilton care for her as she did for him? Surely not . . . but if he did . . .

'Whist,' Riona snapped. 'You've eyes in your head, don't you? At the tea house he could barely do nothing else but watch you.'

'Do you think Alistair noticed?'

'Alistair?' Riona glared at her. 'Alistair? God above! That man can't see anything but you. He's besotted, yet you don't return his feelings, do you? You are in love with Rafe Hamilton.'

Ellen stared out of the window, watching the boys walk down the hill. 'Mr Hamilton will return to England shortly and be gone from my life. Alistair will give us what we need.'

'Will grand things fill your heart?'

'My heart isn't a priority, my children are. For them I have married Alistair.'

Male voices could be heard, and she watched the boys run to join Alistair and Mr Hamilton coming along the vacant field. Her silly heart twisted at the sight of the four males — her sons she adored, the man she married, and the man she loved.

Riona stood and came to Ellen's side. 'You're my sister. I don't agree with what you've done, not that it matters now, but I will stand by you. I've prayed hard every day and spoken with Father Joyce to try and ease my mind over this huge change in our lives. It hasn't been easy for me, so it hasn't.'

'I'm sorry, Riona. I never wanted to hurt you.'

'I know you didn't. But you're too headstrong, Ellen. Mammy always said so.' She gave a grim smile. 'I can't walk away from you or the children. You're my family and all I have in this world. I won't always agree with what you do or what you think, but I will stand by you.'

Ellen hugged her, tears behind her eyes, yet she dare not shed them for the fear of never stopping. This day had been fraught with too much emotion that she was only just keeping a handle on.

'I'll take care of you always,' Ellen said huskily as they broke apart.

As the others came inside, Ellen pasted on a smile and played hostess.

Throughout dinner that included the children, which Alistair insisted upon, knowing how used they were with eating with Ellen and Riona, the atmosphere was jolly and fun. The children were encouraged to talk with the adults, and Austin had a fine way of entertaining them with stories about his friends and observations of the area.

After supper, Riona took the children upstairs to bed, giving Alistair and Mr Hamilton some time to drink port while Ellen went to the kitchen and thanked Mrs Lawson, the cook and Dilly the maid, for their efforts.

Ellen lingered longer than was necessary in the kitchen and then strolled outside for some cool evening air, not wanting to return to the parlour and Mr Hamilton. His arrival had altered her carefully controlled thoughts. How was she to behave with him here? How could she not reveal her feelings? The less time she spent in his presence, the better for her peace of mind and her marriage.

Eventually, not able to stall any longer, she entered the parlour just as Mr Hamilton was collecting his hat.

'Dearest, Rafe is leaving,' Alistair said. 'It has been a tiring day for us all.'

Ellen stood a little behind Alistair. 'I'm pleased you had a safe journey from Liverpool, Mr Hamilton. It is a treacherous voyage.'

'It seems wise for me to experience it for myself so I can be of more assistance to those we take on our ships.'

'Will you stay in Sydney for long?'

His eyes bored into hers. 'No. I should not think so. I have plans to travel to Melbourne. The gold rush in the country there is driving a population explosion, and Alistair and I should expand the business in that growing city as well.'

Alistair took Ellen's hand. 'There may be a reason

for me to travel with Rafe to Melbourne in the next week or so. Would that be very inconsiderate of me as a newly married man?'

She smiled in reassurance. 'I fully understand. I have enough here to keep me busy.'

'Am I not the luckiest man alive, Rafe, to have such a woman by my side?' Alistair grinned.

A pulse throbbed in Rafe's jaw. 'Indeed. You are the envy of most men. Goodnight.' He bowed and left the house.

'What a day it has been.' Alistair took Ellen into his arms. 'Shall we retire, wife?'

Her chest tightened. 'Of course.'

'You go up and I shall lock up the house.'

In the bedroom, Ellen undressed and washed herself by the lamplight. Soaking the cloth in the warm water Dilly brought up earlier, Ellen tried to not think of what was to occur. When she had thought about it in the lead up to the wedding, she'd not worried. The act of sex wasn't new to her, and she liked Alistair and believed she could happily give her body to him. Perhaps it wouldn't be the wild abandonment she had with Malachy when they were young and in love, but she had no doubt that with Alistair it would be pleasant enough . . .

However, that had been before Rafe's arrival.

Climbing into bed, she waited for Alistair and smiled when he opened the door. 'Everything is all right?' she asked.

'Yes, Mrs Lawson and Dilly have gone home.'

Quickly, Alistair undressed and turned out the lamp. In the soft darkness, he took her in his arms. 'I love you, Ellen. Don't say it back to me, for I appreciate you are not ready to.'

'I care for you, Alistair.'

'Then that will be enough for now.' He kissed her deeply and she responded.

He gently pushed her onto her back and kissed her body. Ellen's passion rose and she closed her eyes. It had been so long since she was loved by a man.

Alistair became more urgent, lifting her nightgown up, his breathing short and heavy. He kissed her breasts, growing more excited.

Ellen wanted him to slow down, but he was lost to his own needs and entered her quickly. Eyes closed, Ellen moved to his thrusts, but it was too strange for her. *He* was too strange. Alistair wasn't Malachy, the only man who had aroused her, and Alastair wasn't Rafe, the man whose touch she longed for.

In seconds it was over, and Alistair lay beside her, panting. 'Thank you, dearest. You have made me incredibly happy.'

'I'm pleased, Alistair,' she whispered.

As he slept, she got out of bed and washed herself. Sitting by the window, she let the tears fall.

19

'I believe Mrs Gardner-Hill is extremely interested to meet you, dearest,' Alistair told her a week later as they sat in the carriage on their way to the Gardner-Hill mansion on the other side of Sydney.

'I look forward to meeting her too,' Ellen answered, straightening her silk evening gloves. The silver-grey satin dress she wore was the most expensive she had ever owned, but Alistair wanted her to look her best this evening, the first social outing they were attending as husband and wife.

'She is on many committees for various charities around the city and I am quite certain she will wish for you to become a member of many, too.'

She glanced at Alistair in the passing light cast by a well-lit tavern. 'I'm willing to join a number of charities but I've the children to keep me busy and the house and the estate in Berrima.'

'Indeed. But soon Austin and Patrick will be going to board at King's School in Parramatta, which will only leave Bridget at home. Your time will be freed up a great deal by that until we have our own children.' He smiled.

Ellen stared at the darkened street. The thought of more children gave her mixed feelings. To give Alistair a child of his own would be a wonderful thing after all he'd done for her. Yet, the idea of being with child and giving birth again gave her shudders. She was twenty-nine years old. It had been seven years since she gave birth to Bridget, and she'd been a baby when the potato blight first hit. Ellen's memories of Bridget's baby years were full of suffering and worry.

Of course, being with child while married to Alistair was different, and she knew he would do anything for her, but still, she knew there were other things she wanted to achieve, such as encouraging Alistair to expand his land holdings.

She also had no wish to spend her days having cups of tea with the wealthy wives of Sydney. The very thought annoyed her. How bored would she be simply visiting women she didn't know, day in and day out?

Already in the week since she had been married to Alistair, they had attended two dinners, and she had welcomed four wives on four separate occasions into her home.

She knew being friends with the wives of Alistair's friends was part of her role as his wife, but sitting down to partake in small talk every day was not how she wanted to spend her life. She was used to being busy. Now she felt idle and indulgent. She had a cook and a maid to see to the house and with the boys soon to leave for school, she'd only have Bridget to care for and Riona did more than her share of that.

Her wish was to go to the Berrima property and oversee the building of their new home and to lay the grounds for gardens and plant an orchard and vegetable gardens. She wanted to see fat beasts grazing every time she looked over the land, land that was now hers.

'You are quiet, my dear.' Alistair squeezed her hand.

'I was simply thinking. I heard that the Surveyor-General Sir Thomas Mitchel will be here tonight,' Ellen said. 'I think we should speak to him about surveying the land on the other side of your boundary at

Berrima. We should buy it before someone else does. I read in the newspaper that there are land lots being surveyed in the Argyle country to open it up to more population. We should act quickly.'

'We have plenty of time for that. Sir Thomas is heading to England shortly. Surveying lots will not be his priority.'

'Then we should speak to his assistant. Unless you can have an audience with Governor FitzRoy?'

'Dearest, I have told you. Land grants are not simply tossed out like food scraps to chickens. There is a process. Many are calling for the cessation of grants and instead land should be bought from now on, no matter who you are.'

'Then let us buy some.'

He smiled indulgently. 'We have enough land.'

'We can never have enough land, Alistair.' She held her temper, though every time she mentioned buying land, he cut her off as though the idea wasn't important.

'I have other ventures needing my capital.' He kissed her hand. 'The house in Berrima has begun being built. In the meantime, I shall increase my business concerns here in Sydney and in Melbourne. Buying premises in Sydney have a greater return than land in the middle of nowhere. Sheep farms require enormous capital. I'd rather buy property or land in Sydney and build houses to rent out or sell.'

'But — '

'Here we are.' Alistair unlatched the door as the carriage came to a halt on the drive surrounded by garden beds that even in the dark, Ellen could see were expansive and well-tended.

Outside, Ellen stood and readied herself for the

numerous questions that were directed her way at any function. She was tired of talking about the blight and the famine and her life in Ireland. All it did was make her feel alien to the other women, as though she didn't belong, which she knew was correct. These women had never been hungry, or poor, or desperate. How could they possibly understand? She didn't belong in their society, and every time she spoke with her Irish accent, she only reinforced the notion.

Inside the large ballroom, the wealthy citizens of Sydney gathered in groups, talking quietly and sipping their drinks. Heads turned towards Alistair and Ellen, but she kept her back straight and smiled with a forced warmth. She was doing this for Alistair, for her children, who one day would enter this society that was so at odds to her former life.

'Alistair and Mrs Emmerson. How delightful that you could come to my little ball,' Mrs Gardner-Hill gushed over them loudly, drawing more attention than Ellen wanted. 'And your dress, Mrs Emmerson, beautiful. Who made such a creation? Madame Franklin in Pitt Street who attends me?'

'No, not Madame Franklin, but Mrs Haggerty in Cumberland Street.' Ellen smiled sweetly, knowing full well that her hostess and other society women present wouldn't dream of venturing into the seedy side of Sydney but that's where Ellen had found a grand dressmaker, another Irish woman. Her dress was the stunning result of Mrs Haggerty, the former convict from Dublin.

'Well . . . ' Mrs Gardner-Hill seemed a little shocked. 'You must call on Madame Franklin and sample her skills. She is the best in the colony, I assure you.'

'Thank you, but I shall continue with Mrs Haggerty.

277

She needs the custom more than Madame Franklin. She is a widow with a blind son.'

Distaste turned the older woman's features ugly. 'Indeed? Excuse me, more guests have arrived.'

'Dearest — '

Ellen sighed. 'I'm sorry, Alistair, but she doesn't control me.'

'No, but she likes to *think* she controls all the women of society here.'

'I'm not particularly good at simpering,' Ellen whispered.

Alistair grinned. 'God forbid!'

After rounds of tedious introductions, Ellen made her way to the refreshments table while Alistair spoke to several business acquaintances. Her cheeks ached from smiling and her throat was parched at the constant polite chatter she'd been doing for an hour, always making sure she didn't sound too Irish, or say anything to humiliate herself or Alistair.

'Mrs Emmerson.' A man came to her side with a polite smile. Short with a receding hairline, he indicated to the servant for two glasses of red wine and handed one to Ellen. 'I am pleased to meet you, madam.'

'I'm sorry, but we've not been introduced.' Ellen searched her memory to think if they'd met before.

'Jonas Paynter.' He bowed. 'Your husband and I do business together. In fact, I am hoping to do a little more with him. He has just mentioned in conversation that you are keen to buy more land.'

He had her interest. 'I am, Mr Paynter.'

'I am selling my property and returning to England. I have given Emmerson the first chance to offer for it before I engage a land agent to sell it for me.'

'I see, and where is your land, sir?'

'Balmain. I have five acres on the northern side with views to Goat Island.'

'Oh, in Sydney?' She couldn't hide her disappointment fast enough, and he frowned.

'You do not care for Balmain?'

'It's not that. Forgive me. I had assumed you had land in the country, that's all.'

'Alas, no. My plans were to build terrace houses along the Nicholson Street. If I hadn't been recalled to England due to my older brother's death, then I would have continued with my plans.'

'You aren't returning to the colony?'

'I am not. So, what do you think of buying my five acres?'

She looked him in the eyes. 'What did Alistair say?'

'He said if we, you and I, can work out a deal, then he'll agree to buy.'

'*We* work out a deal?' Ellen stood on tiptoes to look for Alistair. She saw him in the corner of the room. He caught her eye and grinned. He raised his glass to her, giving her the nod of approval she needed.

Excitement rose in her like bubbles in water. Ellen lifted her chin and stared directly at Mr Paynter. 'Well, let us do business then and see if we can make this night one to remember.'

He laughed loudly, causing nearby people to look their way.

Half an hour later, Ellen felt exhilarated and exhausted. After many negotiations and back and forth with offers and counteroffers, Ellen now owned five acres in Balmain. She hoped Alistair would be happy with the price she struck.

'You look enchanting tonight, Mrs Emmerson,' Mr

279

Hamilton murmured behind her.

Ellen spun around, her heart somersaulting against her corset. 'Alistair didn't mention you were attending tonight.'

'I told him I was not going to.'

'But you changed your mind.' She was still delighted by her dealing with Mr Paynter and couldn't help but smile widely at seeing Mr Hamilton here. This was proving to be a wonderful night.

'Yes.' He looked pained, his gaze never leaving hers.

Music began to play, and he held out his hand. 'May I?'

Ellen panicked and stepped back, nearly spilling her drink.

Hamilton frowned. 'Dancing with me is unwelcome?'

'No, no, not that.'

'Then what?'

The heat rush to her cheeks. 'I can't dance, at least not to this.'

He looked behind him to the couples serenely gliding across the floor. Then he nodded, understanding her background. 'Of course. Come, let us walk then. There must be garden paths we can stroll.'

Together they left through open French doors and out onto a wide veranda lit with lanterns.

In the distance, the sound of waves crashing onto the shore of the little cove echoed in the still night.

'This way of life is all vastly different for you, I should imagine,' he said as they strolled past other guests standing by the veranda rail.

'At times, I believe it is nothing but a dream and I'll wake up on my damp straw mattress in my cottage at any moment and smell the rotting stink of blighted

potatoes,' she said softly.

'You have come a long way since then, and in such a short space of time. Now you are married to a prominent man of the colony . . .'

'True, Alistair was one of the most eligible bachelors in the city.'

'Which made him the ideal business partner for me.' Hamilton stared up at the starlit sky. 'He was fawned upon by mamas eager to see their daughters marry him, and fathers also for that matter, knowing he had keen business sense.'

'Yet, it was an Irish peasant who claimed him.' Ellen dared not look at Hamilton. 'How they must hate me.'

'No one could hate you. Men admire you. I have seen them watch you, first at your wedding and then just now in the ballroom. Men are intrigued about you. Women envy you. How did an Irish woman, a beautiful one at that, snare Alistair Emmerson?'

'Snare?' She scoffed. 'I don't like the sound of that. It reminds me of a rabbit caught in a trap. I haven't trapped Alistair.'

'No, and that makes it even more interesting for people. They want to know what it is that is so fascinating about you.'

She shrugged. 'There isn't anything fascinating about me.'

'Not true. From the first moment I met you, I saw something within you. A fight, a determination, a courage that could not be ignored. What is more, there was a sensuality hidden beneath your protective instincts. Such a combination turns a man's head.'

Had she turned his head? She desperately wanted to ask.

Ellen took in his words as they walked down several sandstone steps onto a gravelled path. A couple walked ahead of them. A bird called from the trees while the ever-persistent sound of small waves hitting the sand filled the air.

Strolling beside Hamilton gave her a sense of awareness. Her nerves were tightened, her stomach knotting with something she couldn't name. The man she had dreamed about for so many months stood beside her and she was his equal now, not simply a maidservant. It was a heady feeling.

She cleared her throat, her lips dry. 'I never expected you to come here.'

'When I first met you at Wilton Manor, I never expected to travel here either. Perhaps one day it might have happened, but it was not in my immediate plans to do so.'

'Then why did you?'

'Because my family were driving me to distraction. My sister married a much older man for security, for protection from poverty, and to have the chance of a better life than the one she led with my feckless father in charge of her. Suddenly, I was no longer of need to her or my mother. They were safe and looked after. I felt at a loose end . . . '

They mutually paused at a viewing platform overlooking the harbour.

Hamilton stared straight ahead. 'I also acknowledged that something was missing in my life, something that the business deals failed to fulfil.'

'And that was?'

'A woman.'

She watched a boat tack across the water but didn't really see it. A wave of despondency washed over her

like the tide over the sand below them.

'That woman I had hoped was to be you,' he murmured.

She snapped a look at him, shocked and unbelieving.

More guests walked by, and some stopped near them and took in the view.

Ellen turned back for the path, her head spinning and her heart melting at his words.

'Mrs Emmerson.' Hamilton hurried after her. 'Forgive me, I shouldn't have spoken.'

She stopped and gazed at him in the dim light. 'You wanted me?'

'Yes. I believe I have done so from the first moment I met you.' He ran a hand through his dark hair.

'To be your mistress?' she accused.

'No! To be my wife.'

'A peasant? An Irish peasant who served you tea?' She didn't believe him.

'I saw beyond that. I saw a strong woman full of determination and strength. Someone I admired for her courage and sense.'

She reeled at his words. 'I didn't know.'

'I should have made my intentions clear, but I was uncertain at the time about how I felt.'

'If I had known . . . If you'd hinted or written . . .' Anguish clutched at her heart.

'You feel the same?' He seemed surprised.

'Yes, God help me.'

Laughter drifted from the veranda.

Ellen closed her eyes in bittersweet agony.

'I wish I had said something before you sailed,' Hamilton was saying, 'Then I simply thought to sail as soon as I could put my affairs in order. I wanted to

283

surprise you. I never expected for you to be married within months of arriving here. Naive of me, I suppose. You are beautiful and any man would want you.'

'I considered you to be lost to me . . . a dream . . . Something I could never have . . . Never did I think you would want me.' She wanted to cry but held back the emotions tearing at her. 'I married Alistair for security . . .'

'I understand that, I do. I do not blame you for wanting to better your situation after all you have been through. My sister has done the same thing. I *understand.*'

'Alistair is a good man and he cares for my children . . . ' Ellen couldn't stand still. If she did, she'd reach for him and she couldn't do that.

'What a mess.' He sighed as they turned and walked back to the house as music drifted down to them.

'How would have you found me?' Ellen asked quietly. 'I could've been anywhere in the colony.'

'I was taking a chance that Alistair would have forwarding details on where the passengers went after arrival. I would track you down somehow.'

'All the letters I wrote to you . . . ' Despair filled her. 'You never received them.'

'The letters and I would have crossed on the open ocean. They will be at my office in Liverpool by now.' He looked as heartbroken as she felt. His handsome face seemed full of longing and sadness.

'What will we do?' she whispered, seeing others gathered on the veranda and panicking she would not be able to speak to him privately again.

'You are married to one of my good friends, a man I respect. There is nothing we can do. I shall return to England and we shall forget about each other.' His

284

tone conveyed the pain she also suffered.

She nodded. He was correct. There was nothing to be done.

Rafe straightened his shoulders and took a step back from her. 'Shall we go in?'

'Yes.' She walked ahead of him, the strangling ache in her chest making her struggle to breathe.

On the veranda she turned away and headed for another doorway, leaving him, leaving the man she could never have.

★ ★ ★

'Look, Mammy!' Bridget crowed as she bounced up and down on the white pony, Princess, as it circled the field beside the house.

'You're doing so well, my sweetness.' Ellen clapped.

'Practise the way I showed you, Bridget,' Alistair instructed. 'Go up with the lift of the right leg. Watch it now. That is correct.'

'She'll be galloping like a fiend in no time at all, so she will,' Riona tutted.

Alistair grinned. 'She will be the best horsewoman in the colony, you just watch.'

'She has her mother's determination to succeed,' Rafe said, watching Bridget.

Ellen remained silent. Since their declaration at the Gardener — Hill ball last week, she felt listless and uneasy. Even the purchase of the land in Balmain didn't hold the excitement it should have. She kept busy preparing Austin and Patrick for their start at the school in Parramatta in a few days. Along with Alistair and the boys, she toured the school building and met the schoolmaster and bought them new clothes and books. The boys' excitement covered her own inner despair of loving a man she could only ever be a friend to and who soon would be sailing away, never to return.

'That is enough now, sweet girl,' Alistair called to Bridget. 'We must say goodbye.'

Ellen stepped back as Bridget brought the pony to a halt near them, and Alistair lifted her down off the saddle. 'Go wash your hands, darling,' she instructed.

'Austin, will you turn Princess into the field with Pepper, please?' Alistair gave the pony's reins to Austin.

'Come on, Patrick, you can help.'

Patrick scowled. 'I want a turn.'

Austin patted him on the shoulder. 'Mr Emmerson . . . Papa has promised us riding lessons in Parramatta in the afternoons once our studies have finished. We'll be riding real horses, not a pony like this.'

Ellen watched her boys, who were growing up so fast, lead Princess away. She'd miss them once they left, but their education was important. Already Austin was behaving like he'd been born into Alistair's class. She noticed him copying Alistair's ways and speech.

'We should be leaving shortly, Rafe,' Alistair said as they walked back into the house. 'The captain told me he wants everyone aboard the ship by three.'

'Everything is packed and in the carriage.' Rafe glanced sideways at Ellen.

Her stomach dropped at the thought of him sailing away today. 'Do you have everything, Alistair?' She forced herself to be light-hearted when she felt the opposite.

286

'I shall just go upstairs and check again.' He left them and took the stairs.

Riona stopped at the doorway of the front parlour. 'I'll go and fetch Bridget and the boys to say their goodbyes.'

Alone with Rafe, Ellen could only stare at him. There were only minutes left of him being in her life. How was she to bear it?

'I wish you every happiness, Ellen.' Rafe took her hands and kissed them both.

A small moan escaped her lips. 'Don't go,' she whispered.

'I cannot stay and watch you be another man's wife.' His voice croaked in his throat.

She squeezed his hands, desperate to be in his arms, to have his mouth on hers.

'Goodbye, Mrs Lawson, Dilly.' Alistair was in the hallway.

Ellen sprang away from Rafe, trying to compose herself.

'Are we ready?' Alistair said from the doorway.

Ellen walked out ahead of them and into the sunshine. Higgins sat up on the carriage seat, chatting down to Riona and the children.

While Rafe said his farewells, Alistair embraced Ellen. 'I should be back within a month depending on how well Rafe and I conduct our business in Melbourne. If we are successful in securing contracts, we shall have to set up bank accounts and so forth.'

'I understand. Don't worry about us, we'll be fine. Riona and me will take the boys to Parramatta and I'll write and let you know how they settle once you've written to me the address of your lodgings.'

'Write to me and tell me everything about the

builders you commission for the Balmain land. If it becomes too much, then leave the building of the houses until I return.'

'I'll manage,' she murmured, smiling to ease his worry.

'I know you will. Have I not married the most sensible woman in Sydney?' Alistair kissed her quickly and then turned to the children, who he hugged and kissed and made a fuss over.

Rafe came to her but didn't touch her. 'Farewell, Ellen.'

A single tear tripped over her lashes and she dashed it away. 'Safe journey,' she whispered, gazing through blurred vision at his handsome beloved face.

The children called out their goodbyes as Alistair and Rafe climbed into the carriage.

Riona stood beside Ellen. 'I'm sure Alistair loves those children as though he was their real father.' She smiled fondly. 'I think he married you just to be their father, so he did.'

Riona looked at Ellen and sighed. 'I was jesting. It's a grand thing he loves them so.' Slipping her arm through Ellen's, Riona tutted. 'Stop *crying* for Mr Hamilton,' she whispered. 'It's done, over. *Forget him.*'

Stifling a sob, Ellen nodded. Her heart might be broken but no one would ever know it. She straightened her shoulders and walked back into the house.

20

On a cool day in June, with the wind coming off the harbour to tease Ellen's hair from her bonnet, she walked around the Balmain land with Mr Delahunt, the builder she had hired.

'These plans are detailed, Mrs Emmerson.' Delahunt tapped the rolled plans against his hand. 'We'll have the foundations finished by the end of next week.'

'Very good, Mr Delahunt.' Ellen paused to watch his team of workers dig out the foundations for the terrace houses. She'd instructed the architect to draw a terrace of five houses along either side of Nicholson Street. Each house had two rooms downstairs and three bedrooms above, with an attached kitchen and scullery and a private water closet each.

'Coming into winter there may be weather delays, of course.' He helped her over a drainage ditch.

'By Christmas I'd like to see tenants living here.'

'Christmas?' He scratched his head under his hat. 'It's doable, I suppose.'

'Make it happen, Mr Delahunt, and you'll be awarded a bonus amount. But I want the terraces built solidly to stand a hundred years or more. I don't have time to listen to tenants complaining about leaking roofs and whatnot.'

'I'll stake my reputation on these houses lasting a hundred years or more and no leaks, Mrs Emmerson.'

'Good. For this won't be the last property I will . . . I mean my husband and I will develop.' She headed back to the carriage. 'I will call again next week with the next payment, Mr Delahunt. If you have any concerns, call on me at my home.'

'Will do, Mrs Emmerson. See you next week.'

'George Street, please, Higgins.' Ellen climbed into the carriage and picked up the sheaf of papers on the seat. Today she had meetings with the bank, a land agent and Alistair's solicitor, afternoon tea with Mrs Gardner-Hill and her friends, which Ellen wasn't looking forward to, then she had a dress fitting appointment with Mrs Haggerty and needed to post a letter to Alistair who remained in Melbourne on business.

Alistair's letters arrived every few days, telling her how much he missed her and the children. He also wrote of the frenzied activity in Melbourne. The gold rush had brought thousands of people from all over the world into the fledgling town and created a city within a very short time. Buildings were going up at a rapid pace. Alistair's enthusiasm for the growth of his business shone brightly on every page he wrote. He and Rafe had hired an office and were busy interviewing a prospective manager to oversee the imports Rafe would send there once he was back in England. They were also securing raw materials such as wool to export to England.

In his last letter, Alistair wrote how he was hoping to go inland to the gold diggings to see for himself the fever that gripped men. Apparently, Rafe wasn't too keen on the idea and may return to England earlier than expected . . .

As Higgins drove through the streets into the city, Ellen pulled out of her reticule the letter she had received two weeks ago from Rafe. She had read it so many times that she knew the words by heart.

My Darling Ellen.

This is the only letter I shall write to you.

I am giving myself this one selfish act to put my feelings on paper and then you will never hear from me again.

I love you.

You will forever be my true love, the one I desire above all.

We cannot be together, I accept this, but my heart is yours until it stops beating.

Rafe.

Like the man himself, the letter was short on words and not overly dramatic. He had written what was in his heart without the flowery prose of a poet, but those simple words were enough. She could live with only ever having that letter.

The carriage slowed and Ellen tucked the letter away again. She gathered her things and descended the carriage step with help from the doorman belonging to the bank.

'I'll be an hour, Higgins.' She nodded her thanks to the doorman and was about to go inside the bank when she heard her name called.

Searching the busy street, she couldn't find who hailed her until a wagon passed and on the other side of the wide street, she saw Moira O'Rourke from the ship. She waved and watched in alarm as Moira weaved her way through the fast-moving vehicles and crossed to her.

'Moira!'

'I didn't recognise you at first.' Moira laughed. 'Look at you, the fancy lady.' She stepped back to gaze at Ellen's navy blue and white striped dress. 'You're a picture, so you are.'

'How are you?' Ellen asked, noting the grey in Moira's hair and the haggard look on her thin face. Her brown skirt had a stain on it, and she wore a tatted shawl. She looked just as unkempt as when she first saw her on the ship.

'I'm not as good as you, it seems!' Moira laughed.

'Do you live nearby?'

A weary expression crossed her face. 'I have been lately, at Her Majesty's pleasure.'

Shock widened Ellen's eyes. 'Jail?'

'Aye, sure, and it's not the life I was expecting.'

'What's happened?'

'How long have you got?' Moira chuckled.

'Come, there's a tea shop up the road. Let's go there.'

Before long, they were seated at a table and served tea and slices of lemon cake.

Ellen waited for Moira to finish her piece of cake and then gave her the slice she hadn't eaten.

'You don't want it?'

'No. I've just eaten,' Ellen lied, watching Moira eat hungrily. She poured more tea from the pot as Moira had finished her first cup. 'Why did you end up in jail?'

Moira sat back in the chair and swallowed the mouthful she chewed. 'Prostitution.'

Ellen gaped. 'Why? Where is your husband?'

'Dead.'

'Dead? Oh, Moira.'

'He was sick when I arrived. We had a few months together but . . . ' Moira stared into her tea. 'It wasn't the same. How could it be after all those years apart?'

'I'm so sorry to hear it.'

'Aye well, it's life, isn't it?' She sipped her tea and

then smiled at Ellen. 'It's grand to see you though, so it is. How are the kiddies and Riona?'

'All well. The boys are growing like weeds and Bridget is a right madam.'

'And you're married?' Moira indicated the wedding band Ellen wore. 'Holy Mother, you don't hang about, do you?'

'I married Alistair Emmerson.'

'Emmerson, the blond chap from the lodgings?'

'Yes.'

'Jesus, Mary and Joseph. Who'd have thought? He's a looker, so he is. We all knew he'd taken a shine to you or why else would he ask you to be his housekeeper?' Moira grinned.

'Do you still see anyone from the ship?'

'No. No one. I left the lodgings within days of you leaving. I found me husband from asking around and visiting his old address. He'd only moved to the next street, so he had.'

'I'm so sorry he died, Moira. That must have been hard for you.'

'I've survived it.'

'What will you do now?'

'Try and get a position somewhere. I've been asking around at every inn to see if they want a cook or maid. Sure, and it's a nightmare trying to find work in this town. People say to go bush and find a lonely farmer needing a wife. I'm considering it.'

'Where are you staying?'

Moira glanced down at her filthy hands. 'Wherever I find a spot at night.'

'Oh, Moira.'

'Sure, and I'll get work soon.'

'Well, until you do, you'll stay with us.'

'Nay,' she looked affronted. 'Mr Emmerson won't want me about for sure.'

'He's away. You can sleep in the loft. The boys are at boarding school now.'

'Boarding school?' Moira's eyes widened. 'Will you look at that! You're living the life, aren't you? Not that I'm really surprised, mind. Out of all of us on that ship you were the one who we all thought would do well in the colony.'

'I've only just begun, Moira.' Ellen laughed. 'I'd like it if you came home with me. Riona and Bridget will be happy to see you. I'm so busy now that Riona feels a little lonely, and you'd be grand company for her. Would you stay with us until you're back on your feet?'

'I'll work, mind. I'm not a charity.'

'I have a cook and a maid already, but I could do with a friend.' Ellen smiled.

'Sure, and ain't you got one for life with me?' Tears glittered in Moira's eyes. 'You're a good woman, Ellen, even if you have married a Protestant and sound different than you used to.' She laughed.

★ ★ ★

A few days later, Ellen sat in the drawing room of a grand house on Elizabeth Bay, sipping tea, and listening to the boring conversations going on around her. She had been invited by Mrs Percival, a judge's wife, for tea with some society ladies. Ellen was loathed to go, but she had to play the game. She'd brought Bridget with her, for her daughter needed to learn how young ladies were meant to behave at other people's homes.

294

It surprised Ellen greatly to see Bridget adapt to her new role as a daughter of a gentleman. She played with the other children in the garden just beyond the drawing-room windows and held her own when several of the bigger girls made all the decisions on what they were to play.

Ellen kept a close eye on Bridget, ready for her tantrums. She sat closer to the French door leading out to the garden, listening to Bridget's demanding tones that Cynthia Percival couldn't be the princess again as she'd had two turns at it already.

About to rise and intervene, Ellen put down her teacup but was addressed by Mrs Percival, a tiny woman with a tiny mind.

'Mrs Emmerson, what is your stance on this topic?'

'What topic is that? Forgive me, I was listening to the children.' Ellen gave the ladies her attention.

'Convict servants.'

'I know little about them.'

'Convicts with good behaviour reports are issued with a tickets of leave and can gain private employment. We have employed at least ten of these people over the years, but now they are demanding higher wages.'

'I do not have any ticket of leave servants, Mrs Percival, so I do not have this problem.'

'Be thankful you don't. Ungrateful wretches.' Mrs Percival tutted. 'Why should they, the scum of society, be given more money? Not so long ago they were in chains and working for free. It was annoying enough we had to feed the rogues.'

Ellen tensed at the woman's superior tone. 'Surely if they are now free people, they deserve a decent wage for a decent day's work?'

'A decent day's work? That is just my point, Mrs Emmerson, they do not work. Idle, lazy thieves.'

The other women nodded in agreement.

'I doubt they are all idle thieves,' Ellen muttered, noticing Bridget, who was red-cheeked with temper and wagging her finger in the face of Cynthia Percival.

'But they are, Mrs Emmerson. Do not hire them at all. Learn from me.' Mrs Percival nodded sagely. 'They will rob you while you sleep.'

'Have they robbed you?' Ellen stood, her gaze on Bridget.

'I am sure they have, in many ways by not working hard, or taking more food than they are allotted. Are *you* sympathetic to those scoundrels?'

Another woman gasped, and the woman seated next to Mrs Percival, a Mrs Hinch, whispered something.

Ellen frowned. 'What did you say, Mrs Hinch?'

'Nothing.'

'Yes, you did.'

Mrs Hinch paled. 'I . . . Well, I — '

'She said that you may sympathise with the convicts because of your background.' Mrs Percival's eyes narrowed with barely concealed distaste.

'My background?' Ellen's temper rose just as her daughter's was doing outside. 'I may be Irish, Mrs Percival, but neither me nor any of my family came here in chains.'

'Maybe they were hanged in Ireland instead,' a woman named Mrs Pole sniggered.

A general titter flooded the room.

In that instant, Ellen knew she'd never be accepted

into this society. Being married to Alistair merely glossed over the cracks of the class divide.

Bridget yelled and slapped Cynthia. Ellen rushed outside and grabbed her daughter and pulled her away.

'Make her apologise,' Mrs Percival snapped at Ellen. 'She has no manners, but it is hardly surprising really, is it?'

A cold rage filled Ellen. 'Manners? Look to your own selfish child before you cast stones at mine, you rude, arrogant, narrow-minded fool! I may be Irish, and I may have been poor before my marriage, but I'd rather be who I am, than be either one of you stuck-up, spineless eejits!'

Ellen pulled Bridget behind her as she stormed through the house and out to the carriage.

'Home, Higgins!' she ordered, pushing Bridget into the carriage.

Crying, Bridget clasped her hands in her lap. 'I'm sorry, Mammy.'

Taking a deep breath, Ellen tried to calm down. 'It's not all your fault. Cynthia is a nasty girl.'

Bridget wiped her eyes. 'She pulled my hair and said I was a peasant. What is a peasant?'

'It's a poor person, like we were back home in Ireland.'

'But we aren't poor anymore.' Bridget frowned and stared up at Ellen. 'We have food and clothes and I have a pony.'

'No, we aren't poor any longer. But there will always be some people who won't like us because we were once poor Irish.'

'Well, I don't like them.'

'You don't have to like them, my sweet, you just

have to pretend you do.'

'Why?'

Ellen thought for a moment. 'Because one day you'll want to marry a man who belongs to that society. A man with money and position. I want you to marry well, Bridget, so you'll never have to work or see your babies cold and starving. That's why we pretend to like those people.' As she spoke, Ellen wondered if she had just ruined Bridget's chances of marrying well when the time came. Mrs Percival and her flock of crows would gossip all around Sydney about her outburst. Had she done too much damage?

Should she write and apologise to Mrs Percival? Her heart said no, but her head said yes. She needed to mend those bridges she destroyed that morning. If not for her sake, for the children's. Sydney's society was small, and memories long. She had married Alistair for the children's future. Had she just ruined it?

Sighing, she rested her head back against the seat, annoyed with herself for not playing the game. She had to learn to keep her opinions to herself. Then, suddenly, she dismissed the thought. Why should she change for those stupid women who didn't have a sensible thought between them?

No, she would not bow to their whims. Her children would rise in this society, and she didn't need the likes of Mrs Percival to help her. No, she would do it herself.

Money was what made people sit up and take notice. Money brought prestige. Money brought respect. Money. Land. When she had more land and money than the likes of Mrs Percival, they would not look down their noses at her or her family ever again.

Ellen took Bridget's hand and kissed the top of her head. 'Everything will be all right, my dove. Your mammy will make sure of it.'

21

'Will you look at that?' Moira chuckled. 'Blessed Virgin Mother, you are two handsome young men, so you are.' She hugged Austin and Patrick to her.

Ellen watched on with a smile. Austin and Patrick had returned from boarding school in Parramatta for a week as an outbreak of scarlet fever had erupted at the school. They'd only been gone four weeks, but she was surprised at how much they had grown.

'It's good to see you, Moira,' Austin said.

'Aye, your mammy's been grand offering me a place to live.'

'Shall we eat?' Ellen ushered them to the dining table as Dilly brought out tureens of vegetables.

'I'll go and help Mrs Lawson.' Moira left them and returned to the kitchen where she was the happiest. She and Mrs Lawson got on well and shared the duties in the kitchen.

Riona sat between the boys, lovingly gazing at them. 'I've missed you so much. Tell me everything you haven't put in your letters.'

As they ate the roast mutton and listened to the boys' talk of school, telling stories of their teachers and fellow pupils, the rain lashed down outside the windows.

Austin got up to add more wood to the fire, giving the room a cosy warmth. 'Our riding lessons are my favourite time. We go twice during the week on an evening and for a few hours on Saturdays.' He glanced at Patrick. 'He's so good at it, Mammy. You should see him.'

'I will. We'll all come up for a visit when Alistair comes home.' Ellen added more gravy to her plate.

'We can take a boat up anytime,' Riona added. 'It's not a long trip up the river to Parramatta. We should do it, then we'd see the boys more.'

Ellen sipped her glass of water. 'The boys are in class during the week, but maybe on a Saturday? I'd like to see Parramatta. I have heard much about it. There are land parcels near there which are going up for sale soon.'

As Riona was about to reply, they heard a commotion at the front door.

'What is that?' Ellen stood and left the room.

In the hallway she stared as Rafe came in, half dragging Alistair with him. The shock of seeing Rafe again was soon overcome with concern over Alistair's ghastly appearance.

'Holy Mother of God. What's happened?'

'Send for a doctor.' Rafe carried Alistair into the front parlour as the family crowded behind Ellen.

'I'll see to it.' Riona ushered the children back out of the room, calling for Dilly as she did so.

Ellen rushed to kneel beside Alistair, who looked flushed and drowsy. She stared at the splints on Alistair's left leg.

'Alistair?'

'He won't answer. He is barely conscious. Help me to get him upstairs.'

Together with an arm each around Alistair, they heaved him up the stairs and onto the bed. Moira came up with a hot bedpan and helped them to undress him and make him comfortable.

'I'll make some tea.' Moira closed the door behind

her.

'What's happened?' Ellen asked Rafe as she fussed over Alistair, who moaned.

Rafe took off his hat and wet overcoat. 'Two weeks ago, we were out hunting with some new business associates. A kangaroo jumped out of the trees and straight into Alistair's horse, throwing him off. The horse landed on Alistair and broke his leg through his skin.'

'Why didn't you write and tell me?'

'There was no point. Alistair wanted to come home. I was ready to sail to England, but the morning Alistair was due to sail for Sydney he became feverish. He refused to delay his travel. I knew I would have to cancel my plans and go with him as each passing hour he grew worse. We'd only been out to sea a few hours when his fever became unmanageable.' Rafe's tight expression revealed his anguish. 'I thought last night we would lose him.'

Ellen gasped. 'Dear God.'

'The doctor told him not to travel, but he was determined to recuperate at home.' Rafe ran a hand through his hair. 'I never expected him to become so much worse on the voyage back here.'

'He should have stayed where he was in Melbourne and not risk the journey home. Why did you let him get on the boat in his condition?'

'I tried to tell him that, but he is stubborn . . . '

Ellen heard the tiredness in Rafe's voice. 'It's not your fault. You look exhausted.'

'I have not slept for the last three days. There was no one on the boat to tend to him but me, for we did not know what kind of fever he has and if it would spread to others. I managed to keep him alive and then when we docked just now, I broke the rules and took him straight off the boat and brought him here. If the authorities had come aboard, they would have detained him in quarantine. However, I do not think his fever is contagious, more of an infection of some sort.'

'Thank you for bringing him home.'

'He is my friend. I could not leave him and sail to England not knowing his fate. I had to bring him back to you.'

She wanted to hold him, give him comfort, for he looked ready to drop. 'You need to rest.'

'I shall find lodgings once the doctor has been.'

Several hours later, Ellen sat on a chair beside Alistair, wiping his hot sweating forehead. The house was quiet. Dusk had descended. Riona was downstairs, quietly reading to the children.

The doctor had declared Alistair had a severe fever of the blood and needed complete rest. His broken leg was infected and been lanced, and a mustard poultice applied to the injury. For now, all they could do was nurse him with cool sponges, sips of water and bedrest.

Rinsing the cloth in the bowl of water, Ellen placed it on Alistair's forehead. 'Sleep now,' she murmured, even though he'd not woken up since he arrived.

She sat back in the chair and watched him. He looked thinner than when he had left. She held his hand, wishing he'd open his eyes and smile for her.

The door opened and Moira brought in a cup of tea for her and slices of buttered bread. 'Supper,' she whispered.

'Thank you. Is everyone all right downstairs?'

'Aye, Bridget's a little worried. She's not leaving

Riona's side. Mr Hamilton has gone and said he'll be back in the morning.'

Ellen nodded. Seeing Rafe again when she'd schooled herself to accept that he was gone from her life had opened the wound barely healed.

'How's he doing?'

'He's not woken up yet.'

'Well, may the blessed Lord watch over him and give him a healing sleep.' She made the sign of the cross over her chest.

Ellen gazed at Alistair's dear face. 'He's home now. We can take care of him.'

After a tiring night where Alistair tossed and turned, moaning in his sleep, Ellen finally dozed just before dawn when Alistair's fever finally left him, and he no longer burned and sweated.

As the crows and magpies heralded in a new day, Ellen carefully changed Alistair's sheets with Moira's help and then finally he fell into an untroubled sleep. His leg, although still red and swollen, was not as hot as before and the area the doctor had lanced no longer oozed puss.

Ellen slept late, waking to find Riona had taken the children to see Father Joyce and pray for Alistair's swift recovery. Moira was at the shops and Dilly came up with a fresh bowl of warm water for Ellen to wash. She scrubbed herself clean and then changed into fresh clothes.

She was brushing her hair when in the mirror she noticed Alistair lay watching her.

She clasped his hand to her. 'You're awake.'

'I am home?'

'Yes, Rafe brought you back home. You've been extremely sick with a fever from an infection in your

304

leg.'

'I will get better now I am with my family.'

'The boys are home from school. They are eager to tell you how they've got on there.'

'Send them in . . . ' he croaked.

'Not yet. They'll be back soon. Riona has taken them out. We wanted to keep the house quiet for you so you can sleep.'

He closed his eyes. 'I am sorry to worry you.'

'Just rest. I want you to be your old self again.' She kissed his cool forehead where only hours ago it had been burning hot. 'I'll go down to the kitchen and get you some tea and you must take some of the tonic the doctor left. Mrs Lawson has made you some beef broth, too.'

Soon after, the doctor called and was most pleased with Alistair's fever breaking. He dressed the leg and reset the splints. He left a bottle of laudanum to relieve Alistair's pain.

The little clock in the parlour chimed twice as Ellen saw out the doctor after his visit. She went upstairs to sit with Alistair.

'Now, you heard the doctor. No getting up. Your leg must heal, and it can't while you're not resting. You need to build your strength again.'

'Yes, dear.' Alistair took her hand. 'Has Rafe not called?'

'No. He said he would come this morning.'

Alistair's eyebrow rose. 'This morning? And he has not been?'

'No.'

'He may have my fever, Ellen.' Alistair struggled to sit up.

'Lie down, heavens. Where do you think you're

going?'

'We must check to see if he is not sick with fever, Ellen.'

Her stomach dropped. 'Surely not. Your fever was due to the infection, nothing else.'

'If he said he was calling this morning, and he has not yet done so and it is now the afternoon, then maybe he is ill and with no one to tend to him.' Alistair looked worried.

'All right, settle down. He did look exhausted when he brought you home.'

'Go and see him, Ellen. He saved my life. Without him, I would not have survived the journey home. He may be ill himself now.'

'But where are his lodgings?'

'He would stay at the same hotel as last time. He thought well of them.'

'The Star Inn?'

'Yes. Go there and see if he is well. I could not live with myself if anything happened to him. He should be on his way home to England by now.'

'I'll go. But promise me you'll not leave this bed.'

'I promise.' He closed his eyes, tired and weak from the conversation.

Ellen quickly donned her coat and gloves and pinned on her hat.

Downstairs, she stopped in the kitchen to tell Mrs Lawson she was going out.

On the street, a hansom cab pulled up and Ellen thought it was Rafe at last, but Moira climbed down with baskets of shopping.

'I'll be back soon,' Ellen told her, climbing into the cab.

Through the streets, Ellen's heart raced. What if

Rafe was sick like Alistair? She didn't think she'd be able to cope.

In Pitt Street, the cabbie slowed, and she paid him. The Star Inn was one of quality, and one she knew the upper society often used.

Going to the receptionist's desk, she smiled calmly at the young, suited man who stood as she approached. She used her best voice. 'Good afternoon. I was wondering if I could ask about one of your guests, Mr Rafe Hamilton?'

'Yes, Mr Hamilton is staying with us, madam.'

'He is a dear friend of my husband's, Alistair Emmerson. My husband is currently ill. We are worried if Mr Hamilton may also be unwell, as he has failed to visit us when he said he would.'

'Oh, I see.' The young man scowled. 'I've not seen Mr Hamilton all day.'

'May I go up and inquire as to whether Mr Hamilton is ill?'

'Certainly, madam. We would not like one of our guests to be ailing and in need of assistance.'

'Thank you. I will return immediately if I need your help.'

'Room three, madam. First right at the top of the stairs.'

'Thank you.' Ellen hurried away before he changed his mind, or she was seen by anyone who knew her. Gossip would spread widely if people knew she was entering a man's room.

★　★　★

Rafe frowned as he woke. The knocking sound continued, bringing him fully awake. He cursed and turned over. The knocking sounded louder.

He threw back the sheet covering him and stumbled out of bed. His head was groggy from too much sleep. The room was dim with the curtains drawn. He stumbled over his boots and then banged into his trunk.

He grabbed a shirt and flung it on. Without thinking of his state of undress, he opened the door a crack.

Surprise rendered him dumb. Ellen? He rubbed his eyes to clear his vision. 'Ellen?'

Ellen slipped inside the room and shut the door. 'You are sick?' She touched his forehead, panic written on her face. 'Are you hot? You don't feel hot. How do you feel? Unwell? I'll call a doctor.'

'No . . . What? Ellen . . . ' He rubbed his face, trying to clear his mind from the deep sleep he had been in. 'I am not ill.'

'Are you sure?'

'Yes, I think so.' He did not feel ill.

'Then why didn't you come to the house this morning as you said you would?' Her beautiful face stared up at him. 'I've waited all day!'

'Forgive me. It seems I have slept the entire night and day.'

Ellen peered at him as though he was lying. 'So, you're not feeling feverish?'

'Not in the slightest. I was simply exhausted.'

'Thank the Holy Mother.' She sagged a little, relief on her beautiful face.

'Are you all right?' He held her elbow to steady her.

'Yes. Yes, I'm fine. I thought you were ill when you didn't arrive. Alistair put me in a panic over you.'

'How is he?' He suddenly remembered his friend.

'He's woken. His fever broke and his leg is looking better.'

'Excellent.' Relief flowed over him. He smiled, seeing the colour return to her face. 'You look like you are in need of a tot of something.' He became aware of his opened shirt and the unbuttoned trousers he had slept in. Ellen's gaze flickered to his chest. Desire tightened his groin.

Yearning darkened her eyes as her gaze strayed from his face down to his chest again. She wanted him as much as he wanted her, and the knowledge gave him a thrill he could not hide.

In a heartbeat he crushed her into his arms, kissing her with a passion he could barely control, not that he wanted to. For so long he had thought of this amazing woman. For too long he had ached to have her in his arms. He loved her with every ounce of his being.

'Ellen . . . ' He breathed, pausing for air, then he scooped her up into his arms and carried her to the bed.

He knew she should stop him, but she could not, would not. Nothing and no one mattered at this moment but the intensity of his love as he stripped the clothes from her until she lay naked before him.

He locked the door, then returning he slowly undressed, never taking his eyes off her magnificent body that he had dreamt about. 'You are beautiful. I knew you would be.'

She reached up for him. 'Make me forget everything.'

He needed no more encouragement. He would make her fully his. His woman. His love.

Hours later, the sunset cast shadows across the room. Rafe kissed her. Ellen lay sprawled over his body, as they lay quietly, spent, and drowsy. They had both blocked their minds from anything outside of the room, beyond the bed.

In his arms she had basked in his love, his lust, his quiet pleas for her to touch him, taste him and make him whole. She did. Together they were one person sharing the same thoughts and feeling the same sensations.

However, it was coming to an end, and the thought hit him like a blow to the chest. She had been gone from home for three hours. And no matter how much he loved her, he knew she had to go home.

Slowly, as though they came to the same conclusion at the same time, they held each other tightly, knowing it was the end.

'I love you with all my heart,' she whispered.

'As I love you.' He kissed her deeply, his body wanting her again and forever.

Shaking, with tears flowing silently down her cheeks, Ellen dressed.

'I will come to the house and say goodbye,' Rafe managed to murmur, his voice husky with a pain he had never experienced before. He watched her ready herself to face the world again, needing to capture the moment in his mind forever.

With a last haunting look, Ellen gave him a watery smile and walked out of the room.

When he arrived at the house an hour later to see Alistair, he had his luggage with him. He had managed to purchase a ticket on a ship sailing to England on the evening tide. His own ship with a cargo full of wool and flax had sailed from Sydney within two weeks of him arriving. This time he would sail on a fast clipper which would hopefully see him home in

Liverpool by the end of the English summer.

Dilly opened the door to him, and he walked into the parlour braced to face Ellen, but only Riona was there.

'Mr Hamilton.' Riona stood with a smile.

'I have come to see Alistair if he is awake?'

'He is. He's been listening to the boys' talk of their school. Go on up and I'll make some tea.'

'I will not be staying long. I have been fortunate to purchase a ticket on a ship leaving tonight.'

'Oh. Well, you will be missed, so you will.'

'Thank you.' He wanted to ask where Ellen was but knew he could not.

'My sister is out, I'm afraid. She loves watching the sunset over the distant hills.' Riona's watchful gaze told him more than her words did. Ellen was not going to be saying goodbye.

He nodded stiffly and climbed the stairs. In the bedroom he was greeted warmly by the children. Ellen's boys had grown, and his heart ached at the thought of not seeing them mature into men.

Bridget came to him straight away. 'Will you watch me ride tomorrow?'

'No, my sweet girl.' His voice caught, and he coughed into his hand. 'I am away to England tonight.'

'Tonight?' Alistair croaked from the bed. 'So soon?'

'Yes.' A wave of guilt washed over him. He had dishonoured his good friend and felt a cad. He wished he were a better man, but he wasn't where Ellen was concerned. He loved her, but he should have been stronger and never touched her. Only by working hard on making their business a great success would he be able to make amends.

'An American clipper is sailing for London this

311

evening. At my lodgings I managed to learn that a gentleman would not be able to take his berth, and he offered it to me. Besides, I have much to do for the business, my friend. We have planned a great deal in Melbourne, have we not?' Rafe stepped closer to the bed. 'The sooner I get home the sooner I can put our plans into action.'

'Will you come back, Mr Hamilton?' Austin asked.

Rafe's hearted smashed against his chest as he fought the emotion in his throat as he looked at Austin. 'Not for a long time.'

'Will you write to me?' Bridget slipped her hand into his and looked up at him with her mother's sweet face.

'I will.' He swallowed and quickly turned to Alistair. 'Stay well. I will write once I am back in Liverpool.'

'Goodbye, my friend.' Alistair shook his hand. 'Safe journey and who knows I might take this unruly lot back to England one day in the next few years.' He grinned happily.

Rafe couldn't speak. He heard a door close somewhere downstairs, and his breath stopped. Had Ellen come home?

'I'll walk out with you, Mr Hamilton,' Austin said.

Going out to the hired hansom, Rafe was on edge, desperate for Ellen to suddenly be there so he could see her once more. It was difficult to take another step and leave her.

He shook Austin's hand. 'Look after your mother.'

'I will, sir. Goodbye.'

With a last glance along the darkening shoreline, Rafe ignored all his instincts to run and find her. Instead, with his heart shattered, he climbed into the cab. The horse walked on and he closed his eyes.

312

22

'I like the white sprigged pattern,' Riona said, holding up a bolt of material in Mrs Haggerty's salon.

Ellen turned from studying a pair of kid gloves. 'Yes, that's pretty for the summer.'

Strolling around the shop, Ellen focused on making a choice, but her mind was occupied with other things more important than dresses and gloves.

She had spent the week after Rafe left attending to Alistair's every need, trying to make up for the guilt of betraying him.

But by the following week she believed she would lose her mind altogether if she didn't get out of the house and do something. Then she thought of an idea. Since Alistair's broken leg prevented him from attending his office, she would take over seeing to his paperwork and set up a temporary office in the bedroom.

At first Alistair had been against it, then once he realised how helpful she was and that she had a knack for business, he soon involved her in every aspect of his dealings.

For the last seven weeks, she had visited his business associates of various shops and producers, people who Alistair bought their products to send to England. She collected information from the warehouses and wrote up the ledgers. She met with the builder several times a week now the terrace houses were taking shape and introduced herself to the ship captains who docked in the harbour, and who could potentially take goods in and out of the colony.

She kept so busy she only slept a few hours a night, usually in the chair she sat in while working. The more she drove herself, the less she thought of Rafe and her broken heart and the more money she made for the family.

Alistair was proud of her intellect and sense of business. He guided her and explained things to her, which gave her knowledge to conduct herself with the gentlemen of the city. His patience and encouragement made her want to please him, make him proud.

The shop door opened, and Mrs Percival and Mrs Gardner-Hill walked in, their faces a picture of surprise at being caught out in the lower-class area of the city.

'Why, Mrs Gardner-Hill, I didn't know you were a client here?' Ellen tilted her head quizzically.

'We thought to try Mrs Haggerty's work,' Mrs Gardner-Hill replied. 'After seeing your dress at my ball, I decided to venture here myself to judge the quality. Though this side of town is frightfully rough, and I feared for my life the minute we turned into Cumberland Street.'

'Don't let the area distract you from Mrs Haggerty's fine skills.' Ellen nodded to the needlewoman, who had come out of a back room after measuring another customer. Ellen made the introductions.

'Good day, ladies.' Mrs Haggerty, a large woman of undetermined age, went behind the counter to write in her ledger.

Mrs Percival held a handkerchief to her nose. 'I can smell the sewers.' She eyed Ellen nastily. 'You must feel at home here in this quarter, Mrs Emmerson?'

Ellen gave a small mocking laugh. 'Yes, I do. Being

314

amongst decent, hard-working people who help each other reminds me of home.' She glared at the other woman, knowing she had been spreading gossip about her through the drawing rooms of Sydney. The invitations to tea afternoons had dried up, and yesterday Ellen saw two acquaintances cross the street to avoid her. She had lost so-called friends because of her outburst and may have damaged the future of her children being accepted into the first-class society but feeling so low over Rafe's departure she didn't seem to care as much as she should.

'Who may I assist first?' Mrs Haggerty broke the tense atmosphere.

'My sister and I will return tomorrow, Mrs Haggerty,' Ellen said suddenly. 'Do attend to Mrs Gardner-Hill and Mrs Percival, I understand they are in more dire need of your expertise than we are at the moment, for our wardrobes already hold your fine workmanship. Good day.'

Outside the shop, Riona started to laugh.

'That was mean, Ellen.'

'Oh, they deserved it, especially Mrs Percival, the overbearing witch. She looks down on me, but she'll rue the day she took me on, for the time will come when I show her and them all that I am worthy.'

'You were the one who wanted to enter their society,' Riona said as they walked towards home.

'I want the best for my children. What those women think of me doesn't bother me.'

'It's one and the same, Ellen, and you know it.' Riona side-stepped a pile of rubbish outside an inn. Two idle men leaning against the inn's wall gave them a whistle as they passed.

Ellen grabbed Riona's arm, knowing her sister

reacted badly in such situations after her attack from Lester. 'Keep walking.'

They stopped at the end of the street to allow a herdsman to steer his flock of sheep down towards the harbour. Sheep manure smeared the cobbles, and, on the breeze, the distinct stink of urine came from the tannery a few lanes away.

'Holy Mother Mary. This city is foul.' Riona lifted her skirts high to not soil them from the filthy street. 'We didn't have to put up with this in the country lanes back home.'

Ellen remained quiet, trying to keep the contents of her breakfast down.

'We should go to Parramatta and visit the boys on Saturday. Take the river boat up to see them, so we should.' Riona skipped over a rainwater ditch which doubled as the neighbouring houses' toilet.

'What do you think?' Riona asked when Ellen didn't answer.

The smell of the open sewer was too much, Ellen turned and vomited into the bushes in front of a small hut.

'Holy Virgin, Ellen.' Riona patted her back.

Ellen heaved, wanting to cry at the same time for feeling so wretched.

Riona passed her a handkerchief. 'Jesus, Mary and Joseph, are you all right?'

Straightening, Ellen wiped her mouth. 'Sorry.'

'Was it the smell, or something you've eaten?'

Ellen began walking along the street, fighting the need to be sick again.

Riona took her arm. 'You'll feel better once you're away from the stink. No wonder Mrs Gardner-Hill turns her nose up at this area. It's not pretty. I suppose we can bear it more easily than them.'

While Riona prattled on about the advantages of living in the country compared to the city, all Ellen could think of was she'd not had her monthly show. Not since that glorious time in Rafe's bed.

It was just over nine weeks since he had left. She had counted every day.

Nine weeks of aching with need for him.

Nine weeks of living her life without him.

If she was with child, it was his. The thought thrilled and terrified her. She'd had her monthly curse when Alistair was in Melbourne, so the baby could not be her husband's. With Alistair's broken leg and his weakened state after his fever, they had not slept in the same bed since his return. Ellen had shared Riona's bed instead.

A cold sweat broke out on her forehead despite it being a chilly winter's day.

Rafe's baby.

Once back at the house, she went straight upstairs to wash her face and pour herself a drink from the water jug.

She looked at herself in the full-length mirror, but nothing showed under her bodice, corset, and wide skirts. However, she knew she couldn't hide it forever.

'There you are, my dear.' Alistair limped into the room, using a cane. The doctor had removed the splints a week ago, and he was getting used to walking properly again. 'Did you have your dress fitting?'

'No. Mrs Percival and Mrs Gardner-Hill arrived, and we let them be seen to before us.' Ellen fiddled with her toiletries on the dressing table.

'That was kind of you. Though I am surprised they ventured to Cumberland Street. It's a poor area.'

'Mrs Haggerty's skills will outweigh that inconvenience.' She turned and looked at him.

The fever had taken weight off him, but he was slowly regaining it. Mrs Lawson fed him daily with all the favourite things he liked to eat. He was dressed in a suit and last evening he'd allowed Moira to cut his hair and Ellen had heard them laughing the whole time while she did it.

'You are staring at me.' He broke into her thoughts. 'Do I look pitiful with this cane?' His dimple appeared when he grinned.

'No, not at all.' Impulsively, she went to him and wrapped her arms around his waist. It was the first time she had done such a thing.

'What is this?' He chuckled but held her tightly.

She raised her mouth to his and kissed him. 'It's time I moved back into this room, our bed.'

He kissed her. 'There's nothing I would like better.'

'And I have a favour to ask you.'

'Oh, and what might that be.' He rained kisses down her neck.

'I want us to move to Berrima.'

He leaned back in surprise. 'Go to the country?'

'Yes. I'm tired of the city. I need the fresh air to breathe, and it would do you good, too.'

'You have been pale for the last couple of months. I have been worried it was all becoming too much for you caring after my business interests and me while I have been laid up in bed.'

'The business has been a delight. I've enjoyed it very much, but you're much better now and will want to take over again and I want to see the Berrima house as it's getting built.'

'I cannot be away from the city too long, dearest.

318

Now I am better I need to pick up the reins again, so to speak.'

'You can come back to the city and I can stay in the country.'

'For how long? I do not want to be without you. I need you here as my wife, my hostess.'

'I'd like Berrima to be my permanent home.' Now she had said it out loud, it made perfect sense to her. She needed to be away from Sydney and the memories of Rafe and the society women's gossip. 'I can't breathe here, Alistair. I'm a country girl.'

'You are so unhappy in the city?'

'Yes.'

'Though not with me?' He seemed a little anxious for her response.

'You? No, not with you at all. But the dinners and the garden parties and the tea afternoons . . . It's not for me. I want to walk our land, see the beasts grazing, plant vegetables . . . '

'A simple farmer?' He looked incredulous at the idea. 'But you are my wife and as such there is so much more for you to be a part of. It is expected that you will accompany me to dinners and balls, the theatre and so on.'

'There's nothing I want more than to be in the country. I know you want me to be here, but I can't do it, not permanently. I want a simple life in the country.'

'I very much doubt you will ever be a simple farmer, my dear.'

'No, maybe not. And I will join the society in the country gladly, for hopefully they will have the same interests as me and it will benefit the children. I'll even learn to ride.'

He grinned again. 'We could go riding together

319

then?'

'Yes!' she answered eagerly. 'Please, can we go?'

He kissed her. 'If it will make you happy, then we shall go.'

Ellen embraced him. 'I'll make our property in Berrima the best in the county.'

'Of that I have no doubt. But first I would like a promise from you.'

'Yes?'

'That you will split your time between Berrima and Sydney, so that I have you here to take to dinners and balls.'

She thought for a moment and then nodded. 'I will spend three months every year here in Sydney, will that do?'

He kissed her. 'I would have preferred six months, but I know better than to argue with my wife!' He grinned. 'Come, Bridget wants to show us her drawing. She is the cleverest little girl. She must get it from her mama.'

She halted him. 'Thank you for loving my children.'

'How could I not when they are a part of you, the woman who makes me so happy?'

'I will always try to, Alistair.' She cupped his cheek. 'I'm not perfect, but I'll try to be the best wife.'

'Then who can ask for more?' He kissed her hand, and they walked out of the room.

Acknowledgments

Writing a novel set in Ireland during the famine has been something I've wanted to do for some time. My grandmother Mary's lineage comes from Louisburgh area of County Mayo, Ireland. Mary's father, Patrick Kittrick was born on his father's farm near Louisburgh just like his father, Michael. In fact, Michael Kittrick, my great-great grandfather was born in 1845 and must have been a lucky baby to have survived the famine. His father tenanted land from the Marquis of Sligo, and many of his relations emigrated to distant lands. My grandfather, Patrick left Ireland in 1900 as a young man and went to Yorkshire, England.

My ancestors were Roman Catholic and could speak and write the Irish language as well as English. I am not a Roman Catholic and I had to do some research about the religion. However, I did not want to bog down the story with prayers, mass, ceremonies, etc. I hope I sprinkled enough of the religion in the story for the reader to understand the strength of their beliefs and why Ellen thought as she did about changing her religion when she married Alistair. I could not include all the visits to church and the acknowledgement of feast days, etc, because it would have made the book too long.

Miller's Point, Dawes's Point and Elizabeth's Bay were the original names of those places along Sydney Harbour, but I've taken the 's' off for modern notability.

Passages read by Patrick from the handbook on

the ship were taken from a real handbook written in 1850s to help passengers prepare for the voyage to Australia. The newspaper advertisement Ellen read was also taken from real advertisements of the era.

As always, I want to sincerely thank my readers for their continued support of my stories. I love every happy message they send me. I truly appreciate it and the lovely messages and reviews make the months of hard work worthwhile.

My thanks also goes to Deborah Smith for her support in her Facebook groups and for creating the AnneMarie Brear Facebook Fan Page.

I am very fortunate to have the love and support of my family. I could not do it without them — well, I could, but I'd rather have them beside me listening to me when I stress about deadlines and covers than not!

Thank you.
AnneMarie
Southern Highlands, NSW, Australia.
May 2021